MW01517084

Zion's Promise

CHRIS JEFFERIES

ILLUSTRATIONS BY
PAUL PARTON

© 2002, 2005 by Chris L. Jefferies
All rights reserved.
Published by Jefferies Books

No part of this book may be reproduced, stored in a retrieval
system, or transmitted by any means, electronic, mechanical,
photocopying, recording, or otherwise, without written permission
from the author.

ISBN: 1-4033-9129-7 (Paperback)

Library of Congress Control Number: 2002095520

Printed in the United States of America
Salt Lake City, UT

This book is printed on acid free paper.

Cover design by Jeanette Andrews
Cover image: *The Bay and Harbor of New York*
by Wamuel B. Waugh, ca. 1855.
Used with permission of the Museum of the City of New York.

Dedication

To the late Lucile Crowton Jefferies,
my mother, who early in my life instilled
in me a love of family heritage

And

William Martin Jefferies,
my father, who kept the love alive
as we explored together the old Trails

Author's Note

Dr. Jefferies is a direct descendant of twelve ancestors who traveled the Mormon trail from 1847 through 1862. A self-described "rut-nut," he has spent years tracing the "westering" emigration trails and studying contemporary accounts of those who traveled over them. Foremost is the emigration journal kept by his great-great grandfather.

Although Zion's Promise is his first work of fiction, the author is an accomplished writer who has published in professional journals over the past thirty years. His meticulous research and engaging writing style are clearly evident in his novel. A retired Air Force colonel, he is a career administrator and educator. He holds an undergraduate degree from Brigham Young University, a master's degree from the University of Pittsburgh, and a doctorate from the University of Oklahoma.

Foreward

I met Chris Jefferies in the summer of 1999 as he explained to me the significance of ruts rising up a slope from the broad plains in front of us. The subject of his description was the Chisholm Trail over whose storied ruts we stood, and how the trail changed the West and the entire country as a roadway of commerce and culture. From where we stood just north of the Red River in Stephens County, Oklahoma, the cattle culture spread from the plains of Mexico and South Texas throughout the Trans-Mississippi west.

In like manner, Jefferies' novel, ZION'S PROMISE, explores the trails of the mind and heart as the author's ancestor, William Jefferies, departs his native England for the frontier settlements of the Salt Lake Valley in distant Utah Territory. The journey itself covers not only an ocean, teeming cities, dangerous rivers, deserts, and mountains, but also represents a universal voyage of Spirit and Faith experienced by emigrants of all ages and motivations.

Frontier towns, American cities, river ports, and the vast American landscape, all come alive in this fascinating story of emigration. Jefferies gives us a glimpse of a time long past, with sufficient detail to paint the picture and still maintain the pace of the story. His characters come to life in this panorama of this emigrant family's journey to Zion. All readers, whether Mormon or not, will enjoy and learn from this compelling saga.

—BILL NEELEY, author of *The Last Comanche Chief: The Life and Times of Quanah Parker*.

Acknowledgements

Since beginning this novel, I've struggled with how to categorize it. Is it history with a little fiction, or is it fiction with a little history? I'll settle by calling it history-based fiction. It is, after all, a work of fiction, but it is based on real people and real events.

I began the novel as an effort to stimulate my children's and grand-children's interest in their rich Mormon heritage. They are, after all, seven and eight generations removed from the events I describe. So rather than leave them copies of family group sheets and records, dry and impersonal unless they've been bitten by the genealogy bug, I leave this dramatization. I hope it brings their ancestors alive as real people facing real challenges and opportunities not unlike their own. And, I hope it helps them appreciate the sacrifices and achievements of their forebears that yet shape their lives after seven and eight generations.

But as my writing progressed, I got caught up in the tumultuous, exciting, and historically momentous events themselves, particularly in the fascinating details of how our forebears met and overcame their myriad challenges. Each event is entertaining history on its own, from the early and subsequent Mormon migrations, to Federal efforts to bring the new Utah Territory under control, to the Civil War, and on to the inter-mountain region as part of the Western frontier. It is a fascinating period of history, filled with fascinating characters. So the novel expands into the culture and environment of the times.

In the end, I wrote this work to be entertaining and educational, no easy challenge. To me, history has always been fascinating, perhaps because I believe we are products of our heritage far more than we appreciate.

My great-great-grandfather's journal has been my primary source material. My father gave me a copy many years ago, and as I read it, I felt drawn to William and to his period of history. Finally, I was compelled to write about him. Additional context was provided by other contemporary journals, some available for reference at the Church History Department of the Church of Jesus Christ of Latter-Day Saints, at the Harold B. Lee Library, Brigham Young University, and on-line at the Church's Genealogical web-site. The Church's marvelous magazines, particularly the *Ensign*, contain many articles about the Church's pioneer heritage that proved most helpful, in particular, a series written by the well-known historian, Bill Hartley. I am also grateful to Bill for providing me copies of his original research and allowing me to draw from it.

The Utah Historical Society's journals also contain information I found useful. For information about Porter Rockwell, a major character in this work, I relied on the late Harold Schindler's fascinating book, *Orrin Porter Rockwell: Man of God/Son of Thunder*. My primary source for early Grantsville information was a fascinating thesis published in 1959 by Alma A. Gardner, who served for many years in Grantsville as an LDS seminary teacher. The Oregon-California Trails Association's publications are full of useful information from emigrant journals and other contemporary accounts that helped answer many questions of detail about early emigrant travel. And, I must mention the Crossroad's Chapter of the Oregon-California Trails Association. Individual members, particularly George Ivory, have been most generous to me with assistance and information. Finally, I am indebted to Eric Jamison for his superb editing skills.

In the end, though, I am responsible for what I write. I have made every effort to be as historically accurate as possible. If I err, it is my fault. I sincerely hope the reader enjoys the book as much as I enjoyed writing it.

Chris Jefferies
Duncan, Oklahoma, 2002

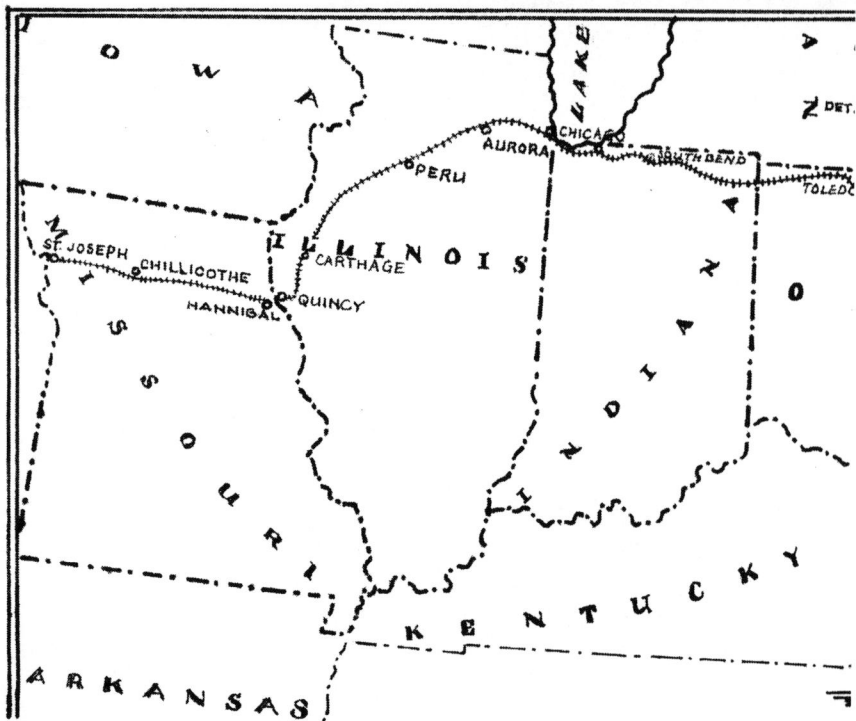

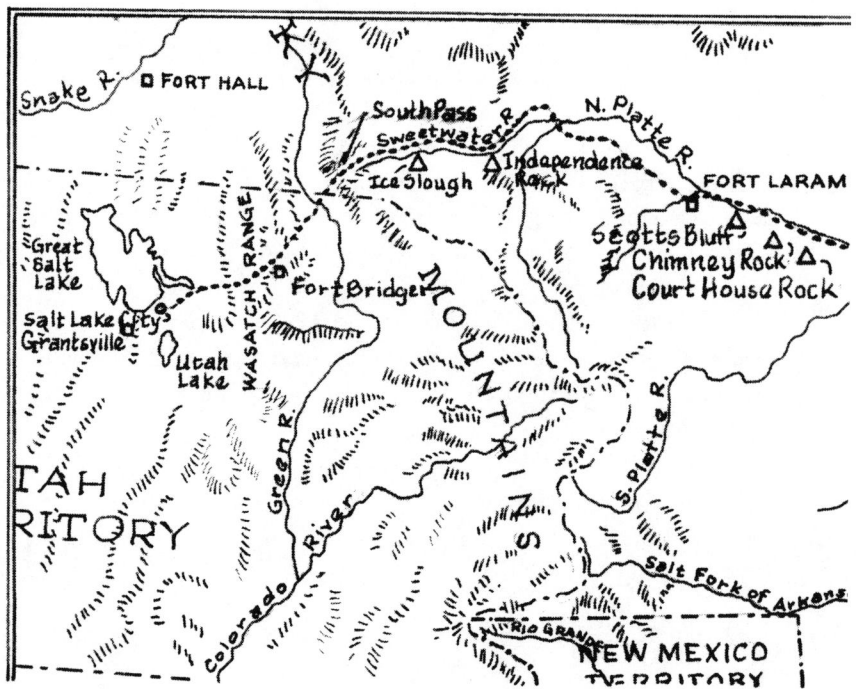

FORT HURON · DETROIT · FORT ERIE · DUNKIRK · ELMIRA · BINGHAMTON · ALBANY · MAS · CON · LAKE ERIE · ERIE · NEW YO · LEDO · CLEVELAND · PENNSYLVANIA · O HI O · PITTSBURGH · WHEELING · PHILADELPHIA · MARYLAND · DELAWARE · NEW JERSEY · VIRGINIA

Missouri R. · IOWA · AIE · Ash Hollow · OMAHA · COUNCIL BLUFFS · NAUVOO · Platte R. · Big Blue R. · FORT KEARNEY · Little Blue R. · Ft. LEAVENWORTH · Kansas River · o Council Grove · MISSOUR

PROLOGUE
1833–1834

CHAPTER 1
Porter and Weldon

Twenty-year-old Porter Rockwell began poling his ferry across the Big Blue river in Jackson County, far western Missouri, as soon as he heard horsemen approaching from the west. From the high, wooded limestone bluffs lining the river's west bank they were descending the long hollow to the crossing. They would cross here, pass through the small settlement spread across the river bottom, and climb a similar hollow up the limestone bluffs on the opposite side on their way to Independence, the rough frontier village about six miles beyond.

Though of average height, Porter was stocky and powerful. His well-developed arm and shoulder muscles kept the ferry easily under control this cool evening as he poled in smooth, broad strokes across the river, angling upstream to allow the current to work for him. Twilight had fallen, and this would be the last round-trip before he closed down for the night and retired to his home in the growing settlement. He and his father had settled and built the ferry at this ancient river crossing after they arrived with their families from Kirtland, Ohio just over two years earlier. It was the second move the Rockwells had made with their Church at the behest of their prophet, Joseph Smith. Joseph had been Porter's boyhood friend, and he admired, respected, and loved the Mormon leader.

The Rockwells, and the Church, had settled in Jackson County where the land was fertile, inexpensive, and the scattered local inhabitants appeared peaceful and friendly. Out on the very edge of the west-

1

ern frontier, Jackson County had seemed to be the answer to their prayers, a place where the Church could establish settlements and practice its beliefs without interference from envious and suspicious neighbors. Well over a thousand Mormon settlers were now scattered across the County in several settlements, and they had prospered. Porter, his father, and his brothers-in-law had cleared the fertile river-bottom upon arrival, and built sturdy log cabins for their families. Soon, other settlers arrived on the Big Blue, and now Blue Settlement numbered some twenty families. Porter was anxious to get home, eagerly anticipating a hearty supper and his young wife's warmth.

The riders, almost a dozen, had arrived at the bank and were impatiently awaiting Porter's arrival. As he grew closer, Porter could see and sense nervousness among both horses and riders.

"Hurry up, you damned fool Mormon. We ain't got all night."

Now alert and suspicious, Porter carefully and slowly approached the shore. Doesn't look right, Porter thought. Despite the coolness of the late October evening, the men were shirtless and each had smeared his torso with paint, Indian-style. A few carried muskets or pistols; the others large clubs, horsewhips, ropes, and as-yet unlit torches. Porter was uncertain about how to react as he stepped ashore and secured the ferry in its moorings. Clearly they knew who he was, but he was as yet unable to recognize any. He didn't like their looks, or their manner.

"'Bout time. Now, if you have any sense at all, you'll forget you seen us," growled one of the riders, dismounting. The others followed suit and began leading their horses aboard the ferry.

Porter was reluctant to begin the trip back across. Though not sure what they were up to, he knew it was no good, not for him nor for any of the Mormon settlers in Jackson County. Porter knew an increasing number of non-Mormons in the area were beginning to resent the growth and prosperity of the Mormon settlements, but so far resentment had been limited to disputes over slavery, trade prices, and the Mormons' reluctance to trade with non-Mormons.

Sensing Porter's hesitation, the leader approached. Leaning close, he drew a knife, and placed it against Porter's throat.

"If you value your life, you'll get on with the crossing. We know who you are, and we'll come back."

Shaken, Porter did as he was told. As he poled the ferry across, the group was silent and tense. He could hear whispering between the leader and one or two of the others. Their discussion was animated as they glanced toward Porter, then turned again toward one another. Porter could see he was the subject of their deliberations. He tried to look closely at each of the men for any kind of distinguishing characteristics, but it was getting too dark.

Porter guided the ferry into its moorings at the opposite shore, careful to keep from turning his back toward any of the riders. He secured the lines and approached the leader.

"That'll be seventy-two cents. Six cent each horse and rider."

The leader said nothing, but motioned for the group to disembark. As the horses and riders began moving off the ferry, Porter again addressed the leader.

"Seventy-two cents. Six cent each horse and rider!"

"That what you charge your Mormon friends?" he replied, belligerently. "Bet you let them cross free! Well, just make like we're Mormons."

As he spoke, the leader moved toward Porter's left, toward the riverbank, and before Porter realized it, he had begun to turn toward him, exposing his back to several of the men.

Porter sensed the blow before it came, and ducked his head. The club glanced across Porter's shoulders, momentarily stunning him, but before the assailant could swing the club again, Porter turned and barreled into the man, knocking him to the ground. Porter paused just long enough to land a powerful blow to the man's face with his fist, then leaped into the river and dove under the ferry. The confusion left the men momentarily disorganized and no one pursued. Porter surfaced quickly, hiding close alongside the ferry.

"Damn you, Weldon! You half-wit! How could you miss him so close?"

Weldon, still dazed by Porter's blow, struggled to his feet. "He is a slippery one. Let's get him before he gets away."

"No! We got too much to do! It'll be late enough tomorrow as it is before we get back to Independence. Let's get on with it. The rest will be here soon and we don't want to miss 'em. We'll wait for 'em on the other side of the settlement, then take care of business."

With that, the group mounted and rode off eastward at a gallop, straight through Blue Settlement.

Porter's settlement!

They're after us!

Thoroughly shaken now that he realized what the mob was up to, Porter began to fear for his family's safety. Galvanized by fear and anger, he scrambled out of the water and began running through the settlement after the raiders. By damn, they'd have to stop him first!

On the other side of the valley, about a half-mile distant, he could see the new arrivals' torches as they rendezvoused with those he had ferried across the river. Now numbering about fifty, the mob was anxious to get on with its work. The leader! If I can get to the leader and take him down, Porter thought, maybe the others won't be so anxious!

At a dead run, he spotted two horsemen conferring at the head of their respective groups and headed directly at them. There! That's the leader of the ferry group! He would jump him, knock him off his horse, and hold him hostage. He doubted any of the mob really expected any resistance, and hoped this might make them reconsider. By now, however, several of the mob noticed his approach and began to yell.

"Look out! Here comes one of those Mormons now! Stop him!"

So intent was Porter on reaching his man that he didn't see the horseman crossing his path from the left. Running full-speed, Porter's and the horse's momentum were enough to send Porter flying as they collided, stunned and breathless. The next thing he remembered was standing in a cluster of men, his arms pinned behind him.

"Well, well. If it ain't Rockwell the ferry-keeper again." Porter couldn't see who was addressing him. "He's one of the ring-leaders, and one we came to see tonight. Weldon, you missed your first chance. See if you can do it right this time."

A paint-smeared figure silhouetted against the torchlight approached Porter. Bringing his face close to Porter's, he spoke quietly but intently.

"You're jes' the first. Soon's I finish with you, we'll take care of the rest, you damn Mormon. This'll teach you!"

The man raised his club and hit Porter squarely on the side of the head. Porter collapsed, knocked out cold.

As Porter slowly regained consciousness, he first became aware of a strong pungent taste in his mouth. It was filled with dirt. Stirring, Porter coughed, spit, and immediately felt a sharp pain in his right shoulder. Leaning on his left arm, he struggled to his knees, feeling numbness on the right of his head. He couldn't feel his ear as he reached up, and his hand came away wet. Blood, he thought. Then the noise and confusion in Blue Settlement flooded over him. Riders were moving between the cabins, throwing torches indiscriminately, firing their muskets and pistols, and pulling down cabins. Finally regaining his feet, he began running toward his own cabin.

Porter passed Brother Bennett's cabin first, and saw that it had been torn down. Bennett was lying in front, his wife and children huddled above him trying to provide comfort. No time to stop! I'll come back, he thought as he ran past. Finally approaching his and his father's homes, he could hear the mob yelling obscenities at his wife and his mother. Oh, dear Lord, I'm too late! He agonized as he approached the neighboring cabins, unprepared for the devastation visible in the flickering torchlight as the raiders rode through what was left of both cabins. The raiders knew what they were doing and had destroyed the dwellings quickly and efficiently. Tying ropes to the ends of roof rafters, the marauders tied the other end to saddle pommels and spurred their horses. When the roofs collapsed, it had been simple and quick to pull down the walls and chimneys. The cabins were in ruin, possessions scattered about.

Depredations complete, the raiders rode off toward Independence as quickly as they had come. As he reached the compound, Porter ran directly to the remains of his house, fearful he would find Luana and the baby injured in the rubble, or worse. There he found his young wife in a corner of the ruins, huddled in fear and hysteria, holding tightly to crying Baby Emily.

"Luana! Luana! Are you hurt?"

Porter kneeled and comforted her and Emily while looking for injuries. He could see none in the flickering remains of the fireplace fire. After a few minutes, Luana's sobbing began to subside.

"I . . . I don't think we're hurt." She paused. "They came so quickly! They stopped at your father's first. I saw the torches and hid." She began sobbing again. "Why would they do such a thing!" Porter continued to comfort Luana and the child until both began to calm. "You better see to your mother," said Luana finally. "They were pretty rough on her."

Porter released Luana and Emily and ran quickly through the ruins to his father's cabin. His mother was sitting silently among the debris, head bowed, silhouetted against a small fire ignited by a broken lamp. She looked up at Porter as he approached, then lowered her head again. In the faint light, Porter saw tears, anguish and resignation on his mother's face.

"It's starting again, Porter. All our hopes and dreams . . ." She didn't finish the thought. "They came after your father. Thank God he'd gone. When they saw he wasn't here, they shouted terrible things at me, then unroofed the house. They want us and all the others to leave. It's going to get worse, Porter. Just like last time." She paused, looking toward Porter's cabin. "I'll be all right. Look after Luana and the child."

As Porter walked back to the ruins of his cabin and the still softly sobbing Luana, his rage began to grow.

"It ain't right! It just ain't right!" he said aloud. "No one can treat me and my family this way!"

The more he thought of how he and his father and the others had worked and sacrificed, and of the abuse they had suffered, the angrier he became. This time I'm going to do something about it! he resolved.

Reaching Luana, he took her again in his arms. Comforting her once more, Porter swore silently that never again would he be unprepared. Next time he would meet force with force! Two names burned into his consciousness: Weldon, a man; and Independence, the county seat. His anger grew. No! I won't wait for the next time, he vowed. I'll have vengeance this time!

That night in late October had been the most serious yet in a growing number of depredations in Jackson County against the Saints, as members of the Church of Jesus Christ of Latter-day Saints called themselves. It had begun late summer. Now, in what appeared to be the first organized and coordinated effort by local and neighboring-county Missourians to drive out the Mormon settlers, many other Mormon homesteads and settlements along the Big Blue were attacked and looted. Homes were thrown down, inhabitants beaten, and men tarred and feathered. But the worst was yet to come. The next week and a half was a nightmare of violence for the Saints that ended only when, driven from their homes into a cold, blustery wind, more than a thousand gathered on the banks of the Missouri river to cross to its north side. There, in Clay County, they hoped to escape persecution. The Saints tried to organize a defense, Porter one of the foremost among them, but they were too poorly armed and the marauders too numerous to defend themselves successfully. With the Governor and Jackson County officials either indifferent or openly hostile to the Saints, they had little choice but to flee. Vengeance, if it were to come, would have to wait.

But for Porter, only a little while.

The cold, raw, late-February wind came from the northeast, almost directly at Porter's face as he journeyed toward his destination. He was wrapped in a heavy woolen cloak, hunched over against the wind, his broad-brimmed hat pulled low. The winter sun was low in the west, casting long, eerie shadows through the bare branches of the patch of woods through which he rode. Be dark before long, Porter reflected to himself, grateful he was almost there. Be damned glad to get out of this wind! He was armed with a Bowie knife and a Hawken rifled musket taken from a mobber several months before. That had brought some satisfaction. But it wasn't vengeance. Not yet.

Porter had been on the road steadily now for over ten hours, and both he and his mount were tiring. The horse was beginning to strain against the wind. Porter had left their new cabin in Clay County well before daylight to avoid questions or speculation about where he was headed. He told Luana only that he would be gone a few days. His business ahead was personal.

Upon being displaced the previous November, Porter had worked feverishly with his father and the other Saints to build shelters for their families from the already cold, late fall. Living first in tents, and then in small log cabins as soon as they could be built, the pace and intensity of activity limited the time Porter had to make good on his vow. It didn't stop him from trying, however. On several evenings, soon after they crossed the Missouri, Porter slipped away to Independence, a little over an hour's ride, to gather information. He was determined to find Weldon, and Independence was the place to start.

Independence had been settled a little over six years before, and already it was a prosperous, bustling, frontier town. Its square was the marshaling area for wagon trains preparing to travel to Santa Fe along the route blazed not long before by William Becknell, and the rude log buildings surrounding it were occupied by a mix of merchants, outfitters, blacksmiths, and saloons. It was in the saloons that Porter knew his greatest chance lay in finding Weldon. He visited one saloon after another on his trips to Independence, just sitting unobtrusively, looking, and listening silently. These were skills at which he was becoming increasingly good, skills destined to serve him well.

Listening was particularly important to Porter. He remembered voices. It was a gift; once he heard someone speak, he would recognize the voice the next time he heard it. And he would know Weldon when he heard him. The events and sounds of that night at Blue Settlement were burned into his memory, particularly the voices. On his third trip to Independence, he listened carefully again through the babble and laughter at each saloon, trying to single out individuals. This time, he found him.

It hadn't been hard, really. Weldon had made it easy. Loud and boisterous, Weldon seemed to delight in boasting over the voices of his companions, especially after he had a few drinks. He was about Porter's age, a little taller, and stockier. After several judicious inquiries, Porter had learned that Weldon came from northern Ray County, about sixty miles to the north. There, he lived with his father on a homestead on the east bank of the Grand River, not far from a small trading post, saloon and ferry crossing. Major north-south and east-west roads in that part of the sparsely settled plains intersected at the ferry.

The trees began to thin out as Porter approached newly cleared fields, and the road began a descent as he neared the trading post situated in a ravine about a quarter mile up from the ferry. By now it was dusk, and the noise and light ahead told Porter that the saloon was occupied and busy. He reigned-up cautiously, but didn't dismount yet, pausing to listen to the voices. There! That was Weldon! Four horses tied at the rail suggested how many were in the saloon. No need to hurry, he thought. Got to be careful. Want to do this right! Finally dismounting, he tied his horse among those already secured and approached the door, pausing once more before entering.

Though cold and uncomfortable outdoors in the wind, the door was open to let fresh air into the smoke-filled, dirt-floored, dimly lit and overheated trading post and saloon. Porter entered a room about twenty feet wide and about the same distance deep. Along the wall to Porter's left, opposite the bar, was a large fireplace. At the rear of the room, a single door covered by a hanging blanket led to what appeared to be living quarters. Trade goods were stacked on shelves and in barrels at the back, and two rudely made tables stood near the door, not far from the bar. Both were occupied by single diners eating meals. Three others were standing at the short bar, Weldon among them. Porter recognized him as soon as he came in the door. All were holding drinks, one of many judging by their conversation. None at the bar noted Porter's entrance. In fact, none of the room's inhabitants seemed to be paying any attention to him at all. Porter sat down on a vacant chair at the nearest table and nodded to its occupant.

"Even'n," Porter said. He would try not to say too much. Like most of the Saints who had come to Missouri from Ohio and further east, he had an eastern accent. If these men were mobbers, he didn't want them to connect his accent to the Mormons and arouse their suspicions. Not until he finished what he came to do. "Name's Brown."

The man was eating eagerly, and only glanced at Porter. "Where're you from, stranger?"

"Independence. On my way to Quincy to fetch my family. Now the Mormon's been driven out, there's plenty o' cleared farmland."

"That's a fact," his tablemate replied, still intent on his food. "You get in on the festivities?"

"Yup. Right in the middle of it." But not like you think, Porter thought. "Got a place staked out. You?"

"Naw. Got nothin' against 'em. That bunch at the bar, though. They was recruited by the Jackson County militia. To hear 'em talk, they ran 'em all out themselves. You want to eat, gonna have to fetch it yerself."

Porter stood, went over to the bar, and ordered a plate. While waiting, he listened closely to the three, paying particular attention to Weldon. No doubt about it. It was him. The three were laughing drunkenly. Weldon began speaking as the laughter subsided.

"Never seen nothin' s' funny as a Mormon try'n to hold on to a rail, bein' rode out o' town, all covered with tar and feathers. Buck nekkid, bouncin' up and down, feathers just a flyin'! Must a put a dozen on rails m'self!" The three broke into laughter again. Weldon continued once more. "And the little nits! Damn, how they scurry and fly when y' chase 'em! Wish I was that quick when I was their age. Not all 'o them, though. Caught up with a few of 'em."

"What'd y'do when y'did?" one of the four asked.

"Why, what else do ye do with nits? Just stomped 'em some. They'll learn!"

Their laughter began again.

Porter struggled to restrain himself. Not time yet, he thought. His plate arrived and he returned to the table. Beans, cornbread, and fatback. Nothing fancy here, he thought, but after his long ride, it was welcome fare.

"I see what y'mean," Porter nodded. "Who's the big one. The loudest one?" he asked.

"Aw, that's ol' Dick Weldon. Kind of a loudmouth bully around here. Not many folks like him much."

Porter finished eating and ordered a drink, returning to the table to bide his time. He sipped slowly. Don't want to get all fogged up, he thought.

After about an hour, all but the three at the bar left. The liquor had taken its toll as the three swayed and struggled to remain erect. Finally, one slid to the floor, unconscious, and another staggered out the door. Weldon alone remained, standing unsteadily at the bar. Porter arose and walked over.

"Come have a drink w' me," Weldon slurred. "No fun drinkin' alone."

"No. Don't think I will. Don't drink with your kind," Porter replied. His hands were clenched as he restrained himself.

"Oh? What kind is that?" He seemed genuinely puzzled by Porter's remark, too drunk to sense it's sinister implication. "As' anybody here. I'm jes' a good ol' boy who likes a drink."

"I mean, I don't drink with bullies and cowards! That's you!"

"Why, tha's an insult! Bully, y' say! I'll show you!" Weldon staggered back to take a swing at Porter, and now off balance, fell to the floor and passed out.

Porter was deeply disappointed. He wanted vengeance, but he also wanted the object of his vengeance to understand why. No satisfaction in whipping an unconscious man. The saloon owner, hearing the commotion, came out of his back-room quarters.

"Damn that Weldon! Does that near ever night lately! His paw will come lookin' for him 'fore long and carry him home. Them two don't get along well at all anymore, not since Dick here knocked up his cousin and brought home that bastard boy of his'n. Only a matter of time 'fore he kicks him out for good."

The owner prodded Weldon with his foot to confirm he was passed out. "He's turnin' out to be a real bad seed," he continued, nodding toward the prostrate man. "When he went down to get in that there Mormon trouble, most hoped he'd get knocked in the head, or stay there." The owner paused and looked at Porter. "You lookin' for a place to bed down? For two bits, you can stretch out your bedroll over there by the fireplace. Includes breakfast. My boy will take care of your horse for another two. We'll leave Dick layin' there 'til his paw comes or he sleeps it off."

Weldon's father did come to claim his son several hours later, clearly in a bad temper from having to come out on a night like this. None too gently, he half dragged, half walked Weldon out the door and dumped him in the back of a wagon. Porter didn't interfere, rolling over to fall asleep again once the two had left. Plenty of time tomorrow to set things right.

Morning came quickly. After eating breakfast and getting directions, Porter headed to the Weldon homestead, about three miles north and east of the ferry. The weather front had blown through during the night, and the morning was bright with sunshine with hardly a breeze. It was the kind of rare winter morning Porter loved, a welcome respite from the dreary winter kill, suggesting spring was not far off. The broad river bottom stretched almost a mile to gently rising hills on the opposite side, and the tall grass indicated the soil below was fertile. The road forked and Porter took the road running north, hugging the base of the low hills as it skirted along the edge of the bottom. In the soft, warm sunshine, the area seemed pleasant indeed. Not a bad place to settle, he thought. Time to think about that later. Porter wished he had more time to enjoy the morning, but he had a task at hand and focused all his thought on what he needed to do.

After about forty minutes, Porter began to pick out a small collection of buildings snuggled in a hollow up against the rolling hills. Must be the place, he thought. Familiar butterfly sensations returned to his stomach as he anticipated the confrontation ahead. Drawing closer, he saw a small cabin, a corral in which two cows were feeding, a pig-pen, a rude shed in which two horses were also feeding, and a chicken coop. The homestead looked none too prosperous, indicating the inhabitants were still struggling to get established. A young boy carrying eggs in his cap just entered the cabin, and a man was chopping wood in front. It was Weldon.

Porter drew up his horse about twenty yards from Weldon, the rising sun at his back. Weldon stopped chopping wood as Porter approached, shading his eyes with his arm, squinting intently at Porter while leaning on his ax. He was disheveled, haggard, and irritated at the interruption. Porter could see his blood-shot eyes, guessing the man was suffering the results of his drinking bout the night before and unhappy with his wood-cutting chore. Good, Porter thought. He'll be slow to react.

"You Dick Weldon?" Porter asked.

Weldon continued to squint at Porter, and after a pause, answered belligerently. "Who the hell are you, and why'd ya want to know?"

Porter dismounted slowly, leaving his Hawken secured to the saddle, and reassuring himself by feeling the knife in his belt. He approached Weldon, careful to keep the sun directly at his back. He sensed nervousness in Weldon as he drew closer. Just then, another man appeared in the doorway of the cabin, curious at Porter's approach. The man was older, and looked to be Weldon's father. Porter glanced quickly, reassured at seeing the man's hands were empty. The man spoke to Porter.

"Mornin' to you, stranger. Don't see many folks through here. Lookin' for directions?"

"No." Porter replied, keeping his eyes on Weldon. "I come to whip your boy, here."

The man paused a moment before he spoke. "Oh? That a fact? What's he done now?" The man paused again, then spoke. "Dick, why's this gent here?"

"Don't know, Pa, but git the scatter-gun."

The elder Weldon remained standing in the doorway. "Knowin' you, son, I expect this here is one you already tangled with, but were too drunk to remember!" He paused once more. "That right, stranger?"

"Not quite," Porter replied. "He wasn't drunk." Alert to his peripheral vision for any sign of movement from the doorway, Porter kept a steady gaze at the younger man. Weldon slowly began trying to move out of the glare of the morning sun to get a better look at Porter, the ax hanging from his hand, but Porter matched the movement with his own.

"Y'er mighty brave when y'ride and mob with others," said Porter. "I expect y're really jest a bully and a braggart. Don't take much bravery to beat-up on defenseless women and children, or to pull down cabins, or tar and feather an old man, when y're ridin' with others. You brave enough to stand up to me on y'er own, y'bastard?"

"Paw, this's one o' those nigger-lovin' Mormons! Git the scatter-gun!"

Picking up the ax in both hands, Dick was nervously trying to reposition himself as Porter continued to match his movement, step by step, still trying to keep the older man in his field of vision. The man did not move.

"Pa, you goin' t'help me?"

Still no movement from the doorway. At the question, Porter stopped moving with Weldon, and began a slow, deliberate backward retreat toward his horse, hoping to draw the man into a rush. The ruse worked. Weldon raised the ax over his head and lunged at Porter. Expecting it, Porter easily ducked beneath the ax and drove his shoulder into Dick's mid-section, sending them both sprawling. The ax fell away harmlessly. The two grappled, each trying to gain the advantage by climbing astride the other. Neither was able to land a solid blow as they continued to wrestle. But Weldon's drinking and dissolute living began to take its toll, and he started to tire. Growing desperate, Weldon struggled to find an advantage as he realized Porter would soon best him if he couldn't shake him off. Out of the corner of his eye, Weldon saw the ax lying well beyond his reach. Exerting one last effort to break free, Weldon succeeded. He quickly scrambled for the ax, and picking it up, turned to square off again with Porter. This time, Weldon thought, he wouldn't be so quick to attack.

Again facing the ax, Porter quickly picked up a stout length of wood lying at the base of the pile Weldon had been splitting and turned to face him. The two circled slowly and cautiously. Porter thought again of the older Weldon, worried that by now he might have the shotgun and, as the two were apart, take a shot. But he didn't have time to dwell on the possibility. Weldon, seeing Porter momentarily distracted, lunged and swung at him. This time, Weldon was not off balance, and it took all of Porter's agility to dodge the blade. Nevertheless, Weldon's swing was spent, and in the seconds before the man could raise the ax again, Porter stepped in and landed a solid blow with his makeshift club to the side of Weldon's head. He went down, thoroughly stunned.

Immediately Porter was astride him, pinning his arms. Reaching quickly for his knife, Porter pulled it out and pushed it against Weldon's throat, just hard enough to draw a drop or two of blood. Porter's mind flooded with scenes of his home in ruins, Luana in tears, his friends being tarred and feathered, and his vow of vengeance. But he paused. What's stopping me! he thought. Why not just thrust the blade home? It would be so easy and quick, and then it'd be over. He'd have his vengeance!

The pain of the knife prick at his throat revived Dick, and he awoke, fear showing in his eyes. "No. No. Please don't do it," he stuttered. At the same time, Porter heard the distinctive clicks of the shotgun's two hammers being cocked.

"I reckon he deserves the beatin', stranger, particularly if he done half of what he brags about," said the older man. "But you ain't goin' to gain anythin' more by killin' him."

The elder Weldon approached to within a few yards of the two men, the shotgun leveled at Porter.

"I'd sure hate it if I had to empty this buckshot into you. 'Sides, if you was a killer, the deed'd be done."

Slowly, Porter drew the blade back and stood up, releasing Weldon. Standing in the doorway of the cabin, beyond the elder Weldon, he saw the young boy he noticed earlier.

Fully revived, and exhilarated he had been spared, Weldon jumped to his feet and scrambled once again for the ax. "Go ahead, Pa! Finish him off! No! Let me do it!" He began to raise the ax.

"Dick, put that ax down! You'll do nothin' of the kind!" As he spoke, the elder Weldon turned the shotgun toward his son. "I don't take no stock in the way you been drinkin' and carousin' and runnin' off with your no-account gang of thugs and bullies. The only reason I ain't run you off 'fore now is cause of the boy, and I need help with the farm, though it's mighty little you do! You been my only hope to make a go of it since your maw and brothers took the fever and died. But I swear, I won't let you kill anyone at my home."

Keeping the gun pointed steadily at Dick, the elder Weldon spoke to Porter.

"You better git. He won't be goin' anywhere soon."

Porter walked over to his horse, and as he mounted, he looked intently at the younger Weldon. "If I ever see you again, Weldon, I won't hesitate. I'd take pleasure in putting a ball in your gut. I'm Rockwell. Porter Rockwell. Remember the name and steer clear o' me!"

Turning his horse abruptly, Porter galloped off toward the river and home. Some day, he hoped, he'd run into Weldon again. Next time he wouldn't let his conscience get the best of him.

CHAPTER 2
William, January 1843

"Frederick! Up with you both, now! Ye can't afford to be late again or they'll dock more of your miserable pay."

Thirteen year-old William Jefferies stirred at the widow Gane's call, not wanting to believe it was already 2:30 in the morning. Hadn't he just fallen asleep? He felt Frederick, next to him, do the same. In the attic loft in which he and Frederick shared a sleeping pallet, he could hear the soft sigh of the wind blowing over the thatched roof just above his head and feel its cold dampness. It would be another miserable January morning. Probably still raining. Oh, to roll over and go back to sleep! But he couldn't; he and Frederick had only an hour and a half to dress, eat, and walk the three miles to the Huish mine and clock in before their shifts began at 4 A.M. They both stumbled off the pallet, quickly dressed in their coal-stained work clothes, and splashed cold water on their faces. He could feel heat coming up through the door below, but it didn't help much. Even in the dim light they could see one another's breath. At least they'd have time to eat the hearty porridge he could smell simmering on the fire. Widow Gane was always prompt and reliable about that, and about seeing they were up in time for their shifts at the mine.

"Ye'll want to dress warmly. It's still mistin' out there," she said to the boys as they sat down at the table.

The bowls of porridge were steaming in the cool air of the kitchen, even though the stove was giving off welcome heat. A large pad of butter atop the porridge in each bowl was beginning to melt. The boys ate quickly and heartily. It would be the only food they'd have until the noon meal at the mine.

"No more sugar left to sweeten it 'til I can get to market. I put an extra large helping of butter to help you get it down."

The boys finished quickly, licking the last grains of porridge their spoons could not pick up. They moved to the door, put on their slickers, and wrapped scarves about their necks.

"Ye'll have to walk quickly to keep warm," the widow Gane said after them as they departed. "Keep safe, boys. Don't take no chances!"

They walked briskly over the narrow, well-trodden lane toward Huish, but were both soon chilled deeply by the wind-whipped drizzle gusting over the Mendhip Hills, laden with moisture from the Bristol Channel just twenty miles to the northwest. Even in the dead of night, with dawn hours off yet, the lane was familiar to William as they leaned into the wind. Walking the lane both ways in darkness since October, when the days began to shorten, he knew every large stone and wheel-rut between the widow's cottage and the mine. Beginning his shift at 4 A.M., and coming out of the mine when the shift finished at 6 P.M., William saw daylight only on Sunday when the mine closed for the day.

And oh, how William yearned for Sunday! Sundays were special to William, and not just because it was a day when he could escape the rigors of the coalmine. It had been just two years since his beloved mother had died and he yearned deeply for her! His mother's lingering illness had taken just about all his family owned to pay the seven doctors attending her, and all to no avail. His father had sold their last cow, with a calf by her side, just before his mother died. His father, having never been close to William and his three sisters, was unwilling or unable to offer much solace or comfort after their mother's death; in typical English tradition, he had been distant and uninvolved in their day-to-day upbringing and nurturing. William thus found his only comfort in Sunday School, where his mother had taken him each Sunday for as long as he could remember. Even with her gone, he seemed close to her there, both because it was something they had done together, and for the spiritual comfort and messages of encouragement he received studying the Scriptures. He had inherited his mother's spiritual nature, and, unlike most boys his age, felt confident and comfortable pondering and studying things spiritual. So many unanswered questions, though!

William's father had remarried within three months of his wife's death, but his new wife, having younger children of her own, never took to William and his sisters. The financial stress of his mother's lingering illness, and an uncomfortable awkwardness at home, led to the family's break-up. His older sister went to service at a near-by manor, his two younger sisters were placed in a neighbor's family, and William himself went to lodgings. He supported himself, not unusual in that day and time, even for a boy of his tender years. But life was hard.

After working for awhile as a hod-carrier for masons, and then tending to thatchers, William found work at the Huish coal mine. Work there paid the best wages in the area, low though they were, but it was tough work and still difficult to make ends meet. Two-thirds of his wages went for lodging and food, leaving him the small remainder for shoes, clothes, and incidentals. He had hoped to earn sufficient to help his sisters, but there just wasn't enough. There seemed no way to get ahead of his expenses.

He had labored in the coal mine for about a year now, lodging with his co-worker, Frederick Gane, and his widowed mother. Toiling in the mine day after day, life had grown hard, dreary, and seemed hopeless to William. Nothing ever changed. Nothing to look forward to, except for a day off on Sunday. Even if there was better work available, there was no opportunity to look for it with the long hours he spent in the mine.

They were both walking briskly now, and in the exertion began to warm. William, hoping to pass the time more quickly, and to avoid the familiar melancholy that always threatened during the long walk to the mine, spoke to Frederick.

"What d'ye think they'll have us doing today, Freddie? Sortin' the coal lumps again with the boys, or d'ye think we'll have a chance to go down into the mine with the men?"

"Ah, who knows? Time goes a little faster down in the mine, but it's harder work. Damp and cold, too. We get more dinner, though, workin' with the men. Guess it just depends on how many's out sick or injured."

"Aye, hard to tell. Sortin' coal's so much drudgery." William pondered on that a few minutes, then spoke again to Frederick. "How long d'ye suppose we'll have to keep workin' like this? I mean, up at half-past two in the mornin,' workin' till six, trudgin' back home just in time to clean up a little and eat a bite, then to bed, just to do it all over again. It's a sad thing when the only things we have to look forward to is goin' down in the mine with the men instead of sortin' coal lumps, and the comin' of Sunday. Surely the Good Lord intended us to have more happiness than that in our lives!"

"Startin' that again, are ye, Willie? I keep tellin' ya, it don't do no good to keep thinkin' on that stuff. It's just the way it is! Me Da' worked in the mine all his life till he was killed in that accident there, and it seems I'm goin' to do the same. 'Sides, the Good Book teaches that if we endure now, our reward'll come in the next life. That's why it's so hard now, ain't it? So's we'll have somethin' to look forward to?"

"Ah, Freddie. I wish I could accept it all like you. Be a lot simpler for me. I just know there's more to life than this. Surely the Lord wants us to have a little happiness! A little happiness now! There must be more to it! We just have to trust in the Lord, I guess."

"Aye, maybe so. Right now, though, all we can trust in is the superintendent," Frederick replied. "Maybe he'll let us go down with the men today. We'll know soon."

For some time they had been picking up the soft chug-chug sounds of the steam engine powering the mine lifts, and now, through the mists, they were just able to begin seeing the soft glow of the lamps at the mine works a half-mile or so away. Soon they'd be out of the wind, but probably still not warm.

Frederick was right. Today they were assigned to work down in the mine. Being in their early teen years, and above average growth for their ages, Mr. Bull, the superintendent, saw that William and Frederick would soon be more productive down in the mines than at the picking and sorting bins with the young boys. Whenever he needed extra hands down below, he had begun to rely on William and Frederick, along with other boys about the same age. Good training for them, the superintendent reasoned. And, it helped condition and toughen them to the rigors soon to come from working down there daily. Last evening there had been another accident down in the shafts, and two men were off work, injured. William and Frederick weren't quite large enough yet to wield a pick and shovel at the coal face, but they were strong enough together to push a coal hopper along the parallel iron rails running up the slight grade of the horizontal mine shaft to the vertical shaft. There, the coal would be loaded on conveyor buckets for the trip to the surface. That was their job today. Both were assigned to the same hopper.

The morning did pass quickly, as they had hoped. Too soon, though, the dinner break was over, and they were back at their labors. By late afternoon, however, working in the dim light of the lanterns worn on their heads, the boys were noticeably tired. The hoppers seemed heavier and heavier. The short breaks at each end of their run, as coal was loaded or unloaded, no longer seemed long enough for them to recover their stamina. Pushing the hopper was particularly difficult up over the slight ridge that separated the horizontal shaft from the more level base of the vertical shaft.

Water seeping down the walls of the vertical shaft pooled at its base before running down the drainage ditch along the lower side of the horizontal shaft. Bits of coal, however, dropping as the coal was loaded from the hopper into the buckets, created a slight dam that caused the water to run directly between the rails instead of in the ditch. No one had taken the time to correct the course of the drainage, requiring at most a few minutes work. This caused the hopper pushers to move to either side of the track to maintain secure footing for the last few yards up and over the ridge to the level unloading area. William and Frederick were approaching this last stretch of track with a full load.

"Willie, this'n is goin' to be hard," grunted Frederick. "Seems like we got a little more load this run. We'll have to give it an extra push to get over the lip this time. Think we got it in us?"

"Don't know about you, but I'm about done in," William replied wearily. "Guess we got no choice. How much longer d'ye think we have 'fore quittin'?"

"Don't know. Seems like it can't be much longer. Maybe we can get a little longer break after we dump this load. Here we come to that damn water. Why can't they fix where it flows? Careful now, Willie. Steady, as you move aside . . . Here's the lip . . . Now!"

With an extra burst of exertion, William and Frederick pushed at the hopper to get it over the slight ridge. In the dimness, neither noticed the water was running broader at this point than before, and even the sides of the shaft, previously dry, were now slick with water. Frederick slipped first.

"Willie! I'm slippin'! Push!" Frederick exclaimed as he struggled to regain his footing.

William didn't need to be told what was happening. As Frederick lost his footing, the weight on William seemed to double, and as he strained under the increased load, he too began to lose his footing. His feet began sliding along the wet floor.

"Don't think I can hold it, Freddie! Too slippery!"

"Then set the brake!" Frederick grimaced as he continued to struggle to keep from sliding. The brake lever was on William's side, just beyond his reach.

William stretched to reach for the lever with his right hand, but just as he grabbed it and began to pull, he lost his balance and his feet slipped entirely from beneath him. Not daring to let go of the lever lest the hopper get away, he reached down with his left hand to steady himself, and instinctively grabbed the only handhold he could feel, the rail. Struggling at the same time to pull down on the brake lever as the hopper began to roll backward, he didn't even feel the hopper wheel run over his left hand, crushing the fore-palm and part of his thumb, severing his fingers. It wasn't until after help arrived, and the hopper was stopped, that he discovered his wound.

William grabbed for the side of the hopper with his left hand in an attempt to pull himself up. But he couldn't grab it! He tried once more, again unsuccessfully. Then, in the dim light of his helmet lantern, he saw his hand.

"Freddie! Freddie! Me hand's gone! Me hand's gone!"

Frederick rushed over. Seeing the bloody stump of William's hand, he began to yell. "Help us here! Help us! For God's sake, help us!"

Two men rushed over to assist. One of them wrapped William's hand in a dirty kerchief, and helped him up to the vertical shaft where the lift carried him, William, and Frederick to the surface. They went quickly to the infirmary where an attendant attempted to clean the wound, and re-wrapped it until a surgeon could be sent for.

Four hours later, Mr. Morgan, the Company surgeon, arrived. By then, the shock had begun to wear off, and William grew faint from the loss of blood and throbbing pain. He struggled to maintain consciousness, though, anxious about the consequence of his injury. Mr. Morgan's examination and subsequent report helped clear William's mind.

"Mr. Jefferies, there is not enough of your hand left to save. You've lost all your fingers, and the tip of your thumb. Even if I repair your thumb, you won't have fingers to use with it. Your best course is to allow me to amputate the remains of your hand at the wrist. That would, at least, allow the fitting of a prosthesis that might be of some use to you. Is that acceptable?"

"No! No! Never!" William exclaimed. "I won't lose the rest of my hand!"

"But surely, you can see that's best for you! By the time I take off the crushed tissue and bone, you won't have enough hand left to be of any use! What good is only a thumb?"

"I don't care! I want you to save every particle of my hand that's possible to save! It's my hand. I'll risk the use it will be!"

"Very well, young man," Mr. Morgan concluded. "If that is your decision, I'll do the best I can."

William was laid down on a table and given chloroform. The doctor worked quickly. He cut the crushed bone away at mid-palm, and amputated the thumb at the first joint. William was left with only half a hand, and a stump of a thumb.

The chloroform wore off slowly, allowing William most of a full night's sleep. By daybreak, the throbbing pain in his hand brought him to full consciousness. He saw he was occupying one of five beds in the infirmary. Two were occupied by the men injured the day before. William groaned as his head began to clear, and noticed Frederick sitting near by. Frederick, seeing him awake, moved over to the bed and spoke.

"Dear God, Willie. Ye didn't have to go and do that to get out o' the mines," he said in a half-hearted attempt at humor. William looked terrible.

"Ah, Freddie, it all happened so quick, I can hardly remember it. Ow! My Lord, how my hand hurts!" He looked fearfully at the bandaged stump of his left hand. "Freddie! Did the surgeon leave my hand? Did he?"

"Aye, Willie. I watched. Ye've got half a hand and part o' your thumb. That's what ye asked him to do."

"Thank the Lord for that!" He paused, still groggy and in pain, reflecting a few seconds. "Maybe I shouldn't have been so ungrateful for the job in the mine," he mused. "Maybe the Lord thought so too, and this is my punishment!"

"Who knows, Willie. Maybe He allowed it to happen so's you can find somethin' better in life. You're always goin' on about how life should offer more. Ye'll sure not be able to do this kind of work anymore."

In pain, William grew silent for several minutes, then spoke, grimacing. "Ye may be right, Freddie, though it's hard to think of this as much of a blessing, it hurts so!" He paused and grimaced again. "Oh my! How much longer will it hurt?"

As if in answer to his question, Mr. Morgan and Mr. Bull came through the doorway.

"Mr. Jefferies! Good to see you awake," exclaimed Mr. Morgan. "Hand hurt? Of course it does. My apology. I'll give you some laudanum to take the edge off. The surgery went quite well. I was able to cut away all the damaged tissue and bone, and sew you up quite nicely. I think you'll heal without complications. Expect to stay here in the infirmary for the next couple fortnights. The nursing sisters will want to change your dressing frequently, and I'll want to keep an eye on your hand. But

I wouldn't expect a future in any kind of manual labor! Have you had any schooling? Can you do any kind of clerking?" He administered the laudanum to William as he spoke, and within a few seconds, the pain began to deaden.

"Aye," replied William, "a little. I learned letters and numbers before my mother died. Attended school 'til I was ten. Never thought about clerking, though, or any job like that. Not much like that open around here. Mostly they go to family apprentices."

Mr. Bull spoke up. "Mr. Jefferies, I want you to know how sorry we are about your accident. Seems like the cause was some of our own neglect, and we've taken steps to correct it. The mine, of course, will pay for all the surgical fees, and you'll stay in our infirmary. As for after your recovery, your co-workers, as is the custom, have taken up a collection to help you until you find suitable employment." He placed a sizeable bundle on the table next to William's bed. "There's a tidy little sum, there. In addition, I think we will be able to help you find a situation that will account for your disability when you recover."

The throbbing pain in his hand had begun to lessen, and William expressed his gratitude. More comfortable now, he began to doze off again, the pain receding in his consciousness as he gave himself over to the laudanum's narcotic effects.

DECISIONS
1860–1861

CHAPTER 1
Love Requited

The meeting had not gone well. It was growing increasingly difficult for William and his missionary companion, Edward Hanham, to give their messages. The small assembly hall William rented for the occasion, to his surprise, was crowded; all thirty chairs were filled, and the overflow stood at the rear and along the walls on either side. As usual, a few had come out of a sincere desire to listen to the Mormon missionaries preach, but more had come out of curiosity. Also, as usual, several had come to heckle, and they had been at it since the meeting began just less than an hour before. Hecklers were not new to William and his companion; typical and expected at public meetings such as this, heckling was usually good-natured, and a few well-chosen scriptures and repartees prepared in advance would give the hecklers the recognition they wanted. Indeed, William had come to know and even respect several of the regular hecklers.

The crowd outside, however, was unusual. The late-fall evening was wet and cold, a continual series of rain showers blowing over the city from the Bristol Channel. Yet outside a growing, unruly crowd surrounded the hall. The crowd had been jostling the curious going inside the hall as the meeting began, and shouted faint but still audible obscenities at the two missionaries as they tried to preach. During the last twenty minutes, however, the obscenities had grown louder and more frequent.

The Latter-day Saint Church was well-established in Bristol in 1860, and missionary efforts had been particularly fruitful. Many had heard and been impressed with the message of Mormonism and joined the Church, including William. He first heard the Missionaries some five years earlier through acquaintances, and joined the Church soon after his introduction. While converts often chose to emigrate to America to build "Zion" by joining the fellowship of the Saints in the Salt Lake Valley of Utah Territory, a sufficient number remained to provide a support structure and a measure of respectability in this part of England, William among them.

As soon as William had heard the Mormon Missionaries' messages, he knew he had found the religion and church he was looking for. The Heavens were not closed, they proclaimed; God and His Son continued to speak to mankind through prophets. To increase mankind's understanding of God and life, they taught, the Lord had provided additional scripture to complement the Bible. Most important to William, the Church's doctrines taught that joy, happiness, and prosperity were desirable and achievable even now, in this life; it is not God's plan, after all, for mankind to suffer silently and miserably through life until a better world comes. William felt he had come home; since joining, he enjoyed a peace and serenity he had yearned for since his mother's death years before. Indeed, he had come to believe so fervently in the gospel and the doctrine it offered that he desired to share it with as many as would listen. Within a few years of joining, then, William accepted a call to remain in his homeland and serve as a missionary. He and Edward had been serving and preaching together in Bristol and the surrounding countryside now for the two months since he returned from Norwich.

Ever conscious of the crowd outside and the now restless audience inside, and growing apprehensive, William began his sermon's conclusion.

" . . . and I bear fervent testimony of the reality of the living Christ, that He is in every way directing the affairs of this Church, that the Book of Mormon is the word of God, and that Joseph Smith . . ."

A large rock crashing through the window at his left interrupted William. A man seated near the window grimaced in pain, grabbing his head where struck by the rock. Soon another rock followed, then another through the windows on the other side of the room. Those seated jumped to their feet, and the audience began to mill nervously, finally pushing toward the door at the rear of the hall. They ignored William and Edward, who crouched behind the podium.

"Had a bad feelin' about that mob soon as we started," said Edward nervously. "Didn't think they'd go this far, though. You think they're after us?"

"Could be," replied William, himself nervous, and uncertain at the moment about what to do. "I've noticed several of this same group at our meetings over the past weeks, and hoped they were sincerely investigating the Church. Seems now more like they were settin' us up."

"Aye," said Edward. "That happened last month up in Liverpool. A mob took Elders Dillie and Martin out of their meetin' and down an alley where they thrashed them thoroughly. What're we going to do?"

"Best run for the police station. Not likely they'll follow us there. But we should split up soon's we're out the door. You go left; it's the most direct. I'll go right and circle round to the station and meet you there. Quick! Let's get in with the crowd before they're all out the door."

They both rose, leaving their stove-pipe top-hats behind, and forced themselves into the departing audience, jostling with them to reach the door. William was first out and sprinted off to the right as soon as he was free of the crowd. He could see several of the outside mob stretching and straining to look at the exiting audience, assuming they were looking for him and Edward. He was right. One of them recognized William as he began running down the narrow cobblestone street, slick with rain.

"There! There goes one! After him! Quick!"

William could hear running feet chasing after him, but didn't look back for fear he'd lose his stride and any advantage he had over his pursuers. He was worried about the slick street stones as his foot occasionally slid on one or another, but he continued apace, willing to risk falling to being caught and beaten. He fervently hoped, and at this moment prayed, that his pursuers might not be as determined. There! There's the corner! Slowing only enough to be confident he could maintain his footing as he rounded the corner, he successfully made the turn and sprinted on. As if in answer to his prayer, William heard one of his pursuers slip and fall upon turning the corner, and he risked a look back just in time to see a second pursuer trip and fall over the first. The ensuing profanity convinced William he had gained little advantage, and that they would continue their pursuit. He frantically began to look for an alley or shed into which he could dart.

His pursuers, now just two, were up and after him again. After their fall, he knew they would be more determined than ever to catch him, and continued to look for a place to hide. He wouldn't have much time! But the light was much dimmer on this narrower street, away from the main thoroughfare from which he turned, and ahead he saw the silhouettes of a series of small garden sheds. Perhaps in the dim light they wouldn't see him dart into one! Or, if they did, maybe not the one he picked and, with no windows, they would all be black inside. He approached the sheds at a dead run, and picking one at random, slid to a stop and grabbed the door handle. Now if it were only left unlocked! He was in luck! It was. He opened the door, quickly ducked in, and closed it quietly. In the dark, he crouched behind what seemed to be a tool crib.

He no sooner crouched than he heard his pursuers slow as they approached the sheds. They knew he was in one of them, but not which. And they had no lantern. They stopped at the shed next down the line, and conferred quietly. He couldn't hear what they whispered, but was sure they would try to search each shed in turn. He thought there were four sheds in this series, each standing a little apart from the other. William heard the door of the neighboring shed open, then the door to his. The man paused a moment before entering, probably listening for a sound, like breathing, that would indicate someone's presence. William struggled to quiet his labored breathing. For several agonizing seconds, he held his breath, difficult after the exertion of running. He could hear the pursuer breathing heavily from his own exertion as he stood in the doorway, and hoped it might help cover whatever breathing sounds of his own he could not control. After a few seconds, the man entered, stumbled against the tool crib, shuffled a few steps in each direction, paused again for a few seconds, and apparently satisfied, turned and left. William tried to exhale softly, not trusting his air to expend quietly enough to avoid alerting the departing pursuer. Two more doors opened, and after a few minutes each closed again. The two conferred once more, and William hoped desperately they would leave. He was soaked through to the skin by the rain and began to shiver with the cold. There! The footsteps led away and after a few seconds faded as the pair returned down the narrow street up which they had pursued William, cursing as they gave up their search.

Thank the Lord! He seemed to be safe for now. With relief, however, came a heavy, disabling fatigue as his anxieties, fears, and physical exertions caught up with him. I've got to rest, he thought as he sat against the wall, his legs outstretched. Just a few minutes and then I'll leave. But his fatigue was greater than he appreciated. Although he was cold through-and-through, and still shivering, a comforting numbness allowed him to fall asleep.

William awoke with a start.

"Who's there?" he exclaimed.

William was certain a hand had shaken him gently by the shoulder, but he could sense no one near in the dark. He shook his head to clear it. How long had he slept? William attempted to bring his legs up to stand, but they wouldn't move! Reaching down to rub them, he could feel nothing! They were numb. Immediately, he began to shiver violently. "I've got to get up," he mumbled. "Got to get circulation going."

His shivering was almost disabling. But he rubbed his legs vigorously, and struggled to stand. Finally, William managed to get to his feet. As he stood, a church clock struck one o'clock. "Must have slept at least three hours," he mumbled. "Could have been dead by morning!"

Silently, William prayed his thanks for his narrow escape from the mob, and for awakening in time to seek shelter and warmth.

As customary for Mormon missionaries of the time, William and his companion traveled "without purse or script," a phrase describing the faith-testing experience of relying upon the Lord to provide food, shelter, and the inspiration necessary to preach. Indeed, few missionaries had the means to support themselves, whether from England or from Utah. William had earned a comfortable living as a clerk since his accident, but when he entered the ministry full-time, he gave up his income. This meant depending upon the beneficence of others, both members and non-members alike, to provide a meal or shelter as he and his companion traveled from village to village seeking those willing to hear their message. In the villages, they depended largely on the kindnesses of non-members. And with success; they found many people to be surprisingly charitable and generous, offering food and shelter whether or not they sympathized with the missionaries' beliefs or were receptive to their message. In the larger cities where the Church was relatively well-established, like Bristol, they were able to depend upon Church members for assistance, and most gave it happily. It was in the home of members, Sister Mary Ould, her two daughters and son, that William sought shelter that night.

Sister Ould had long provided assistance to the missionaries, and William had been a regular visitor whenever his activities brought him to Bristol. A woman in her early fifties, she, her husband, two daughters, and a son, had moved to Bristol from Cornwall, the south-western-most part of England long regarded as the kingdom of the ancient King Arthur. She heard the missionaries soon after arriving, and joined the Church shortly thereafter. Her husband would not even consider joining the Church, but her two daughters and young son followed her within a few months. Mr. Ould ignored his family's participation in Mormonism, not difficult since, like most of his contemporaries, he spent his evenings and Sundays in the local Pub. Missionaries had long been assured a warm welcome, a hot meal, and a place to sleep at Sister Ould's. William hoped his arrival soon after one o'clock on that cold, bitter, rainy evening would meet with the same welcome to which he had grown accustomed.

The door to Sister Ould's and the neighboring row houses opened directly onto the street. The narrow street was dark, and the wet pavement stones glistened from a lamp down the street. William had to tap softly several times before he saw the light of a lamp through a small transom above approach the door. The door opened, and Sister Ould stood in her nightclothes, holding the lamp.

"Elder Jefferies!" she exclaimed. "My, how we worried about you! You've given us a terrible start! Elder Hanham has been almost frantic since you didn't meet him at the police station! He's been by here twice since then, hoping you might come. Are you all right? Come in, quickly. Why, you're soaking! You'll catch your death of cold!"

Closing the door, she escorted William to the sitting-room door just to the right, off the narrow hall leading from the front door. She opened the door and quickly went to the small fireplace in which banked coals were glowing dimly. Setting the lamp on the mantle, she stirred the coals, adding several new pieces as the sparks drew up the chimney. She sat William down on the settee and wrapped him in the afghan folded nearby.

"Now, take off those wet shoes and let your feet warm by the fire. Soon's you warm up some, we'll get you out of those wet clothes. I've got a stew simmering on the stove for Mr. Ould, and I'll bring you a bowl."

William hadn't realized how hungry he was until his shivering began to subside as the chill wore off, and the wonderful fragrance of the stew registered. Sister Ould soon returned with a tray holding a bowl filled to the brim, a glass of milk, and a large slice of fresh bread. "Eat this while I run upstairs to get you something to wear while we dry your clothes. I've sent James off to tell Brother Hanham you're safe."

William began eating heartily as she left the room and heard her ascend the stairs. How delicious it was! It didn't take long to finish everything. He was setting the tray on a nearby parlor table when he heard footsteps descending the stairs. The door opened behind him.

"Hello, William."

William's heart seemed to skip a beat, and he softly caught his breath. Mary Frances! It had been six months since he had last seen her, and that was in Bath, thirteen miles to the east where she was visiting a cousin. He had been preaching in Bath at the time, and after a Church meeting, the three of them had strolled together along the city's beautiful Royal Crescent promenade on a lovely mid-summer evening. How often he had thought of that occasion, and how he had missed her since!

"Sister Ould!" he stammered as he turned toward her, careful to address her properly. I must look pitiful to her, he thought, my suit wet and wrinkled, my hair disheveled, and bare-footed. "I, ah, I didn't know you had returned. Excuse my appearance, please! It's been a long and difficult night."

"I know. Mother told me. She sent this down to wrap yourself in while we try to get your clothes dry. We mustn't let you catch cold!"

She handed William a large patchwork quilt. He took it, and shyly glanced at Mary Frances as he wondered how to ask her to step out while he disrobed, but not wanting her to go. She understood his embarrassment.

"You get out of your things while I step out. I'll hang your clothes in the kitchen where they'll dry quicker."

She left, and William took off his suit and shirt. He left his underwear on as it had already begun to dry from his body heat and would soon be completely dry wrapped as he was in the quilt. He wanted to take no chance to offend Mary Frances, and feared his wet underwear might. In a few moments she tapped lightly on the door and reentered.

"Let me have them. After I hang them, I'll come back to visit for a few minutes if you'd like."

"I'd like that very much, Sister Ould. Please come back."

"I will only if you will stop calling me 'Sister Ould.' Isn't it about time you called me Mary Frances?" She collected his clothing and left.

William sat down on the settee near the fireplace, nervously awaiting her return. She wants me to call her Mary Frances! he thought excitedly. Mary Frances was Sister Ould's older daughter whom he first met just over three years ago when he first began his missionary work in Bristol. Then 17 years old, she struck him as quiet, reserved, and just about the prettiest girl he had ever met. But he had been a missionary for only a year at the time, and so put out of his mind any further thought of developing a courtship. Besides, he thought, it was unlikely such a pretty young girl would ever have any interest in him, he was so plain and ordinary, particularly with his maimed left hand. And, nine years her senior, she would think him too old. She would surely marry one of those handsome, eligible younger missionaries from Utah long before she would even notice him.

But she hadn't. Over the years, as Sister Ould offered hospitality to the missionaries, William stayed there frequently when he was in Bristol, but he was always careful to treat Mary Frances with proper deference and courtesy. He was extra careful not to let it appear he was even remotely attracted to or interested in her as anything other than a sister in the Gospel. She seemed to respond in kind. As she matured, however, she became even more attractive to him, and he tried even harder to keep thoughts of her far from his mind, but without success.

And then they had run into one another in Bath. The service was particularly inspirational; one of the Twelve Apostles from Salt Lake City had visited, and William felt particularly good about his part on the program. It was such a lovely evening! Upbeat, inspired, and full of confidence, he invited Mary Frances and her cousin to accompany him on an evening stroll. To his surprise, they both quickly accepted, and before he knew what had happened, Mary Frances took his arm and together the three spent a delightful evening. My, how he enjoyed being close to her! And she even seemed to enjoy being with him! Although nothing was said or, as it seemed to him, even the slightest thing implied, he began to entertain just a flicker of hope that someday, if she didn't marry someone first, she might think of him as more than just a brother in the Gospel.

And now! She had asked him to call her by her first name! Even more important, she had called him William, and not Elder Jefferies, as usual! Did he dare think she cared deeply for him? Here he was, though, sitting in his underwear, wrapped in a blanket while his clothes dried—nervous, anxious, and embarrassed by his appearance, yet sweetly anticipating her return.

As she promised, Mary Frances soon returned. She entered the room quietly and sat down on the settee beside William. William's heart pounded at her intoxicating closeness, and he dare not move lest she sense his nervousness and move away. To his surprise, and to his delight, she reached over and took his hand. She spoke softly as he turned toward her.

"Forgive me, William, for being so bold. But I feel I need to take this time to visit with you now because you're always so busy with your Church responsibilities, and constantly traveling. After tonight's events, it may be another six months or more before we see one another again."

William's heart seemed to leap to his throat. After daring to hope for as much, he could now scarcely believe that Mary Frances might reciprocate his feeling. Staring straight ahead, he tried to speak.

"I, uh, I . . . ," he stammered.

"Shush, now, William," she said as she softly placed her fingers against his lips. "Let me finish while I still have the strength. I have begun to despair that you might never notice me as a woman. You are always so proper and formal with me! But we've known one another for over three years now, and you've been a guest in our home many times. Yet despite your formality, I've sensed you like me. Your eyes betray you. I've tried carefully to let you know I feel the same toward you, knowing as a missionary you must be single-minded about your work. And I thought we had broken the ice last summer in Bath, but I have heard nothing from you since. Sooner or later, William, you will have a personal life again, and surely you'll want to have a family. It's the Lord's pattern, after all. Forgive me again if I've presumed too much."

William hesitated, his mind racing as Mary Frances's words registered their meaning, yet scarcely allowing himself to accept his fondest hope about Mary Frances being real. The pause grew longer, and Mary Frances started to withdraw her hand, fearful that she had read him wrong. She began to feel embarrassment at her declaration. But William wouldn't let her hand go. Turning again toward her, William looked into her eyes.

"My dear, dear, Mary Frances! How often I've dreamed you might feel toward me as I do towards you! Since our walk in Bath I've been almost afraid to return here, fearing I might betray my feelings, to your embarrassment. Yet I return whenever I can, scarcely hoping for such a thing. I . . . I'm so unattractive, so ordinary, and an old bachelor nine years older than you. I have so little to offer! I thought surely you'd find someone more promising than me."

"Oh, you men always seem to worry about the least important things! You severely underestimate yourself, William. I find you attractive. I see in you a steadiness, a maturity, a determination to do your best, to do what is right. I admire your faithfulness, your love for the Lord and His Gospel and your dedication to its principles. But most important to me, I see a kind, gentle man who would be a kind, gentle husband and father."

William could scarcely contain his joy.

"Are you saying you would marry me?"

"Yes, William. That is what I am saying."

Excitedly, William's mind began racing through the possibilities and opportunities now beginning to open before him. Mary Frances was right. He needed to think beyond his missionary work. He had been serving, after all, almost four years. The work had been fulfilling. It had been the world to him, and brought him great joy. But perhaps it was time to move on in his life. And Mary Frances had declared her willingness to be his companion! He knew immediately it was right.

"Mary Frances, you bring me more happiness than I dared think possible. I promise you will find me an attentive husband and father, and determined to provide well for you. I will travel immediately to London and speak to President Cannon about a release from my missionary duties. Then I'll return and we'll plan our future."

They embraced tightly, holding one another until William felt a stirring in his loins. He quickly released his embrace. He would not do or even think anything improper to bring even a shadow of impropriety to their emerging closeness. Mary Frances, sensing where things could go, did the same. They sat looking at one another for a few more minutes, both a little nervous, but exhilarated and exhausted by the intensity of the last few moments. William spoke.

"It's late, Mary Frances. I need to get some sleep before I depart for London."

"Yes. Of course you do. Sleep here, before the fire where it's warm. It's almost closing time, so Father will be here soon. I'll awaken you with breakfast so you can get an early start."

William tried to settle down to sleep after Mary Frances left, but his mind was still racing over this evening's events. Is all this real? The Lord had truly blessed him, beyond what he thought he could ever deserve, and seemingly beyond his ability to comprehend. And Mary Frances was such a precious blessing! That much he knew was real. And he was deeply grateful.

William was just beginning to doze when he heard a commotion in the hallway outside the parlor. The front door slammed and he heard unsteady footfalls. Then a loud, slurred, voice.

"Damn ye, Mary. Where are you? Where are you? Fix my supper!

It was Mr. Ould, Mary Frances's father. He was drunk, stumbling down the hallway to the kitchen at the rear of the house and mumbling obscenities. William heard footfalls rapidly coming down the stairs, and a voice, Mother Ould's, as she hurried to the kitchen.

"I'm sorry, dear. I fell asleep waiting for you. Here. I'll serve your supper."

William heard the sound of a chair scraping on the floor as it was drawn up to the table. Then quiet for a few seconds. Suddenly, William heard the loud crash of crockery thrown against the wall, and Mr. Ould's loud voice again.

"Why, you old witch! That slop is cold! You know I want you down here when I come home, and I want my food hot!" A pause. "Bloody hell! Whose clothes are these? You got another of those damn missionaries here again?"

William then heard the chair clatter to the floor, and the unmistakable thump of a blow. Then another, and another, and a barely audible whimper. Then Mr. Ould's voice again.

"I've told you and I've told you! Why do you make me do this? You know better! Clean this mess up. I'm going up to bed."

Alarmed, William struggled to his feet, wrapped his blanket about him, and started for the parlor door as he heard Mr. Ould unsteadily ascend the stairs. William flung open the door only to see Mother Ould standing there with her finger to her lips, motioning for William to keep silent. The left side of her face was red, already beginning to swell. She guided him back into the parlor and closed the door.

"Forgive Mr. Ould, Elder Jefferies. When he drinks too much, he sometimes gets this way. Not often. Only when things don't go well at the mill, and he gets an early start at the Pub. I can usually control him, but not tonight. He does seem to be getting worse lately. The rumors of redundancies at the mill worry him."

"I'm very sorry for you, Sister Ould. I had no idea. Can I help with anything?"

"No. I'll be all right. Mr. Ould will soon be asleep. You need to get your sleep. Mary Frances will bring your breakfast and clothes to you before he gets up for work. Please! Get some sleep."

Sleep was elusive, however. Too much was happening in his life. First the mob at the meeting and his subsequent flight, then the joy at discovering Mary Frances's feelings for him and the prospects of marriage, finally the ensuing trauma at Mr. Ould's drunken return. Mr. Ould's behavior was a surprise. As a guest over the years, William had often heard Mr. Ould come home late at night, but he had never heard an altercation. He had even visited with him on the odd occasion when Mr. Ould returned early from the Pub. He seemed agreeable, even polite and friendly! How long had this been going on? The thought that his beloved Mary Frances and her family were subjected to Mr. Ould's abusive behavior at first angered him, then filled him with sadness that such a thing could happen to those to whom he felt so close. What could he do? He would take Mary Frances away when they married, but what of her mother, sister, and brother? Could he provide for them, too? Would they come?

William realized he had finally fallen asleep when he awakened at the sounds of Mary Frances opening the door and the rattle of a tray. He sat up. She approached, set the tray down before him, then sat down next to him and kissed him lightly on the cheek. On the tray were a pot of tea, a cup, a large slice of buttered bread, and jam.

"I'm sorry you witnessed Father's behavior last evening, William."
Her eyes were red and moist. She had been crying. "But perhaps it is for
the best you know our family secret if we are to wed. Please forgive him."
She paused, then continued, hesitantly, her head bowed. "I . . . I would
understand if you wouldn't want to marry me after this." She raised her
head and looked imploringly, anxiously, at William. "Does this change
anything for us?"

Reaching out and gathering her into an embrace, William
exclaimed. "Dear Lord, no! My love for you is deep and abiding, Mary
Frances. I have loved you almost since we first met. I truly want to take
you away from all this and make you happy! You and your entire family,
if they'd come!"

Reassured, Mary Frances lowered her head to William's shoulder
and sobbed softly for a few minutes. Then finding new resolve, she
squeezed William firmly, and arose. "Don't worry about us. We'll be fine.
Now hurry down to London and secure the release from your missionary
duties. Then we'll plan."

As he ate, she returned with his clothes and, with a parting
embrace, left him to dress and depart for London.

The train journey to London was passing quickly. Traveling by train
was much more costly than by coach, but it was much faster; he wanted
to secure his release quickly so he could take Mary Frances away from
her father's abuse. Her family, too, if they'd come. The compartment was
full, and the two young children seated opposite William were restless
and fussy. They and their parents were Dutch, on their way back to
Holland after landing at the port of Bristol, and traveling across England
by train to catch a ferry on the North Sea coast. The overhead luggage
racks were full, with wraps stuffed above the luggage and dangling irri-
tatingly before the ten passengers crowded within. It was stuffy. Rain was
splattering against the window, streaking the soot from the engine's
smoke, so the window remained closed.

Yet William was deep in thought and scarcely noticed the passage of
time. Now that he had time to reflect on the realities of his quickly
changing situation, the challenges they presented began to settle heavi-

ly upon him. Could he support a wife and family? Living as a missionary for almost four years at the beneficence of others left him nothing save his clothes and a few books. Would his father help him get started? Not likely. He resented William's joining the Church, and often told him he should be gainfully employed rather than foolishly proselyting others to join in such nonsense. William felt confident he could obtain employment again as a clerk, but where? Would it pay sufficiently to support Mary Frances's family as well? How far away from Bristol would they have to go to be free of Mr. Ould? Did Mary Frances have a dowry? Not likely, though it made no difference in William's love for her. Yet deeply concerned with these matters, he never doubted his decision to marry Mary Frances or his desire to help her family. His faith had grown strong and unwavering over the past four years. He knew the Lord had blessed him with Mary Frances's love, and had confirmed in his heart that they should marry. But the rest of her family? He knew he would do the best he could and, with faith, things would work out.

The rolling hills of Gloucester steepened as they passed through the Cotswold vales and then on to the gentler countryside of Wiltshire and Berkshire. He scarcely noticed the wait at the station in the grimy mill-town of Swindon as additional carriages were added to the train, or the longer reststop at Reading. It wasn't until the train entered the Thames valley and the outlying towns surrounding London that he began to notice his surroundings once more. How full the luggage racks were above the seat opposite! How had they kept from tumbling off? As he looked at the baggage, the germ of an idea began to penetrate William's consciousness. The more he thought about it, the stronger it became, until it seemed to penetrate his very bones! The luggage! It had come from afar, and now it was on its way to the Continent and Holland!

Travel! That was the answer to his dilemmas! They would emigrate to America, to Utah, to Zion! There, they would be free to practice their beliefs without opposition, without fearing a mob would interrupt Church meetings. There, Mary Frances and her family would be free of Mr. Ould's influence. And, was it not a land of opportunity, of prosperity, open to settlement, where a hard-working person could establish himself and his family? Thank thee dear Father, for this answer, he silently prayed.

But how would they emigrate? He had little doubt President Cannon would approve his release, particularly after he had served faithfully for so long, but would he approve and support his emigration? In the twenty-one years since the Prophet Joseph sent the first missionaries to England, thousands had emigrated. William knew many had been assisted by the Church's emigrating fund, established just over ten years ago, but would that opportunity be open to him? The fund was reserved to assist worthy emigrants too impoverished to pay their own ways to Utah, but William didn't know if he would qualify. He doubted, though, that any had been more impoverished than he. But what about Mary Frances's family? Would they qualify? There must be a way! The spirit of emigration rested too strongly on him to doubt a way would be provided if it was the Lord's will.

With these thoughts and resolves in his mind, the train pulled into Paddington Station in the early evening. The Church's European Mission headquarters were on Islington Street, not far away. He hoped fervently that President Cannon would be there. Soon, perhaps he'd have his answers. Disembarking the train with a prayer on his lips, he hurried to the street and hailed a cab for Islington.

William's timing was good. Not only was President George Cannon present, but also his two counselors, Amasa Lyman and Charles Rich. It was not often the entire Mission Presidency was together, given the far-flung geography over which they presided, and they were working late. Most of their time, separately and together, was spent ministering to missionaries and new converts spread across the United Kingdom and northern Europe. Most important to William, however, they also presided over the Church's emigration programs. William was asked to wait in the outer office while the Presidency concluded its meeting.

Thirty minutes passed before the door to President Cannon's office opened. President Cannon himself strode out the door and over to where William had just arisen from his seat.

"Elder Jefferies. Welcome."

He shook William's hand heartily, and putting his left arm around William's shoulder, guided him back toward the open door.

"Come. Join us in the office. I'm sorry you had to wait so long, but I have to take advantage of the limited time that both my counselors are in town."

As they entered, President Cannon motioned to an empty chair at the end of a rectangular table, and walked to his own chair at the opposite end. His counselors, Elders Lyman and Rich, were standing on either side of the table. Both shook William's hand before the four took their seats.

"Well, Elder Jefferies," President Cannon continued, "what brings you to London?"

"President Cannon, I've come to ask for a release from my mission. I've served four years this month, and I believe it is time to marry and begin a family."

President Cannon thought for a moment.

"Why, yes! Of course!" He paused. "You are quite right. It is time. You have served faithfully and well, Elder Jefferies. We are particularly pleased with your work presiding over the Norwich Pastorate. The Church made important strides there during your stewardship. Of course we'll release you, with our gratitude and congratulations for a mission well served. I'll prepare the letter of release before you leave."

Conversation paused while President Cannon made notes on the pad in front of him. Then Elder Rich, to William's right, asked a question.

"Elder Jefferies, have you thought what you'll do once you marry?" A pause. "Have you considered emigration?"

William's heart raced as he heard the question. *Are they reading my thoughts?*

"Why, yes. I have indeed, though I have yet to discuss the subject with my intended. In fact, I would like to take her mother, and younger sister and brother, if they agree. Is that possible?"

Again a pause, while the three leaders thought it over.

"What's their family name, and where do they live?" This question came from Elder Lyman, on William's left.

"The family name is Ould. They live in Bristol. Mary Frances, my betrothed, is the eldest of Sister Mary Ould's three children. A younger daughter, Laura, is 17 years, and a son, James, is 15 years."

"Yes! I know the family," Elder Lyman replied. "Sister Ould has been a stalwart member in Bristol for years. I've stayed in their home. So Mary Frances is your intended, eh? You're a fortunate man, Elder Jefferies. She is highly eligible. I thought for some time one of our young missionaries from Utah would find favor in her eyes. But it appears the Lord has raised her up and reserved her affections for you. Congratulations!"

"I thank you," William replied. "I truly have been blessed. But as much as I believe emigration is right for the two of us and her family, we have two problems. The first results from my four-year mission. I have not the means to send myself to Zion, let alone my future wife and her family. Second, though I believe they would be disposed to leave, Mr. Ould would not. And, I'm not at all certain Mr. Ould would allow his family to go."

The Presidency sat silent for a few moments.

"We can help with your first concern, Elder Jefferies," President Cannon interjected. "The Emigrating Fund was established to assist just such worthy members as you and your betrothed. Your faithful service to the Church more than qualifies you for assistance. Moreover, if her family conclude they want to go, your eligibility would extend to them as well, although from what I know of Sister Ould, she and her family would qualify in their own right. The way the Fund operates is this: If you can pay your ways to Florence on the Missouri River, where the Saints will gather for the onward trek to the Valley, we'll advance you credit for travel to the Salt Lake Valley. Ordinarily we would offer passage for the entire trip, but demands on our limited funds have been especially severe this year. You'll agree to repay the money to the Fund over a reasonable time as you become established to support others coming after you. Would that serve your needs?"

William was almost overcome with gratitude and humility. "Yes. Yes, it will. I am grateful to you and to the Church. I assure you, I will make good on the debt."

"I'm sure you will, Elder Jefferies," President Cannon continued. "As for your second concern, we can only advise you to exercise your faith and be patient. The Lord has a way of working things out for those who earnestly seek His assistance. If it is His will, then it will work out. I'll prepare the authorization and related correspondence and send it to Elder Blackburn at the Church emigration office in Liverpool. We've chartered two packet and one clipper ships to depart from there in April. Contact him in about three weeks to confirm the arrangements. The first emigration companies should depart mid-April. This being December, you should have adequate time to complete your Church and personal affairs before you leave."

Concluding, President Cannon stood, and the others followed suit. He walked around the table and took William's hand, shaking it firmly. "Brother Jefferies, you have our blessings, and our prayers for prosperity and happiness in a bright future. I can think of no one I'd like more to see in Zion, helping us build it up. Now if you'll wait in the outer office, I'll prepare your release papers."

Elders Lyman and Rich likewise shook William's hand, and he departed for the outer office, closing the door behind him. Tears of relief and joy came to his eyes as he contemplated how blessed he was.

William's return to Bristol the next day didn't seem to pass as quickly as his trip to London the previous day, but that didn't bother him. He basked in his happiness. After a sound night's sleep at the London missionary lodgings and a good breakfast, he felt like a new man. Even the cold, dreary continuing rain that pelted the train compartment's window did not dampen his soaring spirits. He felt a calmness, an assurance, a joy, unlike any he had ever experienced, save at his decision to join the Church four and one-half years earlier. Now, as then, he knew he was making the right decisions, and that the Lord was confirming it in his soul. What an eventful two days it had been! From time to time, William had wondered what the Lord had in mind for him after his missionary service. And he could not have planned a better or more exciting outcome himself! He had thought about emigration, but it seemed too far away a possibility to dwell much upon. But now here it was, all laid out before him, and he savored the prospects as the train journey continued.

By late afternoon the train pulled into Bristol's Temple Meads Station. The sky had cleared, and the setting sun bathed the town in gold colors. It was a good omen, William thought, and it served to further gladden his spirits. William decided against a cab, as Sister Ould's house was just a half-hour's walk. He arrived just as dusk was turning to night.

Lights were glowing in the windows of the neighboring row houses as William turned down the narrow street, but Sister Ould's house was dark. His spirits sank. Were they gone? Would he have to wait to share his good news with Mary Frances? He tapped on the door. No answer. Discouraged, he tapped again. Finally, he saw a faint light approach the door. It opened, and Mary Frances stood there holding a candle. Seeing William, her countenance brightened.

"Dear William! I was praying it was you! Come in. Quickly."

She kissed him on the cheek as he entered, and led him to the dark parlor. Entering, she used the candle to light a lamp, and motioned him to sit beside her on the settee. Something was wrong; he sensed it the minute he entered the house.

"Where are your family? Why is it dark in the house?" he asked.

Mary Frances took Williams's hands in her own. "It's Father again. Last night was even worse than the night before, when you were here. He was told yesterday he was redundant at the mill. That set him to drinking even heavier than usual. By the time he returned home, he was in a rage. He beat mother badly. When James tried to stop him, Father turned on him, too. Laura hid upstairs, and I ran to fetch the Constable. He had to arrest Father to get him calmed down. Father's still at the Station. Mother and James are upstairs, and Laura is looking after them. Oh, William, I just don't know what to do! It has been like this, off and on, since we arrived here from Cornwall. And now it's getting worse! I'm not sure we can stand much more!" She lowered her head and began to sob quietly.

William drew her close to comfort her, and rehearsed the meeting with President Cannon and his Counselors. When he finished, Mary Frances seemed to feel much better. She sat up, wiped her eyes, blew her nose, and looked at William directly. She spoke firmly.

"William, I will go with you anywhere you wish. I'm thrilled at the prospect of emigrating. But I have to ask you to consider carefully an invitation to Mother, Laura, and James to accompany us. Are you certain? Are you really certain that is what you want? Do you wish to think upon it? I cannot ask you to do it on my account alone. You must also want it yourself."

William did not need to think about it.

"I'm certain. I've thought and prayed of little else all day. I want them to come with us. I could not, in good conscience, take you away with me and leave them here to suffer continuing abuse at your father's hands. I'm also certain all three would be a great help to us as we establish a new life in Zion. I have no illusions the future will be easy for any of us. But I know it is the right thing to do, and five of us working together will accomplish much more, and more quickly, than just the two of us alone."

Mary Frances flung her arms around William, tears welling again in her eyes, but this time, tears of happiness. "I do love you so, William. I am proud and happy to become your wife. Let's go upstairs and visit with Mother, Laura, and James."

CHAPTER 2
Getting Ready

The next three months passed quickly for William, Mary Frances, and her family as they made preparations for the wedding and subsequent emigration. Mr. Ould, apparently chastened by an extended incarceration, left his family alone. He spent very few nights at home, and none of his family sought to find out where he was staying. It was just as well, for all feared that if he learned of their plans, he would certainly try to prevent his wife and two unmarried children from leaving. None thought it likely he cared if they stayed or went, but they did believe he would try to prevent them from finding the happiness he clearly could not find himself.

William needed to conclude his Church business, and therefore spent little time in Bristol. He returned to Norwich soon after Christmas to introduce Elder Elias Blackburn, his successor, to the Pastorate and assist him in getting established. The tithe accounts at each branch, his responsibility for the past year and a half, needed to be accounted for, cleared, and the proceeds forwarded to Church headquarters. Those tasks took many weeks. He had many good-byes to say, as so many had been kind and helpful to him in his service. He would truly miss those faithful brothers and sisters, many of whom had sacrificed much in the cause of the Lord and His gospel. All were happy for him in his pending marriage and emigration, and wished him well. He found it difficult to leave. He was touched by the outpouring of good wishes, particularly by an ode written to him by Sister Susan Walpole of Norwich:

And now, dear Brother, kind and true, the time is come to part;
But Oh! Before you bid adieu, accept a grateful heart
For all the counsels you have given, for every gift conferred.
I'll pray my Father you to bless, for all your labors here;
And give His Angels charge o'er you, on sea, or desert drear.
Farewell, dear Brother, yes farewell; forgive a Sister's tear.

By mid-March, William returned to Bristol. He tidied up his remaining Church business there quickly, and assisted Mary Frances and her family as best he could with preparations for leaving. Upon contacting Brother Blackburn, the Church's emigration agent in Liverpool, William was informed they would be sailing on the smaller of the two packet ships, the *Manchester*. It was smaller and slower than the other two vessels, so it would set sail first. The departure was set for Sunday, April 14th if the winds and tides were right, and they planned to depart for Liverpool on Thursday, April 11th. That would leave only two days to ensure all arrangements were in order, but they dared not leave any earlier lest Mr. Ould discover their absence and try to prevent their emigration. With the departure date set, William and Mary Frances set their wedding date for Wednesday, April 3rd, just a week prior. A week would give William and Mary Frances a little time alone before what was likely to be a long absence of privacy. As with their departure, they dared not marry sooner for fear Mr. Ould might get news of it and raise his suspicions. With arrangements complete, William determined to bid what he feared would be a difficult farewell. He would go see his family for the last time.

William's father and sisters still lived in Coleford, a village about 18 miles south. It was the village of his birth, and there he had spent a happy childhood until his tenth year when his mother took ill and died. William had written ahead to his father, telling of his plans and of his desire to bid good-bye to him and three sisters before leaving. His father replied, inviting William to visit on the Sunday just prior to his planned wedding. He had also invited his sisters to come.

William arose early on the appointed Sunday, and caught the mail coach bound for Weymouth, a port city about 75 miles south on the English Channel. The journey was bumpy and rough, despite the coach's springs, but it was a beautiful day, and he enjoyed the trip through the familiar hills and valleys greening in the spring. Despite his efforts otherwise, he found himself growing nostalgic for his youth and the simplicity of life as it seemed then. It would be difficult to leave his homeland, he reflected, and he knew he would miss the green hills, the lavender, the lilacs, the honeysuckle, the myriad wildflowers just now beginning to bloom, and the roses. Particularly the roses. Would they grow on the plains and deserts of Utah? From the descriptions of Utah given by the many missionaries coming to England, he knew it would be a much different countryside where he was going.

He had traveled about three hours when he asked the driver to stop as they reached a country lane that ran to Coleford, about three miles to the east. He was intimately familiar with these fields and farms, and with many of the families who still lived there. Yes. It would be difficult to leave. Very difficult. Only the promise of a life with Mary Frances in the new Zion, where they could practice their religion without opposition and interference, sustained his resolve. But even this was tested as he followed the road down into the valley across which Coleford lay, crossed the familiar stream he knew flowed into the river Avon about 10 miles downstream, passed the mill opposite where he had carried wheat with his father to be ground into meal, and climbed the opposing hill toward the crest. Just beyond, on the gently rolling hills, lay Goodeaves, the family farm.

As the lane wound up the hill, it passed the school where he had enjoyed four years of formal education. And there, just up the hill a little further on the right, was the Methodist Sunday School building where he attended with his mother before her death. Many fond memories flooded his mind as he passed, and he thought he might stop for a few minutes if anyone remained after the morning services. But it was deserted; being near one o'clock, services had long since finished. Finally, he reached the top, and as he followed the lane leading along the crest to the right, Goodeaves came into view.

It was a simple farm; the produce of several cows, a good garden, and from additional fields his father leased provided comfortable circumstances. The farm cottage was small, just two rooms down, and two rooms in the half-story above. A thatched roof covered the dormer windows above and the stone walls below. The door was open in the warmth of the spring midday, and he caught the scent of food being prepared. It was good, he thought, to be home.

As he approached the gate to the small garden in front, he heard his name being called.

"William! It's you at last!"

His youngest sister Ann, five years his junior, came out to greet him. William closed the gate just as Ann reached and embraced him. He was pleased at his warm reception.

"We were afraid you might not come. We would all hate it if you left without saying good-bye! Come in," she continued as she led him to the door. "We're all famished and can't wait any longer to eat."

The door lead directly into the main living room. It was furnished with a large table set for a meal, chairs lining the walls, a dish cupboard against the wall opposite the windows, and the old fireplace at the end. The fireplace still served to heat the house and to prepare the meals. His older sister Elizabeth, his sister Sarah, two years younger than William, and his father, all arose as he came in with Ann. Elizabeth and Sarah stepped forward to embrace him. As William reached his father, his father greeted him with an outstretched hand. William took it and they shook firmly.

"Good to see you again, William. I'm glad you could come."

William was pleased with his father's greeting. For his father, the greeting was warm. He and his father had not agreed on much since William left soon after his mother's death almost twenty years before. When William joined the Church, disagreements had been sharper. Indeed, for several years, they had barely been on speaking terms.

William and his father brought the chairs up as William's sisters placed the food on the table. They sat down. Before the food was passed, William spoke:

"Father, may I have the privilege of asking a blessing on the food?"

His sisters looked anxiously at one another, and then at their father, for they knew his opposition to William's religion. After a pause, his father replied:

"No. No Mormon shall ever ask the Lord to bless anything I am going to eat."

An uncomfortable pause ensued. Finally, the silence was broken by Ann. She spoke softly, her eyes misting.

"Father, this will likely be the last time we will ever sit at table as a family. Can't you soften your heart just for this occasion? Can't you look beyond your prejudice long enough for us to enjoy this short time together as a family?"

All eyes were on Father. His face reddened. He remained silent for several seconds. Finally, he addressed William.

"You may ask a blessing for the others, but please don't ask the Lord to bless what I eat."

William proceeded to do just that, being careful to mention the blessing was on behalf of Elizabeth, Sarah, Ann, and himself only. After he finished, the food was served around the table, and the awkwardness passed. Cheerfulness returned as they began to eat.

"Now, William, tell us all about Mary Frances," said Elizabeth. "She must be very special to want to marry you," she kidded.

William responded good-naturedly, and recounted meeting her for the first time, his attraction to her, his growing fondness for her from afar, and how, finally, Mary Frances was the one to make her feelings for him known first. That brought on more kidding from the sisters, and William responded in kind. He did not, however, recount Mr. Ould's abuse. For almost two hours, the meal and visiting continued with good spirits. Finally, William's father, who had been largely silent, spoke.

"William, I know I have spoken often of my displeasure with your joining the Mormons. They are a sect with which I cannot agree. More important, I cannot understand why they appeal to you! But that aside, don't you understand that even their own countrymen don't like them?

Why, just three years ago, their Government sent the army to drive them out of the territory because of their rebellion!"

As he spoke, he stood and walked to the cupboard against the wall, and opening the cabinet below, pulled out a yellowed copy of Lloyds newspaper, and handed it to William.

"See? Just like I told you!"

William took it and read the article his father indicated. It didn't take him long. He had read it before. He laid it down, and bowing his head, spoke softy to his father.

"Yes, Father. I know this. But you haven't kept the subsequent newspapers with accounts about what happened when the army arrived in Utah. They recount how the army discovered there was no rebellion, but that enemies of the Church, and there are many who feel as you do, had stirred up sentiment in the eastern United States with false reports of rebellion and disloyalty. And this after the Mormons, at great sacrifice in a crucial period of emigration west, provided a battalion of troops to fight for the United States in their war with Mexico!

William raised his head, paused, then turned to his father. He continued.

"I'll tell you why I joined the Mormon Church, Father, and why I want to emigrate. Since Mother's passing, I'd been looking for a religion that had answers. A religion that could explain to me why such sad things happen, that could explain where she was, and if she was happy or miserable! I grew weary of platitudes that we must endure misery in this life, and that peace and happiness is ours only in the next! I was seeking answers about where we came from, why we are here, and where we go when we die. I was seeking sense in all the babble of contradictory doctrine I saw in Christendom. Well, I didn't have to look far. As soon as I heard the first Mormon missionaries, I knew I had found the answers I was seeking. More important, as I prayed about it, I felt a peace of mind and spirit that I had never experienced before. The Lord bore strong and unmistakable witness to my soul that what they were teaching was true and correct! I cannot deny or turn away from this witness, Father. It is why I have spent the last four years as a missionary for the Church, why I've endured the persecution and spite I have experienced.

"The Lord bore witness to me that this is His church. That the heavens are not closed. We have a prophet to lead us today, just as in olden times! We have additional scripture to help us understand His nature, and His plan for us, His children! He teaches that we can, and should, have happiness and joy now, in this life. And most important, I'm seeking a place where I can go and practice these principles without the constant heckling, without interference by narrrow-minded bigots, and without threats. My homeland is tolerant of much diversity, but diversity of religion is still difficult. That's why I'll emigrate."

All were silent after his strong testimonial. Then, one by one, his sisters came over and embraced him, tears in their eyes, and wished him well. They understood. William had no illusions that he had convinced any of them to believe the principles to which he bore witness; that comes only through long study and prayer. But he was satisfied they understood and respected his beliefs and decisions.

William knew he had to leave. The afternoon was growing late, and he wanted to return to Mary Frances this evening, even though it would be late. But he didn't want to leave without some kind of reconciliation with his father. He still felt a deep affection for him, despite their many and long-standing differences and disagreements. It would likely be the last time they would ever be together. What could he say? What should he say?

William and his father stood on opposite sides of the room, both looking at the floor, each perhaps afraid of looking at the other and revealing his feelings. His sisters were standing together near the fireplace, likewise solemn and silent. William's father finally broke the silence. He spoke softly, still looking at the floor.

"I don't want us to part with ill feelings, William. I know we may never see one another again if you emigrate. But I don't know what to say. I can say I'm sorry we never grew close. When your mother was alive, you and she seemed so close, it didn't seem you had any time for me. And then when she passed on, things were so hard for all of us that we pretty well went our own ways. And you have always been independent, a trait I admired at first. It just didn't seem as you needed me. And the business with Mormonism. I don't think my objections were so much against it as they were against how thoroughly it took you away from the beliefs you, your mother, and I shared when you were young. It was just another broken tie between us. For all that, William, I am sorry."

Now, he looked up at William. William was looking at him with moist eyes, and his father's began to tear as well. But he continued.

"Under all this, son, I must admire the depth of your convictions and your resolve. As your father, how can I not wish you well as you truly make your own life?"

With this statement, he turned again to the cupboard. Reaching high to its top, he searched for something, and finding it, took it down. He walked over to William, and handed him a small pouch. William felt the weight of a handful of coins as it dropped into his hand. He looked from the pouch to his father's eyes in wonderment.

"I have little to offer as an inheritance or as a wedding gift. It's only fifty guineas. Your sisters will inherit the farm, but this might help you and your new wife get established in your new land. Take it with my blessings, and with my wishes for happiness and prosperity."

His father looked imploringly at William, as though he needed absolution for years of not being a better father. But William could say nothing. His emotions were too full, and tears ran down his cheeks. But he embraced his father warmly, and his father responded in kind. William's tears and embrace were the absolution they both needed.

At this same time at the Ould home in Bristol, Laura was washing up after their own Sunday meal. She usually enjoyed Sundays: the Church services, the scripture study, the warm fellowship, and the Sunday dinner after church. She especially enjoyed dinner. Dining in the afternoon, her father was always at the Pub, so it was quiet, peaceful, even gay when the traveling Elders were invited home for dinner, particularly when the younger, unmarried traveling Elders were in town. Unlike Mary Frances, Laura was not beyond flirting with the young missionaries from Utah who preached in Bristol from time to time. Indeed, she looked forward to and enjoyed such distractions! In fact, several had corresponded with her over the last year upon their return home. One young Elder in particular, Elder Thomas King of Salt Lake City, had taken to writing Laura often since his return. And it was not surprising the young Missionaries had done so; Laura had grown into a very pretty young lady by her sixteenth birthday, and she knew it. She was destined to be a heartbreaker.

Laura and Mary Frances were alike in many ways and they enjoyed a strong bond of closeness. They were deeply religious like their mother. They enjoyed many of the same pastimes, and had similar tastes in many things. Both exuded a sense of strength and determination, surprising given the nature of their family life with an abusive father. But they were also strikingly different. Laura was as outgoing and vivacious as Mary Frances was quiet and reserved. With long, blond hair, Laura's maturing beauty was immediately striking; Mary Frances's beauty grew more apparent as one grew to know her. Laura made friends easily and enjoyed many friendships; Mary Frances made friends more slowly, preferring a few close friendships. It was these differences between the two sisters that seemed to bring a sadness to Laura that Sunday after dinner. She had been uncharacteristically quiet during dinner, even though a young traveling Elder had been invited home to dine.

Mother Ould grew concerned as they finished tidying up.

"Laura, dear. Why don't you join Mary Frances in the parlor and visit with young Elder Ratcliff? It's not like you to be so reclusive."

"Oh, mother," responded Laura. "Mary Frances can entertain him just fine! After all, she's betrothed now, so it doesn't make any difference if he's impressed or not. I . . . I just don't feel like being sociable."

"Why Laura! That's so unlike you!" Mother Ould paused. "What's wrong, dear? Is it Mary Frances's wedding next week? Is it that we'll be emigrating soon?"

A longer pause. Then Mother Ould continued with a quiet, almost hesitant query.

"Is it . . . is it that we'll be leaving Father?"

"Yes. No. Oh, I don't know! Now that the time is almost here, it seems to have come so quickly! Just three months ago, I dare not hope that things would get better for us. But now that it is here, I'm frightened! I will so miss my friends! But no, I will not miss Father's rages. Him, perhaps, just a little. But Mary Frances has William to rely on, to count on, but what about me?"

"I have no doubts whatsoever that you . . . that all of us, you, me, and James, can count on William. He is that kind of person. I'm surprised you seem so uncertain. Why, look at James! He sees this as a great adventure!"

"Yes, I know. But he's still a boy. I'm finally getting men to notice me . . . to see me as a woman, not as a silly young girl!"

"Oh, I see." Mother Ould paused. "So you think there will be no eligible men in Utah? You think there will be no young men on our trek westward? What about Elder King; he writes you often, and he's in Salt Lake City!"

"Oh, Elder King! Yes, he is nice. But now that he's gone, he doesn't seem so interesting after all. Do you really think I'll meet handsome, eligible young men on our trip? Will there be interesting men in Utah? Hm . . . Perhaps I underestimated. Yes. I will join Mary Frances."

Monday and Tuesday passed quickly as the family, absent Mr. Ould, prepared for Mary Frances and William's wedding. Mother Ould had learned her husband had moved in with a widow, so the decision to exclude him was reinforced in all their minds, and any lingering remorse she had about leaving him no longer troubled her. There really weren't many arrangements to be made anyway, for it would be a quiet, private affair. All felt badly about not including extended family members and friends, particularly as they would soon be emigrating, but they wanted to take no chance that Father Ould would get wind of it and interfere. There were, nonetheless, several arrangements required as they would have two weddings.

To comply with the law of the land, they would be married in the Church of St. Phillips and Jacobs, the parish in which the Ould family resided, by the Reverend William Day, a vicar of the Church of England. Because they also desired to be married by the priesthood authority of the Mormon Church, they would be joined in marriage by a Mormon elder in a separate ceremony at the Ould's home later that evening. Elder George Halliday would perform it.

And so Mary Frances and William were wed on Wednesday, April 3, 1861, exactly as planned, without untoward incident. The church ceremony was in early morning, when few who knew the family would be about. The day was gloriously spring: bright sun, warm breezes, fragrant lilacs, and beautifully blooming iris. The ceremony was formal and stilted, but it didn't take long. Immediately afterward, the small wedding party went quickly to an inn on the opposite edge of town for a wedding breakfast: the couple, Mother Ould, Laura, James, and Elder Halliday, who had acted as father to give away the bride. There, secluded from any who might know them, they celebrated the occasion with gaiety and happiness. Their spirits were high. William and Mary Frances, shyly and somewhat awkwardly, began to enjoy their new sense of physical and emotional intimacy as husband and wife. It was heady, and exciting. They could scarcely keep their eyes and hands from one another. To pass the day, William and Mary Frances rode the train to Bath, a short trip, where they visited the ancient Roman baths, enjoyed lunch in a cozy tea room, and walked again along the same promenade where their relationship had taken a subtle, yet important turn the previous summer. It was a glorious day, and they looked forward to its crowning occasion, their marriage by an elder of their own church. Then they would feel truly married.

The ceremony was simple and brief. Young Elder Ratcliff opened with prayer, Elder Halliday gave brief introductory remarks, and then in a ceremony similar to the morning's statutory ceremony, solemnized the marriage of William and Mary Frances by the authority and power of the Holy Priesthood. Where an almost giddy happiness accompanied the morning's ceremony, the evening ceremony was accompanied by a sense of completion, of permanence, and of joy.

CHAPTER 3
On to Liverpool

As William and Mary Frances were enjoying their reminiscent stroll along Bath's Royal Crescent, Brigham Young called a meeting to order in Salt Lake City's Social Hall, some six thousand miles to the west. The building, located on First East street just a half block south of the Beehive House, Brigham's residence, was a classically English-style Georgian structure constructed of adobe that served religious, social, and civic occasions. Its main floor was a large rectangular room with a stage opposite the entrance. Though spacious, the room was full. Members of the Quorum of Twelve Apostles who were in town sat on the stage with President Young. The President sat at the center, flanked by Heber Kimball and Daniel Wells, his Counselors. Other Church general authorities and the Bishops from the territory's settlements sat crowded together on the rows of benches extending the length and breadth of the room. President Young had especially invited the Bishops, as they were the ecclesiastical and civic leaders of their Wards, the parish-like geographical areas into which the territory's settlements were divided. The crowd quieted down as President Young stood at the podium, waiting.

"Brethren, I have just received word from Elder Cannon in Liverpool that he expects over two thousand Saints to emigrate this season from Europe. Most will be from England and Wales, but a large number will also come from Sweden and Switzerland. The first sailing will be within a few weeks, with two additional sailings following soon thereafter. Upon landing in New York City, the emigrants will travel by rail and riverboat to Florence on the Missouri to outfit for the trip to the Valley. In addition, we expect upwards of one thousand more Saints to join them from the eastern states where they have been waiting for a satisfactory resolution of our late dispute with the United States. Some have waited for as long as three years. At three thousand, then, this will be the largest emigration season we have had since '56."

Nods and murmurs of agreement rippled through the gathering. President Young continued:

"We are gratified so many desire to join their faith and works with us in building up Zion. But herein lies the problem. War clouds hang heavily over the States. The Government has already begun to increase their armies and to requisition materials. I have it on good authority that even the troops at Camp Floyd are about to be recalled."

At that announcement, the room erupted in subdued cheers. Although the army had left them alone for the most part since arriving almost three years before, generally avoiding the settlements and confining their activities largely to the camp located about 35 miles south, the Saints still considered the two thousand Federal troops an occupation force. No one would miss them.

"Let us get back to the matters at hand," continued President Young. "My point is that our emigrants are likely to find a shortage of outfitting materials and supplies when they reach Florence. What they do find are likely to carry highly inflated prices and to be of dubious quality. We need to provide assistance. Our successful experiment with last season's emigration suggests how."

President Young paused while he sifted through several papers before him.

"You recall we sent a Church wagon train to the Missouri early last season to pick up indigent emigrants, and it returned the same season with no difficulty. That was a milestone for us. And, the train was a great relief for those Saints who in earlier years would have been required to travel by handcart."

Again, nods and murmurs of agreement. He continued:

"We also realized an important additional benefit. Our down-and-back trains saved the Church about half the cash we have hithertofore expended in bringing the Saints from Europe to the Valley. It costs, in cash, nearly as much for the teams, wagons, materials, and provisions required for their journey across the plains as it does to transport them from Europe to Florence. In other words, by sending everything from here at much lower cost, we avoid purchasing it there at higher cost."

"This season, we will do even better," he continued. "We expect a good portion of the three thousand Saints to form emigration companies independent of the Church. We encourage independent companies among those who are able, of course, as it allows relief from dependence upon Church resources. So, in addition to Church teams and wagons, I propose sending as many loose cattle as we expect the independent trains to require, together with such provisions as we can spare. These we will offer at prices lower than they will find elsewhere. In this manner, we market our surplus, and at the same time, save the emigrating Saints considerably higher costs. I now ask for your sustaining vote. Those who will support this plan, and are willing to help make it happen, please signify by raising your right arm to the square."

Hands all around the room raised in support.

"All those opposed may likewise signify."

No one raised a hand.

"Good. Thank you, brethren, for your support. I therefore issue a call for two hundred wagons, and four yoke of cattle for each wagon, prepared to depart for the Missouri within three weeks. That also includes teamsters for each team. These wagons will form four Church companies under command of Captain Joseph W. Young. I also call for one hundred fifty thousand pounds of flour and other staples to be deposited at four Church stations along the route. These provisions will be for sale to independent companies, and to the Church to support the indigent companies. Bishops, that means at least one wagon, team, and teamster from each Ward in the territory. More from those wards able. In return, the Church will issue tithing credits to those who participate."

"In addition, the territory is cattle-poor. We have a surplus. Encourage your Ward members with cattle to send them along for sale to the independent emigration companies. Finally, whatever space remains on the wagons after Church requirements are met may be used by the owners to contract to carry whatever freight your ward members wish to sell in the East. I plan myself to send ten wagons, teams, and teamsters, and most of my surplus cattle. Elder Kimball plans to send four. Indeed, if necessary, I will cheerfully sell all my property in exchange for teams and wagons and send them back to emigrate the poor. This is nothing more than fulfilling the covenant I made in Nauvoo, together with most of you, never to slacken until all the poor are gathered to Zion. Extend my personal blessing to each who participates for their service to the Lord and His cause, and assure them the Lord will bless them for their efforts. Brethren, that's all I have to say at the present time. If there are questions, please address them to Brother Joseph Young. We are adjourned."

As the meeting broke up and the attendees began to leave, President Wells, Commanding General of the Nauvoo Legion, stepped down from the low stage after conferring briefly with President Young and pushed his way through the departing crowd toward a figure standing unobtrusively in a corner at the rear. The figure was dressed in a dark cloak that hung below his knees against the chill of the early spring evening, and held the wide brim of a low-crowned hat before him in both hands. Long dark hair flowed to just below his shoulders and he wore a short beard flecked with gray. His alert, piercing eyes crinkled as he broke into a smile as President Wells approached, hand extended.

"Porter! Good to see you after so many months!" President Wells exclaimed as the two shook hands heartily. "Thank you for coming."

Porter Rockwell replied. "Always happy to oblige. Sounds like we got a big emigratin' season this year."

"We do, indeed. Brigham apologizes he doesn't have time to visit with you this trip, but he sent me to ask if you'd be willing to run an errand for him."

"As I say, always happy to oblige. Where's he want me to go this time?"

"We have no recent intelligence about possible depredations against our emigrants along the road from the Missouri. Last year's down-and-back trains were the first of any size in several years. We saw no sign of trouble against the Saints last year, but we were small compared to the traffic we expect this year and didn't attract much notice."

"You mean Injuns?"

"No. Not so much from them. Ever since the Harney expedition they've been quiet. No, I mean from renegades who prey on travelers. We've had reports of trouble along the Humboldt to the west, so we need information about the road between here and the States. We'll attract a lot of attention this year with more than three thousand outfitting in Florence. Will you make your way east, maybe as far as Fort Kearny, and see what you can find out?"

"Sure will. I expect with war comin' on a lot of riff-raff will take to the roads. Give me a few days to wrap things up at the Inn and I'll be on my way."

The appointed day, Thursday, April 11th, arrived quickly. But it had been a difficult week. No one experienced second thoughts about leaving, but deciding what to take and what to leave behind created many an emotional moment for the Oulds and for Mary Frances. William's instructions from the Emigration Office were quite explicit. Unless they were prepared and able to pay for excess baggage, they could take no more than one luggage trunk each, weighing no more than fifty pounds. Knowing they would be starting households in Utah with only what they could carry caused much thought about what to take and what to leave. In the end, their practicality prevailed. They would take three changes of clothes and an extra pair of shoes each, bed linens and blankets, extra fabric, basic tools, only a few of their most prized books, a few choice pieces of china and porcelain, and tinware for dining. Crockery and tableware would be left behind; it was heavy and breakable. So too would prized items of furniture, some with particularly strong family and sentimental ties for Mother Ould. But it couldn't be helped. These she gave to close friends who, she knew, would give them a good home.

The morning dawned cold and foggy. Sleep had been fitful and restless, and all were awake early. They arose and dressed in their Sunday finery for the long journey as English custom dictated. Mother Ould prepared and served a substantial breakfast, not knowing when they would have time or opportunity for the next meal, and packed the leftovers with food they would be carrying. James and William loaded the trunks on the cart engaged the previous day, and William sent James ahead to the train depot with the luggage. The others followed soon after in a cab. William had purchased the tickets several days earlier, so they went directly to the platform to await the train's arrival and William went to help James with the luggage. But James was resourceful, and already had it unloaded from the cart and stacked neatly in the baggage area. William checked the luggage with the porter, and was assured there would be no danger in it being left behind. Still, William instructed James to keep a close eye to be certain it was placed safely aboard when the train arrived. James needed no persuading. Of all the family, he was the one who seemed to have the fewest regrets about leaving, and was anxious to be a part of what he called a "grand adventure."

"William, d'you think I can ride in the baggage car with the luggage? The porter said it'd be all right long's I got a ticket."

"Why, I suppose so. Why would you want to?"

"It'll be more of an adventure than sittin' in a stuffy compartment. Besides, I want to learn what happens."

William could certainly see the advantage in having the luggage looked after so carefully, as he was sure Mother Ould would, too. William had grown very fond of James since his engagement to Mary Frances and the family's decision to emigrate. In many ways they were quite similar. Both were quiet and independent by nature, and both liked to be helpful. But even more than himself, William reflected, James took genuine pleasure in doing things well. And he was dependable and quite resourceful. There were few tasks he couldn't duplicate after watching them done once or twice, and once he agreed to do something, he would do his best to get it done. No question about it, William thought, James would be of great assistance to the family during their "grand adventure."

The train pulled into the station at 6:14 am, precisely on time, with a mighty noise and hiss of steam as the locomotive's great drive wheels slowed to a stop. It's periodic release of steam while idle added to the excitement and anticipation of departure. William stayed on the platform long enough to see James assist the loading of trunks, then joined the others in their compartment. In the excitement and confusion of imminent departure, however, William almost missed seeing Elder Halliday and Elder Hanham, his old missionary companion and friend, as they searched along the platform for William and his family. He opened the compartment door, shouted their names, and waved. Seeing him, the Elders rushed up breathlessly.

"Elder Jefferies! So glad we caught you!" exclaimed Elder Halliday as he embraced William. Elder Hanham followed suit. "We didn't want you to leave without someone here to send you off."

Mother Ould, Mary Frances, and Laura followed William on to the platform, eagerly embracing them in fond farewell.

"Thank you for coming," said Mother Ould. "With so many here sending off friends and family, I was beginning to grow a little sad we had no one. You've made an old lady feel much better!"

"We knew it would be difficult for you with no family to bid you adieu, so as representatives of your Gospel family, we have come," responded Elder Halliday. "Besides," he continued, turning to his companion, "Elder Hanham has news for you, don't you Elder?"

"Yes! Exciting news! Sister Hanham and I will be joining you in Liverpool on Saturday! Our emigration approval came through just yesterday. So, look for us. Let's try to get on the same ship, perhaps in the same emigration company when we depart Florence!"

"We'd like that very much, Edward," replied William. "It will be good to have an old friend along. We'll watch for you."

With one more quick round of embraces, they reboarded the train as the locomotive's shrill whistle signaled departure, and at

7 A.M. sharp, the train lurched forward amidst many waves from the platform as friends and family bid farewell to the passengers. Elders

Halliday and Hanham stayed on the platform until the train grew dim in the morning fog, and finally faded out of sight.

All were silent for the first two hours as the train made its way along the river Severn, each engrossed in their own thoughts as they reflected on this momentous event and the changes it would make in their lives. The train stopped first at Gloucester, then Tewkesbury, and finally Worcester, where it refueled, allowing a brief reststop. At each stop, passengers detrained and climbed on, but none joined the family in their compartment. By the time they departed Worcester, traveling across the rolling hills toward Birmingham, the fog dissipated and a bright spring sun brightened not only the green countryside, but the family's spirits as well. William finally voiced a concern he knew all shared.

"Mother Ould, do you think Father Ould will try to stop us?"

Mother Ould continued to look at the passing countryside as she tried to decide how to respond. After a long pause, she replied.

"I wish I knew. By all appearances, he'd be glad to be rid of us. Certainly his behavior over the past three months suggests he would. I've taken nothing with me that isn't mine alone, so he would have no cause to try on that account. But he's a deeply unhappy man, and carries a subdued anger at almost everything. Always has. Lord knows, I've tried to figure out why so I could help him. But he would never share any of his thoughts with me. Never. I thought for awhile the Gospel might provide some solace and understanding to him, as it has us, but he would never make the effort to study and understand it. He just seems to wallow in his unhappiness and self-pity. It's as though he needs the sadness and anger to get through the day."

Both Mary Frances and Laura nodded in agreement. It was clear Father Ould had been the subject of many discussions and commiserations between them. Mary Frances continued the conversation.

"My only fear is that he'd try to stop us because of the shame his family abandoning him would bring. That, or out of spite. I think he feels we should be as miserable as he is. Do you think he knows we've gone?"

"We've tried to be careful so's not to raise his suspicions," William replied. "Unless he comes home today and sees we've left."

"It's hard to know," said Mother Ould. "About all we can do is trust in the Lord. We know we've made the right decision. I think the Lord's confirmed that to each of us. We should be out of Father Ould's reach in a few days."

The train change in Birmingham went smoothly. James' custody of the luggage ensured it, and soon they were on their way once more, on to Liverpool just over three hours distant at the end of the line. A Latter-day Saint family of three from London, the Wards, joined them at Birmingham, together with Elder Claudius Spencer, an older missionary returning to Utah. William had met Elder Spencer during his administration of the Norwich Pastorate and was happy to see him again. The compartment was crowded, but the newcomers provided pleasant company. They, too, expected to sail on the same ship. Their enthusiasm was catching, and before long, all were caught up in the same excitement. The time passed quickly.

William smelled the sea before he saw it. The familiar scent came soon after the train departed Warrington, the last stop, and began its run alongside the river Mersey. The river gradually widened the closer they drew to Liverpool, until it became Liverpool Bay just beyond the city. Nearing the city, they first glimpsed a forest of sail masts. Getting closer, they began to make out individual ships and boats in the harbor: the large, sleek, clipper ships; the broader, tubbier passenger and cargo packet ships; the smaller barks and brigs; and finally, the barges, tugs, shuttleboats, and canal barges. They could see the docks lined with ships, barks, and brigs, with smaller vessels interspersed between them, all busily loading and unloading cargo and passengers. It seemed like hundreds more vessels were anchored in the Mersey, awaiting either a berth or the right wind and tide for departure. Tug boats were busily maneuvering the larger vessels about, taking them to their precise locations. The intense activity was at once daunting and exciting.

Just before three in the afternoon, the train pulled into Liverpool's Wapping station. The Emigration Office had booked lodgings for travelers they knew were coming, and after confirming James had unloaded the trunks, William hired a cab to transport Mary Frances, Mother Ould, and Laura to their rooms at Mr. Powel's on Great Crosshall Street. Though not a member of the Church, Mr. Powel was a friend to it, and was one of a large list of landlords whose rooms the Church routinely booked on behalf of emigrating Saints, confident they would be well treated at fair prices. The Church had learned early in its emigration experience, beginning some twenty years earlier, that the thousands of emigrants coming to Liverpool to wait for ships sailing abroad were fair game for the swindlers and scoundrels who would charge high prices for dirty, overcrowded rooming houses, or offer to carry and deliver luggage, then make off with it.

The family would stay with Mr. Powel until boarding ship. Sending the ladies on ahead, William joined James and arranged to store their luggage at the station until their departure. It was too late in the day to check in with the Emigration Office by the time the two joined the others at Mr. Powel's, so the family remained in their rooms and took a light supper. Learning Church services were scheduled nearby, they sought them out. There, for the first time, they met many emigrating Saints they would get to know well over the next six months. Upon returning to their rooms, no one objected to an early retirement. It had been a long and tiring day.

As tired as they were, however, sleep did not come easily. They occupied two upstairs rooms, William and Mary Frances in the smaller, which overlooked the busy street and the bustle of a port city that did not slacken by night; ships and boats had to be loaded and moved away from the docks to be ready to sail on the tide. The commotion, together with their own excitement, resulted in another fitful night's sleep for the family and they welcomed the dawn when it arrived. James was the first up. His inquisitiveness and curiosity had gotten the best of him; too many new and strange activities were going on about him, and he could hardly wait to get out and explore. Only his mother's insistence that he first have a bite to eat kept him from leaving at first full light, and then, only after promising to check in with her every two hours, did he leave. William's warning to watch out for the press gangs didn't slow James at all; he knew the gangs kidnaped their victims for impress sea duty outside taverns at night, and he did not intend to be anywhere near them day or night.

William was likewise anxious to get on with the day, but it was too early yet. The ladies had no such ambitions. It would be their last opportunity to shop, and they intended to use it. Each had set aside a little money for the occasion, so they prepared carefully, discussing their adventure and intended purchases. Three ladies getting ready for shopping was just too tedious for William, so he passed the time in the sitting room downstairs, studying his scriptures until breakfast was served. The ladies joined him just as breakfast began. William had to admit they looked very comely, and knowing the rigors they were likely to endure in the months ahead, he was pleased to see them happy.

Their lodgings included breakfast, and Mr. Powel intended to see they had a good one. He had hosted many emigrants as they awaited departure, and knew shipboard fare would soon become spare and tiresome. He brought tea first.

"Shall I bring you the full fare? May be one of the last English breakfasts you'll have for a long while. I've got eggs, sausage, kippers, beans, stewed tomatoes, bread, and strawberry jam. Will that do you?"

Without hesitation, all expressed delight at the menu. They may not have rested well, but their appetites did not suffer. As they ate, the ladies rehearsed their day.

"William," interjected Mother Ould, "will you look after James? We're likely to be engaged most of the day."

"Why yes. Surely. I expect to be at the Emigration Office all day, and I'll be happy to take him along. He can help. I'll wait for his return before going on."

The ladies departed after breakfast, and William continued his scripture study until James returned, flushed with excitement. He visibly deflated upon hearing the news he would be accompanying William, but perked up again at the prospects of helping out in the Emigration Office.

The Offices were nearby, right on the Waterloo Docks. James had located them in his explorations, so the two went directly there. The docks themselves, against which the waters of the Mersey and the bay beyond lapped gently, were built of cut stone and surfaced with wide paving stones. The warehouses, running the length of the docks, and likewise constructed of stone, began about fifty feet back from the edge, leaving a broad working space occupied by all manner of cargo being loaded and unloaded. A long line of large and small vessels extending the length of the docks were tied alongside. William and James wound their way amongst the stacks of cargo toward one of the warehouses. At its dock level was a large ship chandler's shop, and adjacent to it, a doorway which led to rooms above. William and James entered the doorway just after 9 A.M. As they climbed the stairs, the pungent odors of creosote, pitch, oil cloth, and hemp from the chandler's shop below combined with the harbor smells outside, and the cacophony of outside sounds began to dampen.

They entered through an open door at the top of the stairs. The Offices occupied a large room. Two clerks sat at tables at the rear of the room, and Elder Blackburn, the emigration agent, sat at a table overlooking the harbor at the front. They were busy registering emigrating Saints and collecting their fares, several of whom were queued up before each clerk. William had served with Elder Blackburn during his missionary labors, so as he and James entered, the agent stood in recognition.

"Elder Jefferies! Good to see you at last! Pleasant trip?"

Blackburn came around the table to greet William with a warm handshake.

"Yes! The trip went quite well. Got everything packed, and James here made it a personal task to ensure it all arrived safely. Ran into Elder Spencer in Birmingham on the way up. He and another emigrating family, the Wards, joined us and we had a grand visit. Looks like you're busy," William said as he looked around at the clerks and registering emigrants.

"We are. Been busy all week. The *Manchester* will be the first to sail," he said, turning and pointing out the window to the packet ship tied just down the dock.

"I expect close to four hundred will register before it weighs anchor. Today is the final registration day we sent out in the instructions. The *Manchester* will be moving out into the Mersey about noon tomorrow, so we'll be busier than ever ensuring everyone gets registered and all necessary arrangements are completed. The fare is three pounds, sixteen shillings each. Would you have time to assist? I know you've got clerking experience and would be a great help."

"I've planned on it," replied William. "James here, my brother-in-law, is available too. Just let us know what you want us to do."

"Splendid! I can use your help here in the office, Elder Jefferies. And I know a strong lad like James will be greatly appreciated aboard the *Manchester*," he said, turning to James. "Would you be willing to assist there?"

The prospect of helping out on the ship clearly pleased James. He nodded his enthusiastic agreement.

"Yes. I would."

"Good. Go aboard and ask for Elder Evans. He's supervising the luggage stowage. Tell him I sent you."

James wasted no time departing, and Blackburn instructed William in the registration procedures. After registering and paying the fare for himself and his family from the inheritance his father had so generously provided, William began assisting with the large group of Saints that soon began to arrive in increasing numbers. Some were from Sweden and Switzerland, and a large number from Wales. But Elder Blackburn had prepared; among the clerks was someone proficient in each language, so registration proceeded smoothly. William was surprised and pleased by the number of English emigrants he recognized and who came up to shake his hand. He had traveled widely during his four years as a missionary, much of the time in a presiding position. Consequently, he had come to know a large number of the Saints. And many more knew him.

William assisted with registrations until just after lunch. As they finished eating, Elder Blackburn turned to William.

"Elder Jefferies, we're caught up for now, and things will be slow until the last train arrives at three P.M. Would you be willing to help us with a few errands? I've just heard from the *Manchester's* first mate about the provisions included in the price of the charter. We'll need to supplement them if you're to have a comfortable crossing. I'll provide a list."

"If that is what you need help with the most, then I'm prepared."

"Good. The items will be easy to locate just off the docks," Elder Blackburn said as he began writing. "They're the basics. Let's start with lanterns. The ships never seem to provide sufficient lanterns, so we'll need at least a dozen more. Also sleeping tics and bedding. We instruct all emigrants to bring their own bedding, but invariably some will forget or have insufficient means to purchase it. Likewise tinware, so we'll buy more. We've already gotten sailcloth for tents and wagon sheets, but we'd better have more of that as well; might be scarce in Florence."

Elder Blackburn paused as he contemplated the list of dry goods, and handed it to William.

"I better make a list of foodstuffs, too, if you don't mind," he said, continuing. "Let's have more vegetables. Never seems to be enough. Leeks and cabbages will stay fresh the longest. Plenty of beef aboard, so we won't need more of that; you'll have your fill of bully beef before you reach New York. Perhaps a few more barrels of pork might help. And flour. Never enough flour. Or sugar. Plenty of potatoes and dried beans, so no more need of those. Oh yes. Oatmeal and rice. Better get more of both. Any provisions left over when you land at New York can be carried with you to Florence."

Midway through his task, William wished he'd kept James with him to help. Most of the goods he ordered would be delivered dock-side in the morning, but he was soon loaded with small items and quantities the vendors would not deliver, and before long found it necessary to hire a cart. Before William finished, it was full of merchandise. He took the cart straight to the *Manchester* and supervised its unloading.

By 6 P.M., he returned to the Offices. Elder Blackburn had just finished processing the last group of Saints, and suggested William join his family to prepare for boarding the next morning. Leaving the Offices,

William went aboard the ship to collect James who, it seems, had been busy all day helping stow the luggage from a steady stream of emigrants. He found James up on the quarterdeck being instructed in the art of tying knots by an old, grizzled, bearded sailor who had taken a liking to him.

The family passed the evening in their rooms with supper, scripture study, and repacking their carpetbag luggage. The ladies were proud of their last minute purchases, and insisted that William and James give their approval. The two obliged quickly and returned to their scripture study. Conversation was otherwise scarce. It would be their last night in their native land. All five were affected by a mix of sorrow at leaving behind family, friends, and familiar surroundings; feeling anxiety at the unknown ahead; excitement at the adventure; and a firm resolution they were doing the right thing.

James seemed the least sorrowful; to him it was still a grand adventure. And Laura seemed the most among the five; she was leaving the largest circle of friends. William and Mary Frances were energized by the prospect of starting life together as husband and wife, and would probably be happy going anywhere. That it was Zion only added to their confidence and happiness. Mother Ould felt truly torn. Relief at escaping an abusive husband was overshadowed by remorse and guilt that perhaps she could have done more to improve things between them, even though she knew she had tried. Nevertheless she was determined to start a new life, and the prospect that it would be where she could thrive in her worship overcame both remorse and guilt.

It was also William and Mary Frances's last night to enjoy a measure of privacy. Shipboard intimacy would likely be non-existent, and they couldn't foresee how it would be possible on the wagon trek. They would be staying in Florence for awhile before the wagon trains assembled and departed, but neither knew what kind of accommodations they could expect-tents, most likely. Indeed, true privacy had been scarce since their wedding, and both felt deprived at being unable to develop a truly satisfying intimacy. So it was William and Mary Frances who experienced the last measure of sadness as they enjoyed one last intimate tryst, not knowing when they would be able to do so again.

Afterward, as they lay closely entwined, enjoying the afterglow of their intimacy, Mary Frances spoke softly to William.

"Dearest William, are you truly pleased with our marriage? I worry I might have been too forward in approaching you about our relationship. I worry you might have felt compelled to respond favorably to me out of politeness. And I worry you might feel overwhelmed at taking my family with us. I do so hope that I . . . that we are not a disappointment and burden to you."

William turned his head and kissed Mary Frances softly and lovingly on her cheek. Tears came to his eyes.

"My dearest, you and your family mean everything to me. If only you knew how desperately I hoped you would become my wife, yet durst not even pray for it, then you would have no doubt or worries about my love for you and your family. Forgive me. Everything has happened so quickly since the wedding that I fear I have inadequately reassured you of my love and devotion. To be able to take you as my bride and partner to Zion is my fondest dream come true. Contrary to your fears, dearest, my fear is that you may find me too dull. Too old. Too . . . "

Mary Frances interrupted William's conversation by placing her fingers on his lips and whispering.

"Shush, now, dearest. You need have no fear about any of that. You know none of that means a fig to me. I do love you so. And all you need do to reassure me is tell me you truly love me, too."

"Then be assured of my deep, abiding, and unfaltering love for you, Mary Frances."

They continued in their embrace until they both drifted off to sleep, then unconsciously separated and fell more deeply asleep.

Fitful sleep the two previous nights finally caught up with the family. Exhausted by poor sleep and a grueling two days, they all slept soundly their last night on land. Even the all-night bustle of the port city did not penetrate their slumber. At dawn's first light, however, James was up and stirring. Soon, Mother Ould and Laura, with whom James shared the room and bed, were also up and bustling about. In the adjoining room, Mary Frances and William awakened at the sounds, but were just too comfortably and cozily snuggled together to venture out any sooner than absolutely necessary. They lay silently together. Then Mary Frances turned to face William.

"You know, my dear, once we go aboard and set sail, there is no turning back. I know we're doing the right thing, but aren't you the least bit afraid of what might lie ahead? Much of Zion is still an untamed wilderness, you know. There'll be savages, wild animals, and perhaps even highwaymen and outlaws. Doesn't that worry you?"

William reflected a moment before answering.

"Honestly, I haven't given it much thought. I suppose you're right. But I take comfort in knowing that thousands of Saints have emigrated over the past twenty years to establish Zion, and that Zion is beginning to thrive. And look how we're being assisted! A grand, organized movement is behind us each step of the way. But even more, I know we'll be safe and will likewise prosper because we've felt the powerful, unmistakable manifestation from the Lord Himself, that this is the right thing to do. Don't you agree?"

Mary Frances paused to reflect before she replied.

"Yes. I do. It's just that when you think of what we're doing by itself, it can be a bit frightening. But you're right, of course. And I have one more thing to be thankful for. A worthy husband, confident, capable, and courageous."

With that, she rolled over and jumped out of bed, anxious to be about their adventure. Soon after, William followed.

CHAPTER 4
Did You Ever See Such Confusion?

Completing their ablutions and dressing, the family tidied up the rooms, put the last of their belongings in the luggage, had morning prayers, and went down to breakfast. Knowing his guests would be leaving early to board their ship, Mr. Powel had breakfast ready early. As on the morning before, the family enjoyed the full-fare meal. They ate heartily, knowing it would be their last English breakfast.

William arranged for a cab the night before to take the ladies directly to the *Manchester*. Soon after breakfast, the single horse-drawn vehicle arrived. William helped the ladies step up into the enclosed interior, and assisted them arrange their skirts as the three squeezed together on the singe seat designed for two. He shut the door, handed the hand-luggage and fare up to the driver seated above the rear of the cab, and waved as they departed.

He and James then walked to nearby Wapping Station to collect their trunks. Hiring a cart to haul their baggage, the two proceeded to the docks where they quickly found themselves bogged-down in a congestion of supply wagons, provision vendors, baggage carts, ship chandlers, and other passengers, like themselves, bringing their luggage to load aboard the *Manchester*. They looked with dismay at the long line of stores, commodities, and luggage ahead of them.

"Well, James, looks like we've hurried for no reason. It'll take all day to get this stuff aboard!"

"Oh, I don't know," replied James. "It'll go quicker than it looks. See? The crew and passengers have started a line to pass things up the gangway and down into the holds. We had things pretty well organized down there yesterday. The second and third mates are down below supervising the stowage."

"Just the same, it'll be awhile. I want to check on the ladies, so if you'll keep an eye on things here, I'll come back when things start to move."

With that, William proceeded up the passenger ramp. At the top, one of the clerks he knew from the emigration office was checking passengers as they came on board. He recognized William.

"Elder Jefferies! I've checked your family in and given them your berths, but Elder Blackburn is looking for you. You'll find him aft on the quarterdeck."

William glanced in the direction the clerk pointed, to the short, elevated deck about six feet higher than the main deck and running to the ship's stern, then turned his full attention to the main deck upon which he had just stepped. It was as congested as on the docks. In a general melee, families huddled together bidding tearful farewells to family and friends. Others looked around, uncertain whether to go below or remain on deck. Children ran and scurried about, their gleeful cries adding to the din as they dodged between huddled families, piles of hand-luggage, and the stores being loaded. Seamen were busy in the rigging, and two lines of handlers, both sailors and passengers, were handing stores down hatches to the holds below, the sailors cursing the ineptitude of the passengers, and the passengers grousing about the sailors.

William wanted to find his family before he reported to Elder Blackburn, and searched with growing concern through the crowded deck when he couldn't locate them after several minutes. Had they somehow gone to the wrong ship? Finally, he spotted Mary Frances waving to him up forward, near the bow. All three women brightened in relief as they spotted William pushing through the other passengers toward them.

"Dear, oh dear!" exclaimed Mother Ould. "Did you ever see such confusion? How are we ever going to survive a month at sea so disorganized! And how will we ever find where we're supposed to go?" She handed William a slip of paper on which was written their assigned berths. He kissed Mary Frances quickly on her cheek as they greeted.

"Well, let's take a look," he said, accepting the paper. He read aloud.

"It says we're between decks, starboard side, berths eleven and twelve. That shouldn't be too hard to find. I've got to check in with Elder Blackburn, so I'll ask him."

Mary Frances grabbed William's arm and pulled him close.

"Oh no! You're not going to leave us in this confusion, are you?" she asked with concern.

William glanced at the three women and saw the anxiety registered in their expressions. He tried to reassure them.

"Just let me check in with Elder Blackburn. You ladies wait right here, and I'll return soon's I can. Then we'll find our berths. I don't expect to be gone long. You'll be fine here. James is helping with the luggage, and as soon as he finishes, he'll join you."

"Please hurry, William," pleaded Mary Frances as William turned to head aft toward the quarterdeck.

Though their worry concerned William, he knew they'd be safe. After all, if they stayed aboard, where could they get lost? The congestion and confusion is, indeed, daunting, William thought to himself as he pushed his way toward the rear of the ship. Mother Ould was right. We are terribly disorganized. How do we change that?

As he jostled through the other passengers, William saw Elder Blackburn standing on the quarterdeck with three other men wearing uniforms. He pushed through the crowd standing just below the quarterdeck, and climbed the short ladder. The quarterdeck seemed like a haven of peace in contrast to the crowded main deck from which he had just come. Other than Elder Blackburn's group and several seamen busily working at the stern end, the deck was empty of people. Seeing William approach, Elder Blackburn called out to him.

"Elder Jefferies! There you are! Will you have time to assist us?"

William approached the small group and Elder Blackburn stepped forward, taking William by the arm. As he directed him toward the others, Blackburn began introductions, starting with a short, stocky, dark-bearded man in a nautical uniform with a captain's markings.

"Elder, this is Captain Trask, Master of the *Manchester*." Motioning to the other two, he continued.

"And this is Dr. Chamberlin, ship's doctor, and Mr. Mustard of Her Majesty's Customs."

Dr. Chamberlin, a lean, spare man, wore a uniform similar to Captain Trask's, but with different markings. Mr. Mustard's uniform was more military than nautical. He was about the same height as Trask, but overweight; his uniform buttons stretched tightly across his rotund belly. William shook each's hand, in turn.

"William, Mr. Mustard and Dr. Chamberlin will be inspecting our passengers to be certain all are healthy enough to survive the crossing. Once you're underway, there'll be no turning back for ill passengers, and the only medical care will be what Dr. Chamberlin can administer. But, as you can see, we need to organize to ensure everyone is checked. Will you help? I've asked Elder Spencer to help us as well. He's crossed several times already, so he will be a great help."

"Of course," William replied. "What do you want me to do?"

"We expect President Cannon and his counselors to come aboard tomorrow and organize your ship's company, but for now, it will expedite matters if we divide the passengers into two groups according to their berth assignments, the starboard and the larboard. To which side are you and your family assigned?"

"Starboard."

"Fine. Please take charge of the starboard Saints. I'll ask Elder Spencer to line up the larboard. After the inspections, have them go below and find their berths. The berths are marked, so once they discover the side to which they are assigned, they should have little trouble. Ah! Here comes Elder Spencer now."

After introducing Elder Spencer to the officers, Elder Blackburn explained the task to him, and after the three conferred for a few minutes, William and Elder Spencer descended to the main deck and began rallying the uncertain and bewildered Saints into their respective groups. All obliged willingly, happy to see order being established. Soon, the ship's company separated into two groups, each lining their respective sides of the main deck. Once the passengers quieted, Dr. Chamberlin and Mr. Mustard began their inspections of the starboard group.

Registered in New York, the *Manchester* was a packet ship, the workhorse of the western world's merchant fleets in the mid-nineteenth century. At 1,065 tons displacement and about 170 feet long and 35 feet wide at its beam, the *Manchester* was of average size, but smaller and somewhat slower than the newer class clipper ships. Built primarily as cargo vessels, packet ships had a limited number of true passenger accommodations. The few available were staterooms located in a deckhouse toward the stern, or as on the *Manchester*, beneath the stern quarterdeck in the same area as the crew accommodations. When packet ships primarily carried passengers, their cargo space was reconfigured into steerage accommodations by converting the deck between the main deck and the cargo holds below, called the between-decks, into a large passenger area. Two-tiered bunks about five feet in length, or berths, were constructed along both sides of the deck, which ran virtually the entire length of the ship. The *Manchester* had sixty-four two-tiered bunks, or one hundred twenty-eight berths, half on each side. Three passengers could be assigned to a berth, so the ship could carry 384 passengers in reasonable comfort. For this trip, 379 passengers were manifested. On non-Church charters, it was not uncommon to crowd four passengers or more to a berth. Although uncomfortable, and sometimes miserably crowded, such crowding kept the fare for steerage passage affordable for the masses wanting to emigrate to the New World.

Down the center of the between-decks, in the space between the rows of berths, tables and benches were built. In the very center was a ladder leading to the hatch on the main deck above, protected from the elements and the seas by a small enclosure structure. The only natural light for the entire between-decks came from the main hatch when it was open, and by smaller hatches forward and aft when opened for ventilation. Lanterns otherwise provided light. On the *Manchester*, only six lanterns were provided by the ship, so the Church emigration office purchased more. At the stern was the galley, generally only a large stove.

A ship this size usually provided one cook for the passengers, but on Church charters passengers were assigned to assist. As a result, and because the Church supplemented the ship-provided provisions, the fare on Church charters was far superior to that available in non-Church steerage. At the end opposite the galley were the sanitary facilities. They were very primitive, nothing more than several large buckets shielded by pieces of canvas strung from the overhead. One side for the men; one for the women. Fastened to the outside of each berth on brackets that allowed for quick removal were metal buckets covered with a hinged lid. These served as chamber pots for occupants of the berth. The ship was also equipped with two privies on either side of the main deck for use by the passengers. These were elongated sheds built to overhang the deck, each having four holes in a bench extending directly over the water.

William felt badly about leaving James to man-handle their luggage, but knew he could handle it as James had spent the previous day assisting in the cargo hold. Indeed, when William did catch a glance of him, James had stowed their luggage and was helping with the large stacks still awaiting on the docks. Mary Frances, Mother Ould, and Laura had calmed down when the ship's company was divided, reassured by the order and by William's patient encouragement. Since William was assisting the other passengers, the ladies remained on deck until all in the starboard group had been inspected and sent below. Already, some who had gone below earlier were now returning on deck. William finally returned and escorted the ladies to the ladder, going down first to give each a hand descending, and to catch their carpetbags as they were tossed down.

"Dear me. How dreary," commented Mother Ould as she reached the deck and looked about her. "Can we survive a month down here?"

Even with the three hatches open and lanterns burning, the light was dim. Their two berths were on the right, just ahead, about a third the distance back from the forward end. As they approached, they saw a young man about 15 years old sitting on the lower berth. He looked up when William and the ladies drew close, concern showing on his face. He was no doubt worried because the occupants of the only two remaining vacant bunks on the starboard side were coming to claim their spaces.

"Are these . . . are these your berths?" he stammered uncertainly.

"Why, yes," replied William. "We have berths eleven and twelve. Where are you assigned?"

William glanced at the berths in each direction, hoping he might see one from which the young man had come.

"I have number twelve also," he said, handing his slip to William. "I'm traveling by myself. I'm sorry if I inconvenience you."

William looked at the slip. The young man was right. Number twelve. William's heart sank. With five in his family, and three passengers assigned to a berth, he knew it likely that they would have to share the space with someone. But as he assisted the other passengers on the starboard side find their berths, William had found no one else assigned to either of his two, and had begun to entertain the hope that he and Mary Frances would have a berth to themselves. But now, since a young man was assigned to them, sleeping arrangements would be awkward. James, himself, and the young man would have to sleep together. If a woman had been assigned the third space, then Mother Ould and Laura could have shared with the woman, and he, James, and Mary Frances could have shared the other berth. At least that way, he and Mary Frances could have been together.

"Not to worry," William said, unconvincingly. "We're not inconvenienced any more than anyone else," William said as he motioned to the crowded accommodations. "What's your name?"

"Franklin Blair," he replied, obviously still nervous. "I'm fifteen. I come from Sussex. My family are sending me on ahead to Zion, so's I can earn money and help them come, too." He hung his head shyly.

Mother Ould's heart went out to the boy, the same age as her James. She sat beside him and placed her arm about his shoulders.

"So young, and all alone! You're welcome to stay with us."

William was pleased that Mother Ould was so accommodating, and looking at both Mary Frances and Laura, saw they shared Mother Ould's sentiments.

"Well, Franklin Blair. You'll sleep with me and James on the upper berth. James is the same age as you."

Relief showing in his face, Franklin threw his traveling bag up to the berth above.

"Thank you! I'll try not to be a bother. And I'll be as quiet as a mouse!"

After placing their hand-luggage on their berths, the family climbed up to the main deck to enjoy the hazy, mid-spring sunlight. Most of the loading was soon complete, and Dr. Chamberlin and Mr. Mustard were just finishing inspecting the last of the larboard group. Seeing Elder Spencer walking toward the quarterdeck, William joined him, and the two climbed the ladder. Captain Trask and Elder Blackburn were standing further aft. Beyond the two, at the helm, was an officer and several seamen. The captain and Blackburn turned toward William and Elder Spencer as the two approached.

"Well done," said the captain. "We'll finish in good order for a one o'clock departure. That'll give us plenty of time to get to our anchoring station in the Mersey before nightfall."

Continuing, the captain turned to Elder Blackburn.

"I must say. You Latter-day Saints are well organized! Very orderly. What you have done in just a few hours would have taken most of a day on any other voyage with this number of steerage passengers."

"Well, Captain, we are united in faith and purpose," replied Elder Blackburn. "Those are the common ties that bind us, even though few of us have seen one another before today. You'll find those same ties will make the voyage much smoother and less tiresome for you and your officers than I'm sure you've experienced formerly."

"Yes! I see that'll likely be the case. It'll be a welcome contrast to the last lot I carried, to be sure! Never did see such an unruly, constantly bickering group of passengers. Always complaining, but never willing to do anything to help themselves. That was a miserable crossing for all. Yes, I welcome your discipline and organization. The rest of the emigration business could learn from your example. Welcome aboard. Now, if you'll excuse me, I must see to getting us ready to cast off."

Touching his cap bill in salute, the captain turned to join the group standing at the helm.

"Thank you, brethren, for your assistance," said Elder Blackburn to William and Elder Spencer. "You'll be departing soon, so I'll get off. I'd be grateful if you two will continue to preside until President Cannon arrives tomorrow. In the meantime, we've got a few more families arriving this evening, so I'll send them out as soon as we process their bookings. One family is from Bristol, Elder Jefferies. The Hanhams."

"Yes! I'm expecting them. Elder Hanham is one of my oldest friends in the Church. In fact, it was Elder Hanham who introduced me to the Gospel! He'll be a great help to us."

"Good. Say, Elder Jefferies, would you be willing to assist the passengers with any last-minute needs they discover after settling in? From what the captain says, I expect you'll be at anchorage for at least two more days before setting sail, and if past experience is a guide, quite a number will find themselves short of one thing or another. If you're willing, I'll make a boat available to you to come ashore."

"It will be my pleasure to do so," William replied. "I'll do everything I can to assist."

By noon, it appeared the *Manchester* was ready to cast off, and within a short time thereafter, a steam-powered tug-boat hoved into view, chug-chugging as black smoke poured from the stack. The crew came to life as the tug came along side, several exchanging tow-ropes with the tug and lashing them to capstans, while others climbed the rigging to secure the lashings. The last of the non-passengers left the *Manchester* and the gangway was pulled on board as the dockside mooring ropes were let go. Passengers lined both railings to witness the departure, a few small clusters waving tearful farewells at the dockside rail to family and friends along the dock who had come to see them off.

Young Franklin Blair was among them. On the dock stood his mother, father, and five younger brothers and sisters. All were in tears, Franklin included. It was a difficult time for the entire family, but the hope and prayers that the family might soon be reunited in Zion sustained and gave them encouragement.

But there were not many others on the dock. Most passengers had come from too far away to allow others to accompany them this far only to bid farewell. Leaving the first mate at the helm, the Captain went aboard the tug to supervise the *Manchester's* departure, and, with a series of toots, the tug-boat slowly and gently pulled the ship away from the dock.

William, Mary Frances, Mother Ould, Laura, and James were among the passengers lining the dockside railing. All were caught up in the excitement of departure, even if it was to an anchorage only a short distance into the Mersey. It was symbolic. They were on their way to Zion! They had left their native land! William and Mary Frances stood arm-in-arm as the ship pulled away.

"William, I'm so excited! Can you believe we've come this far in so short a time? Can you believe it's been only four months since we made the decision to marry and emigrate? Oh, I hope the voyage goes quickly! I'm so anxious to get to Zion and start our new life!"

William gave Mary Frances a squeeze, hardly able to constrain his own excitement at his fondest dreams coming true.

"We have the Lord to thank, my dearest. It's clearly His hand that has brought this all about. The way events have unfolded so quickly, I'm more certain than ever that the Lord foreordained our life together and called us to Zion."

James shared their excitement, though for him, it was still the adventure. And what an adventure it was becoming! He was thoroughly caught up in the ship's routine and the pace of activity, carefully watching everything that went on, from the coiling of the ropes as they were brought aboard, to the activities of the helmsman, the crew above in the rigging, and the hands still stowing cargo and baggage in the holds below. And Laura. She finally seemed at peace with leaving behind her friends, gratified at meeting a number of young women and men about her same age. Particularly the young men; she saw several she thought had promise.

Mother Ould alone continued to reflect mixed emotions as she watched the gap widen between the dock and the ship. Still resolute about her decisions, she couldn't shake the fear that perhaps it had all gone too easily and smoothly. She didn't think she'd feel entirely secure until they set sail and were truly on their way.

Within the hour, the *Manchester* dropped anchor, becoming one of what seemed like hundreds of ships similarly anchored in the broad Mersey. But with their departure from the docks also came the need for a shipboard routine. Almost four hundred souls were now living within a very confined space, as they would for the next four or five weeks. Perhaps longer, depending upon the winds and weather. And, most of them were now between-decks, anxious to get settled.

And there, chaos returned! First, there was the baggage. Most passengers had opted to allow their large trunks and boxes to be stowed below in the hold, keeping with them only the personal items they believed they would need during the voyage. Some, however, were loath to stow away anything they thought might be required, and, not knowing for sure what that might be, kept all their luggage with them. Consequently, the center of the between-decks was crowded with luggage, occupying most of the tables in the center and cluttering the aisles. Then there was the question of who would sleep in which berth. Family squabbles were breaking out on both sides of the between-decks, in English and in Welsh, particularly among the older children who vied with their siblings for a favorite spot. And, true to Elder Blackburn's prediction, many discovered they had brought along too little bedding to sleep comfortably on the berths' wooden planks.

Younger children, not particularly interested in where they were to sleep, and still keyed by the excitement of departure, were again running to and fro, dodging between people and luggage. Adding to the confusion was the cook in the galley, exasperated by the task of preparing a meal for so many, with no one yet assigned to assist with the cooking, trying to start the cooking fires, and looking frantically among the stacks of luggage for the provisions he had previously assembled to prepare. The resulting din and confusion brought William and Elder Spencer together to confer.

"Elder Jefferies, I think our services are needed again."

"Yes. I agree. If we don't step in, there may be more than a few altercations to settle. We may all be brothers and sisters in the Gospel, but we're stuck with our human frailties as well. You've been through this before. What do you propose we do?"

89

"First thing, we've got to get this luggage below. Without room to move about, life aboard ship will soon become intolerable. Let's give each family with luggage here thirty minutes to take out what they need. Then let's get it below. We've also got to assign cook's assistants. We'll be lucky to get one meal a day if the cook doesn't have help. Then, we've got to make specific assignments for a shipboard routine. Emptying the chamber pots and sanitary pails three times a day, washing down the tables and decks daily with lime, getting the bedding up on deck to air out daily. Besides keeping ourselves organized and tidy, the routine will help break the monotony of life confined to a ship."

"That all makes sense. Shall we take our respective sides as a start?"

"Yes. We'll organize that way. I'll get us started. This'll be just like a street-meeting!"

With that, Elder Spencer made his way to the center of the between-decks and stood on a bench to be visible above the crowd and luggage. William accompanied him.

"Brothers and Sisters!" he yelled. No response.

"Dear Brothers and Sisters!" He paused as a few quieted down.

"Please give me your attention!" This time, he hollered as loudly as he could.

Slowly, the crowd quieted down.

"Brothers and Sisters, Elder Jefferies and I are the only appointed leaders remaining on board until President Cannon arrives tomorrow to organize the ship's company. We desperately need your assistance until then. As you can clearly see, we've got much to do to restore order and get ourselves settled in, or it will be a long night. And, we'll be lucky to get a meal. Here's what we need to do."

As he spoke, several of the Welsh Saints who spoke English interpreted, as did others for the Scandinavian and Swiss Saints.

Resolutely, Elder Spencer outlined their tasks as he and William had discussed. They first organized into two messes for eating: the starboard and the larboard. The starboard mess would dine first, then the larboard. The order would reverse for the next meal. With that done,

Elder Spencer asked for two volunteers from each mess to assist the cook to prepare the evening's meal. Four Sisters volunteered with the understanding that the duty would rotate among all the families. Then instructions were given about the luggage. Though a few groaned, most applauded the instructions. When he explained about the need to service the sanitary buckets, the groans grew louder, though all accepted the necessity. Elder Spencer assumed this was a task that would not work with volunteers, so he assigned the task by berth. With thirty-two, two-tiered berths each side, the lower berth would be responsible for emptying the buckets in the morning, and the upper berth would be responsible to do the same in the afternoon. Berth number one on each side would begin, and the duty would proceed sequentially, berth by berth, during the course of the voyage. Unless the voyage lasted beyond thirty-two days, then no one would have the responsibility more than once. Individuals and families would be responsible for obtaining and disposing of their own water for daily ablutions.

With instructions given and accepted, the confusion settled down as all went about their tasks. William and Elder Spencer were pleased with the response, and within the next three hours, the between-decks was cleared of excess baggage, a meal of boiled potatoes and beef was prepared and eaten, and everyone seemed to settle down to a routine, making themselves as comfortable as possible. William and Elder Spencer assisted them as best they could.

By this time, the Saints had sorted through their luggage and, having been aboard for most of a day, were able to assess their needs. Most were short of bedding and tinware for the meals, as well as sundry other items. Anticipating this, and as Elder Blackwell had requested, William went among the Saints taking last minute orders for his trip ashore.

It was growing dark when William heard a commotion on the main deck that suggested the boat with the remaining emigrants had arrived. He went up just as the late arrivals began to come aboard. Among the last was Elder Edward Hanham, his old friend and missionary companion, and his wife, Rachel. William strode up to them as they set their bags down on the deck.

"Edward!" William exclaimed. "So pleased to see you both! Here you are, just as you said!"

William shook Edward's hand and gave Rachel a polite embrace.

"Yes. We've been very anxious to get here, especially to speak to you. Events have been unfolding that have caused us quite an anxiety. They concern you. May we speak in private?"

Puzzled, William led Edward aside where Edward spoke in subdued tones.

"About midday, after you and the family left, I was visited by a detective constable making inquiries as to you and your wife's where-abouts. Seems Mr. Ould had gotten wind of your departure with his wife and family, and claimed you had forced them to go against their will. I told them as little as I dared, but by talking to other Saints in Bristol, they pieced together that you had all come to Liverpool to emigrate. Mr. Ould seems determined to force his wife and two children to remain. The wife and I thought you ought to be warned, so we came aboard as soon as we arrived."

Alarmed, William thought quickly. What was the risk Mr. Ould and the police would get to them before they sailed?

"You think he'll come here to stop us?"

"I gathered he is very determined to stop you from what the detective and the others who had been interviewed said. All I'm sure about is that he wasn't on our train, and I believe it was the last from the south for the day."

"Mother Ould has been afraid something like this might happen from the moment we arrived. Even before. Dear Lord! Do you think he'd know to come out to the *Manchester?*"

"Couldn't say for certain, but there's only one ship in the harbor presently chartered by the Church, and that's the *Manchester.* With the police assisting him, wouldn't take him long to figure it out. And, you're on the manifest."

A flood of thought washed over William's mind as he glanced down at the deck. What were they to do? Was all their planning, their faith, hopes, and emotional turmoil to be for naught? And so close to leaving? Should they try to hide? William knew another Church charter was scheduled to sail in about a week, and they could probably get on it, but where would they hide? William began to feel panic. Dear God! What to do? He offered a silent prayer, asking for inspiration. No sooner had he done so than a calming peace came over him with a silent assurance that all would work out. It was the same assuring witness he received when he first heard the Gospel message. The same calm assurance he experienced when he knew his marriage to Mary Frances and emigration to Zion was the right thing to do. And the same witness that they should take her family with them. No. He wouldn't panic. The Lord had brought them here; He would provide a way. Calm and confident, he looked up again at Edward.

"Good friend and brother, thank you for the warning. I am grateful. But I believe we'll be all right. I'm not sure how, but we'll be all right."

CHAPTER 5
Can We Hide?

William took the Hanhams to Elder Spencer, who had also come on deck for the boat's arrival, and introduced them. Elder Spencer confirmed they were billeted on the larboard side, and offered to show them to their berth. William excused himself and went below to confer with his family, finding them busily assisting other passengers. Mother Ould was at the galley helping with the meal's clean-up. Finding James, he asked him to gather the others to join him on deck as soon as possible.

In about a quarter of an hour, they huddled as far forward on the main deck as they could to find a measure of privacy. It was now fully dark, and cool in the spring evening air. They stood together in the shadows of a lone lantern affixed to the forward mast as William relayed the news. Mother Ould covered her face with her hands and began to sob softly. Mary Frances and Laura stepped forward to comfort her, and after a few minutes, the sobs subsided as she regained her composure. She was resolute as she faced William.

"That man has cowered me for the last time. I will not return with him, nor will my children," she said as she gathered Laura and James about her. "What shall we do?"

William suggested they pray together and then discuss a course of action. He acted as voice as they drew closer.

"Dear Lord, as Thy children seeking guidance, we thank Thee for the blessing of one another, for Thy guidance in bringing us here, and for manifesting so clearly to us that we should emigrate to Zion. We

beseech Thee, dear Lord, now that we are on our way, to guide us, to protect us, and to shield us from those who would frustrate Thy plans for us
as we begin our journey. Give us the inspiration we need to respond to
this danger, we ask in Thy Son's name. Amen."

All of them experienced the same calmness as William had earlier.

"It seems to me our only real option is to remain on board and trust
in the Lord," said William. "If we try to hide ashore until the next charter, we'll just be faced with the same situation then."

"I agree," said Mary Frances. "Let's settle this now. But can't we hide
aboard, too?"

It was a fair question. If Mr. Ould came aboard and couldn't find
them, would he be satisfied? Would he think they'd gone ashore to hide?
It seemed their best hope. James spoke up.

"I think we can hide down in the hold. It's full of passenger luggage,
and lots of hiding places. I know. I've been down there. Besides, it's dark,
and difficult to move about. It would take a week to search all through
that!"

"That's a good idea," replied William. "Let me speak to Elder
Spencer and to the captain. We can each find a place ahead of time, and
one of us can always stay up here on deck to watch for Father Ould.
With a signal, we can go to ground."

They all thought that would be their best hope.

William conferred with Elder Spencer, and together they went to
the captain. William was reluctant to share their family secret with anyone, but Elder Spencer was understanding, as William knew he would
be, and he had no choice but to confide in the captain. William grew
nervous as he and Elder Spencer approached the door to the captain's
quarters at the end of a narrow, dark passageway. What if the captain
wouldn't help? Would he send William and his family ashore? The captain invited them in as Elder Spencer knocked. They entered a small,
sparsely furnished room. As with the passageway, the low overhead gave
bare clearance to their heads as they stood before the Captain seated at
a chart table occupying most of the center of the room. Along the bulkhead to their right was the bunk, a small desk was affixed to the bulk-

head aft, and cabinets lined the bulkhead to their left. Dim light came from the single lantern hung from the overhead's center, and from a smaller lamp on the chart table next to the log in which the Captain was writing. He looked at them expectantly.

"Begging the Captain's pardon," began Elder Spencer, "Elder Jefferies has a matter he'd like to discuss with you."

William briefly rehearsed the events pertaining to Mr. Ould and his family, and their present dilemma. The captain listened politely, but impassively. When William concluded, the captain paused before replying.

"You say your father-in-law believes his family is here against their will? Are they?"

"No, sir. Definitely not. To the contrary."

"Bring them to me. I want to speak to them."

William left Elder Spencer with the captain and hurried below to gather his family. Within ten minutes he was back with Mary Frances, Mother Ould, Laura, and James. As they crowded into the small room, the captain and Elder Spencer stood to accommodate the ladies. Captain Trask looked intently at the four. He spoke to Mother Ould.

"Madam, I'm told you intend to leave your husband."

"Yes. That is correct. I intend to divorce him."

"And, that you are going to take his children." He nodded at Laura and James.

"That is also correct. Except, I am not taking them. They are accompanying me with their own free will."

"Is that true?" He looked directly at Laura and James. They both nodded in unison as they replied.

"Yes."

Captain Trask looked at each of the family slowly and deliberately, as though contemplating what he might do.

"I'm satisfied that you are all here by your own volition. But I cannot prevent your husband from coming aboard if he is accompanied by the Harbor Master or the Police. While we are at anchor in the harbor, I'm still subject to local authority. However, you have my permission to hide anywhere on board you might find appropriate, and I will instruct the crew to keep their mouths shut. It will be up to you," he continued, nodding at Elder Spencer, "to instruct the passengers. But if you're found, I cannot prevent legal authorities from taking you ashore if they have the proper papers. As for me, I won't lie, but I will be non-committal. Furthermore, I will set sail on schedule. It's not likely your husband will have the influence to delay that. As it stands now, we depart Tuesday morning. I wish you luck."

The family was visibly relieved as they received the captain's decision and expressed their gratitude. Elder Spencer left with them.

"Well, Elder Jefferies. If Mr. Ould doesn't find his family aboard, do you think he'll suppose they got off to hide?"

"That's what we're praying for, Elder Spencer. That's what we're praying for."

Sleep did not come easily for any aboard the *Manchester* that night. It was well into the early morning before a semblance of quiet came over the between decks as families and individuals struggled to settle down and get as comfortable as they could on the hard wooden berths. Those with extra bedding shared with those without. A few families chose to endure the hard surface for the sake of privacy as they hung their bedding curtain-like around their berths. And, although the ship was at anchor, the gentle swells of the Mersey created enough movement to cause sea sickness among a few of the Saints, and the evening was punctuated by occasional retchings as those unfortunate souls struggled to the sanitary buckets at the forward end. Infants were fussy, and several cried fitfully throughout the night. When slumber came, it was likely interrupted by the unfamiliar sounds of shipboard life: the bells signaling watch changes every four hours, and the creaking and groaning of the ship's timbers and rigging. Neither William nor James, crowded together with Franklin on the top berth, were aware of sleeping much that night. When daylight began to show through the open main hatch, all aboard breathed a sigh of relief. At least now they could be up and about. It had truly been a long night.

Morning activity seemed to cheer everyone as the company of Saints began their first full day of life on ship. The sanitary assignments went smoothly, if not agreeably, bedding was folded, and the between-decks generally tidied. Breakfast was simple; boiled oatmeal and hot tea. It would become a tiresome staple. As the early morning fog burned away, a hazy sunshine warmed the decks and invited the passengers to the main deck and fresh air. It was Sunday, but William and Elder Spencer decided to delay services until they were joined by Elder Cannon and his counselors, Elders Rich and Lyman. They were scheduled to arrive just after noon to conduct services and organize the ship's company. Meanwhile, James was assigned the task to watch for boats approaching the *Manchester*, and give the alarm to his family if it appeared his father might be aboard.

Elder Cannon and his two counselors, accompanied by Elder Blackburn, arrived on schedule. William and Elder Spencer assembled the Saints on the main deck, while the visitors conferred with the captain and, together with him, toured the vessel. At length, they returned to the main deck. As the small group approached the stairs to the quarterdeck, Elder Cannon stopped and summoned William, Elder Spencer, and Elder Hanham. He waited for them as the rest of his party climbed the stairs.

"Brethren," he said, addressing William and Elder Spencer, "I'm grateful for your service in getting the ship's company in order. You've done a first-rate job of it. I propose calling you two, together with Elder Hanham," nodding to Edward as he spoke, "as the presidency of the ship's company for the duration of your trip to Florence. Elder Hanham, I understand you speak Welsh."

Edward replied that he did.

"Splendid. That will be very helpful as you have a large number of Welsh Saints aboard. Now, each of you has distinguished yourself as a leader in the Lord's service while you fulfilled your late missionary callings. The Lord requires your services once again. Will you accept?"

The three nodded.

"Good. I was sure you would. Elder Spencer, I'm calling you as president. Elder Hanham, you will serve as first counselor, and Elder Jefferies, second counselor. Elder Jefferies, I understand you have clerking experience."

William nodded. "Good," Elder Cannon replied. "I'd like you to keep a record of the trip, and to collect the Saints' fares to Florence. I believe it will be fifteen dollars each for adults. You'll have plenty of time to do it. When you arrive in New York, give the sums to Elder Jones, our Emigration Agent there. Will you do it?"

Again, William nodded. "I'd be honored."

"Well, then, we've settled things, haven't we? We'll ask for a sustaining vote before the company, then set you apart in your callings after the meeting. Elder Spencer, you've crossed before, so you appreciate the need for the Saints to be organized and productively engaged on the long voyage. We'll give you instructions after the meeting. Please join us on the quarterdeck."

Elder Cannon turned and mounted the stairs. The three Elders followed, joining the small group already gathered at the quarterdeck's rail before the assembled Saints below on the main deck. Elder Cannon motioned for Edward to stand next to him to interpret. The congregation grew silent as Elder Cannon paused before beginning.

"My fellow brothers and sisters in the Gospel! I congratulate and bless each of you in your decision to leave your homelands and sail to America to help build Zion. I know many of you do so at great personal and family sacrifice, and with great faith. But I promise you, in the name of the Lord Almighty, that great blessings await if you but persevere, endure, and remain faithful to your covenants. The Lord is indeed gathering His elect from the four corners of the world. You are among them."

He paused periodically to allow Edward to interpret his remarks into Welsh. Several others throughout the congregation's Scandinavian and Swiss Saints did likewise.

"Our purpose here, this afternoon, is to organize you into a ship's company, appoint the company's presiding officers, and provide instruction that will prove providential to both your emigration and to your salvation. But let us first sing a hymn of rejoicing and praise to the Lord, 'The Spirit of God, Like a Fire Is Burning'."

Elder Cannon turned to Elder Rich, who raised his arms and, timing the rhythm, began to sing. The congregation joined in singing the familiar hymn, loudly and often discordantly, but fervently. After the invocation, Elder Cannon conducted the business of presenting Elders Spencer, Hanham, and Jefferies as the company's presidency, asking for and receiving the congregation's unanimous sustaining vote. Elders Cannon, Rich, and Lyman each followed with a sermon, providing both practical instruction and spiritual guidance. In particular, they each emphasized the importance of being friendly, patient, peaceable, charitable, and tolerant to one another throughout the difficult trip ahead. After each had spoken, the congregation sang a hymn. The new ship's company presidency were then given a few minutes each to address the congregation. William's turn came last.

"Dear Brothers and Sisters, I am humbled to be able to serve you as a member of the Presidency. Like you, I am excited and hopeful about living in Zion, where we can worship without interruption and opposition. And like you, I am anxious to begin a new life with my family. But we have much to do before we reach there. We may pass through many trials and tribulations as we journey, and if we remain united in purpose and effort, helping one another, then I have no doubt we will all arrive safely. I and my family pledge our help. We will do everything we can for your convenience and comfort."

William concluded his remarks, and President Cannon again stepped forward.

"My brethren and sisters, I thank you for your patience and attentiveness during our services. Much good advice, both spiritual and temporal, has been given to you to assist you in your journey. I commend it to you. If you follow it, then I promise you a safe journey. I will now lead the prayer to dedicate this vessel for your safe journey."

Elder Cannon paused and looked slowly over the congregation. He then clasped his hands before him, and bowed his head in solemn prayer.

"Our dear Father in Heaven. Acknowledging Thy hand in all

things, and desirous of Thy merciful care and protection, we thank Thee, dear Lord, for the marvelous opportunity this Company has to join with the great number of other Saints Thou hast called from the four corners of the Earth to build up Thy Zion in the mountains of the West. We are grateful for your manifesting it so clearly to each of us that this is, indeed, what we should be doing."

As Elder Cannon spoke these words, a great feeling of spiritual reaffirmation swelled over William, almost bringing him to tears. He listened attentively as Elder Cannon continued.

"Now, dear Lord, by the authority and power of the holy priesthood vested in me as one of Thy Special Witnesses, I dedicate and consecrate this good ship, the *Manchester*, for the express purpose of carrying this righteous company of Thy Saints to their new land. To America, the land Thou hast established and set apart for the establishment of Zion and Thy kingdom on earth. I bless this ship, that she may sail true and safe, her journey sped by Thy protective hand, and that she may weather whatever hazards may befall her. I bless her crew, and especially her captain, that they may perform their duties in a manner pleasing to Thee, that they may receive a portion of Thy spirit to make wise and correct judgments and decisions. And, finally, I bless the Saints aboard her, that they will be righteous, charitable, kind, and tolerant toward one another, and that illness and injury will be rare, and such as there may be, that Thy healing Hand will mercifully attend them for a quick recovery. I pronounce these blessings in the Holy Name of Thy Son, Amen."

The congregation raised their heads, and many an eye was full of tears; clearly, many others had experienced the same spiritual reaffirmation as William. A new sense of unity seemed to come over the newly formed ship's company, and the closing hymn was sung more vigorously and enthusiastically than the others. The meeting concluded with a benediction.

As the assembly broke up and the Saints began to scatter around the deck and below decks, Elder Blackburn came up to William.

"Elder Jefferies, I understand that Elder Hanham has had a word with you about your wife's father."

William nodded. "Yes. Last evening. We believe our best chance is to remain aboard in hiding. The captain is satisfied we're all here willingly, and gave his permission. If Mr. Ould doesn't find us, we hope he'll think we've gone ashore. Then, if we sail Tuesday morning as scheduled, we need avoid him only through tomorrow."

"That seems as good a plan as any. You can very likely expect him to come out to the ship tomorrow. The local police have already made inquiries to determine if you and your family are manifested for Tuesday's sailing. Keep a good lookout."

"That's our plan. We've already chosen our hiding places. It's up to the Lord, now. We believe he'll shield us from Mr. Ould."

"You certainly have my best wishes, Elder Jefferies. You and your family."

Elder Cannon and his counselors remained aboard the rest of the afternoon and into the evening, sharing a meal and visiting with as many individual families as they could to give encouragement, advice, and a blessing. It was after nightfall when they departed. William, in the meantime, continued to take orders for his trip ashore in the morning.

The second night's routine went better than the first. By now, almost all had adjusted to the ship's movement, young children were more familiar with their surroundings, and fatigue from the previous night's sleeplessness resulted in a reasonably quiet night. At least for William, Mary Frances, and James. Mother Ould and Laura again slept fitfully, anxious about what the next day might bring.

William was up earlier than the others. This would be a busy day for him. After joining the company for morning prayer on deck, William made sure James was posted where he could see approaching boats, then checked with the others to be sure they knew where to hide if they received the signal. Without waiting for breakfast, William took the small boat Elder Blackburn had made available to him for his shopping trip, and headed ashore. Three of the crew accompanied him on the boat to attend to last-minute preparations for tomorrow's departure. With a fresh wind, the crossing took less than an hour.

William kept a close watch at approaching boats as he and his group sailed toward the docks, relieved that each vessel showed no sign of Mr. Ould. As they approached the docks, however, his fears were confirmed. There, on a small boat just departing, was Mr. Ould. Short, rotund, his familiar workman's cap pulled low to shade his eyes, he was unmistakable. Two men accompanied him, one a uniformed police constable. Although he had expected it, a visceral fear still rose in his stomach as he saw his father-in-law. William quickly ducked behind the single sail. "Dear Lord," William prayed to himself, "protect my family! I leave them in Thy care!" He quickly reviewed their preparations, satisfied they had done all they might.

The approaching boat passed within a few feet of William's.

Aboard the *Manchester*, James was watchful. In just over two hours, about a half-dozen small boats had approached closely, but all passed on to other destinations. Then he saw the small boat headed directly for the ship. As it neared, he made out the familiar form of his Father. Oh, no! There he is! Time to alert the others!

Quickly, James turned from his vantage point and hurried below decks where he knew his family would be waiting. He found his mother assisting in the galley and, quickly alerting her, hurried on to their berths where Mary Frances and Laura were just finishing breakfast.

"He's here! He's here!" James whispered loudly. "Quick! Let's get below!"

The three arrived at the cargo hold just behind Mother Ould, who had already raised the hatch and was climbing down. James was the last to descend, and left it open to allow just enough light for them to find their way. Reaching their places, each crouched, hiding deeply in the passenger luggage, silent and still, their hearts beating rapidly from exertion and fear. Soon after, someone lowered the hatch, pitching the hold into total darkness.

Up on the main deck, Mr. Ould and the two constables had just ascended the ladder from their small boat tied alongside to the small boarding platform extending from the main deck. Captain Trask, in anticipation, stood at the rail at the head of the ladder, his first mate with him. The man accompanying Mr. Ould and the uniformed constable addressed the captain.

"Captain, I'm Detective Constable Morse." Motioning toward the other two, he continued. "This is Police Constable Lewis. We're here with Mr. Ould, of Bristol, to find his family. Mr. Ould has cause to think they've been abducted by Mormons and are being forced against their will to emigrate. May we come aboard to look?"

Captain Trask looked at each closely before replying.

"What are their names?" he asked.

"Ould. His wife, Mary Ould, his younger daughter, Laura, and young son, James. They'd likely be here with his oldest daughter, Mary Frances, and her new husband, William Jefferies."

"What makes you think they're here against their will?"

"My beloved wife would never leave me willingly!" answered Mr. Ould, weasely. "Nor my children. I'm a devoted husband and father! I love them dearly!"

Captain Trask looked long again at Mr. Ould, taking his measure. He didn't like what he sensed. Not after Mrs. Ould's description of their relationship.

"If you find them aboard, what do you propose to do?"

"We intend to take them before the magistrate, and let them answer to him," replied Morse.

"And if they choose not to go?"

"We have a writ, requiring they appear," said Morse, handing a paper to the captain. Captain Trask studied it, then returned the paper to Morse.

"I won't stop you from searching, but you'll have to do it yourselves. My crew is too busy getting ready to set sail tomorrow morning. Are you certain they're aboard?"

"Why, yes!" said Mr. Ould. "They're on the manifest!"

"Well, I wouldn't rely on that alone. We often have passengers changing their minds just before we sail. Won't know absolutely for sure until the tug takes us out into the bay. Even then, the tug may bring out last-minute passengers or take ashore some deciding to leave. You may search, but I'll not delay our departure! Not even for the Royal Navy!"

Captain nodded to the first mate, who allowed the three to come aboard. They conferred, then began looking over the passengers on the main deck. Detective Morse asked a few if they'd seen Mrs. Ould and her son and daughter. In reply, all he got were shrugs. After satisfying themselves that their quarry was not on the main deck, they went below to the between decks, with Mr. Ould looking closely at each passenger they passed.

Between decks was dim, with natural light coming down the main hatch and the two ventilation hatches at either end. The few lanterns, though lit, did little to add to the light. They had to search slowly, the quarters being crowded, starting first on one side, and then the other. They took pains to look at each individual, though the two constables relied on Mr. Ould for identification. After a thorough, fruitless search, including each berth and the curtained-off sanitary facilities, the three conferred again.

"I don't know, Mr. Ould," said Detective Morse. "We've searched all the passenger areas and seen neither hide nor hair of 'em. And none of the other passengers will even admit to knowing them."

"Well, they wouldn't, would they?" replied Mr. Ould. "Damn Mormons! They all stick together. They're here somewhere. They've got to be!"

"How do you know they haven't gone ashore to wait for a later sailing?" replied Morse. "Two more Mormon charters are scheduled over the next month, you know."

"No! I know how determined Mrs. Ould is. Once she makes up her mind, nothing will change it! If she's manifested on this ship, then this is the one she'll be on!"

Detective Morse looked hard at Mr. Ould. "If she's determined, you say? Doesn't sound like someone being held against her will to me! Now what's the story here?"

"Doesn't concern you. You've got the writ. All you have to do is help me find them and get them before the magistrate! That's your duty," replied Mr. Ould, testily.

"Well, hell's fire! We've done our duty! If you wish to search more, then go ahead. Constable, let's go on deck. We'll wait for you there, Mr. Ould."

Morse and Lewis turned and walked to the ladder, curious passengers scurrying out of their ways, and climbed to the main deck. Mr. Ould looked carefully around the between-decks once more, finally returning to the ladder. As he stood there, contemplating his next move, he noticed the hatch leading down to the cargo holds. He turned to the nearest passenger.

"What's down there?" he said, pointing at the hatch.

Caught off guard, the passenger stammered.

"Why . . . why that's the luggage hold. Nothing but luggage down there."

"Luggage, you say? Well, we'll see about that!"

Mr. Ould reached down and lifted the hatch. Immediately, the four fugitives involuntarily gasped and held their breaths. Seeing it was dark below, Mr. Ould walked over to one of the masts, took the lighted lantern hanging there, and began climbing down. As he reached the bottom of the hold, he paused to allow his eyes to adjust to the dimness. The entire hold was crammed with luggage in irregular stacks, from deck to overhead, and it smelled strongly of creosote and pitch. There was a single aisle running roughly down the center of the hold, with barely enough room to squeeze between the stacks of luggage on either side. Mother Ould and Mary Frances were the closest to him, and they fought hard to still their breathing.

Holding the lantern as high as practical, Mr. Ould began forcing himself between the stacks, knocking a steamer trunk loose with his second step. As it came loose, it fell over onto Mother Ould crouching behind it. She winced in pain as it struck her bowed head, but she bit her lip to avoid crying out. Mr. Ould continued moving through the hold, climbing atop the lower stacks to look beyond, holding the lantern in that direction. He searched methodically.

When he reached the stern end, he returned to the ladder and began searching toward the bow. Laura and James were in that direction, and they hunched as small as possible as they saw the flickering lantern light approach. Laura was sure her father would hear her rapidly beating heart and discover her hiding place. But the lantern came, casting a faint glow all around her, then moved away. They had hidden well. A good hour passed when, sweating from the exertion, and apparently satisfied, he climbed up to the between-decks, closing the hatch behind him. He returned the lantern to its hook, and climbed up to the main deck. Detective Morse and Constable Lewis were standing at the rail near the landing platform.

"Did you do any better this time?" asked Morse.

"No. But I'm still certain they're here, somewhere. If you aren't inclined to help me further, then let's go ashore. I'll have another word with the magistrate."

"Suit yourself. I'll do whatever he says."

The three then departed the ship, and sailed away toward the shore.

William completed his shopping errands, loaded his purchases aboard his boat, and was returning to the *Manchester*. As coincidence had it, William had just left the dock when he saw Mr. Ould's boat approaching. He looked closely, trying to determine if his family was aboard with Mr. Ould and the detectives. Once again, he hid behind the sail as the boat passed, peering intently around the mast. No sign of Mary Frances and the family! Joy and relief flooded over him, and he silently prayed his thanks. They had made it!

Buoyed by relief, the trip to the *Manchester* passed quickly. As they reached the ship, James was waiting to give William the good news and help with the unloading.

"How are your mother and sisters!" William called out as they tied alongside.

"None the worse for wear! Only a few bruises!" James replied. He came down and began to assist William in carrying the purchases up to deck. Several other Saints climbed down to lend a hand, and soon all the cargo was up on the main deck. Mary Frances, Mother Ould, and Laura were waiting a short distance away. William walked quickly over to the group, embracing Mary Frances warmly. The joy of relief shown on all their faces.

"Well, how was it?" William asked.

"Horrid!" replied Mary Frances. "It was dark and cramped and smelly down there! Father came down by himself to search. He passed right next to me! Good thing the ship was creaking, or I'm sure he'd have heard my heart pounding!"

Mother Ould, still looking pale, nodded in agreement.

"Do you think he'll be satisfied we're not here?" asked William.

Mother Ould shook her head, slowly. "I'm just not sure. I think the detectives were satisfied, but not Father Ould. I just don't know. Let's pray he gives it up."

It was mid-afternoon, and William was distributing the goods to those who had ordered them. Mother Ould was aft in the galley helping with the evening meal. Thinking the danger was passed, James joined Mary Frances to assist William. So intent were they in their tasks, that none heard the approach of a small boat as it scraped alongside the vessel, nor the scuffle of feet climbing the boarding ladder. It was not until Mr. Ould, Detective Morse, and Constable Lewis descended the ladder to the between-decks that any of them were aware of another search. Mary Frances, standing toward the stern with William and James, saw them first. She blanched as she recognized her father.

"William!" she whispered frantically, tugging on William's shoulder. "William! It's Father again!"

William and James turned together in time to see the three men reach the deck. Laura, sitting on their berth nearer the ladder, saw them also. Fortunately, the between-decks was crowded, shielding the fugitives from immediate discovery. The three men began searching forward, giving Laura time to move behind a group of Saints standing nearby. Mother Ould still didn't see them, her back toward the direction in which they were approaching.

"William! What are we going to do?" Mary Frances moved behind William, as though seeking his protection. William looked around them, seeking somewhere they might hide. Nothing presented itself. But the crowd of Saints milling about as they prepared themselves for the meal offered hope.

"It's too late to go down into the hold. Our only recourse is to mingle in the crowd. See? Like Laura."

They watched as Laura, slowly and unobtrusively, wound her way from group to group in a direction opposite the searchers.

"We'd better separate," he whispered. "If we're together, there's no way he can miss us. Dear, you go further aft, then work your way up the side opposite from which they're looking. James and I will do the same after you're away from us. But act calmly! You don't want to stand out!"

The three separated, and tried, as casually as possible, to become first part of one group, then another. But still Mother Ould did not seem to sense her danger! She continued, her back to the three searchers, intent in her task. Slowly and deliberately, the searchers looked at each passenger as they worked their way along the starboard side toward the galley. When they reached the galley, they glanced at the galley workers, including Mother Ould, her back still toward them. But they recognized no one, and moved on. Then they began down the larboard side, toward the bow, again looking intently at each face. As they moved forward, the family members moved aft, on the opposite side, at one point passing just a few feet from the searchers. Indeed, they were so close, that the hem at the back of Mary Frances's dress came within inches of her father's legs as she faced away from him and continued her slow movement!

Time seemed to pass slowly, as Mr. Ould, Detective Morse, and Constable Lewis continued their search. After what seemed like hours to William, Mary Frances, and her family, the three came again to the ladder leading up to the main deck.

"Well, are you satisfied yet?" Detective Morse asked Mr. Ould.

Mr. Ould looked around once more in the dim light. "No! I know they're here, somewhere! There," he said, pointing down at the cargo hatch leading to the holds below. "We haven't looked down there again!" He lifted the hatch and the three peered into the darkness below.

"Good God, man!" exclaimed Morse. You want to climb through there again? Then go to it! I'm satisfied they're not aboard. I agreed to one more search at the Magistrate's insistence, but as far as I'm concerned, we've done it. Now, Mr. Ould, Constable Lewis and I are leaving! Come with us if you like, but otherwise, be prepared to spend the night here."

Reluctantly, his face flushed and angry, Mr. Ould followed the two officers as they ascended the ladder, still looking intently at the passengers below as he climbed. Finally, he was out of sight.

William, Mary Frances, Laura, and James each breathed a sigh of relief, and sat down where they were. The stress of the last hour had taken it's toll on their nerves. Mother Ould continued with her duties in the galley, seemingly unaware of their close call.

A festive mood embraced the ship's company after supper, knowing the tedium of their long, three-day wait aboard the anchored ship was soon to be over, and that tomorrow morning they would finally be on their way to Zion. The mid-spring evening was warm and pleasant, the sea breezes having died with the twilight. Most of the company was promenading on deck, and soon, the sounds of a violin playing a cheerful Welsh melody began to waft over the deck. The rhythmic sounds of a tambourine then joined in, and before long, several Welsh couples began an impromptu dance. Others soon joined in, and before long most of the company assembled on deck were either dancing or clapping in rhythm. William and Mary Frances were in the latter group, the festive mood adding to their relief at having avoided Mr. Ould. Laura and James joined the dancers. Few non-Welsh Saints knew the dance's movements, but no one cared. English, Scandinavian, and Swiss Saints joined enthusiastically, moving rhythmically with the beat. Soon even William and Mary Frances joined, losing themselves to the mood and to the music's rhythm.

Dancing continued for several hours, the rhythms gradually slowing until, pleasantly exhausted, the dancers began to drop out. But the joyful mood prevailed, and the versatile violin player switched from dance melodies to folk songs, first Welsh, then English, and on to Scandinavian and Swiss, with each group joining in turn. Finally, the mood began to grow somber as, eyes misting, each began to realize they were leaving behind, probably forever, their native lands, family, friends, and many a treasured custom. Seeming to sense this, and before melancholy could set in, the violinist changed tempo yet again and began playing "Come, Come, Ye Saints," a favorite Mormon hymn each group knew in its own language. All joined in enthusiastically.

We'll find the place which God for us prepared,

Far away, in the West,

Where none shall come to hurt or make afraid;

There the Saints will be blessed . . .

Then came "The Spirit of God, Like a Fire Is Burning," another favorite, vigorous hymn.

The Spirit of God, like a fire is burning!

The latter-day glory begins to come forth;

The visions and blessings of old are returning,

And angels are coming to visit the earth . . .

and each seemed to realize that though they were leaving behind treasured memories and traditions, they were joining together in a new heritage as they made their way to Zion, sharing in common their faith, their beliefs, and their hopes.

Porter Rockwell had been on the wagon road heading east for a week. It had taken him a little longer than he had anticipated to prepare for the trip. After his meeting with President Wells, Porter returned to his Hot Springs Inn at the far end of the Salt Lake Valley, just up the hill from the Jordan River, sited along the wagon road between the Salt Lake Valley and the Utah Lake Valley to the south. Here the river leaves the narrows between the two valleys as it flows northward to the Great Salt Lake. From the Inn's stores, Porter outfitted himself with provisions, then continued south to Lehi to visit Mary Ann and their children. He wanted to be certain they had everything they needed for the next month or so until he returned, and discovered they needed provisioning themselves.

But he was making good time. Traveling on Brown Sal, his choice mare, Porter was averaging about fifty miles a day, much better than the twenty miles typical of ox-drawn wagons and the thirty-five miles of mule-drawn freight wagons. Stopping only for short breaks during the day, and after dark in the evening to sleep, he had outdistanced the Church's down-and-back trains two days ago. Last night he overnighted at Independence Rock along the Sweetwater, and tonight he expected to make Fort Casper and its overland stage station. He was looking forward to the stop. The station was roomy, clean, and served good food; he hadn't eaten a hot meal for three days. Porter knew the stationmaster at Casper and expected a warm welcome. If the weather holds out, he thought, he'd be able to make Fort Laramie in two more days.

Traffic along the road had been light. For the last two days all he encountered were the daily eastbound and westbound stages and Pony Express riders. None of them had noticed anything unusual as they traveled, no surprise to Porter who reasoned that renegades, if there were any, would wait until the wagon trains took to the roads and look for stragglers.

Two days later in the late afternoon, Porter descended the rocky Guernsey Hills to the south bank of the swift-flowing North Platte River. He continued along the road running at the base of high bluffs for several miles, then ascended the bluffs at Mexican Hill to the plateau which would soon put him in sight of Fort Laramie. Sure enough, within thirty minutes there was the fort, stretched out in a large rectangle along Laramie Creek just upstream from its confluence with the larger North Platte River. The setting sun cast long shadows from the fort's buildings and brightly illuminated their whitewashed exteriors. It was a pretty sight for road-sore eyes!

It was too early in the year yet for the fort to be busy; at the height of the emigration season in July and August, the fort would be a beehive of activity in a sea of white wagon sheets. Now, besides the activity within the fort as soldiers returned from patrols and work details and tended to their evening chores, the only other activity was in the small Indian village of tepees along the Laramie just upstream from the fort as the squaws prepared evening meals. The smoke rising from cook fires in the barracks buildings and the Indian village hung over the settlement in a low thin layer, undisturbed in the stillness of early.

Porter was hoping he'd catch Bill Moore here. Moore was the US Marshal for the Nebraska Territory, and Porter had worked with him on occasion several years earlier tracking down fugitives from Utah Territory when Bill was Deputy Marshal. He knew Bill's information would be reliable. Porter decided he'd try to find Bill first, and then, depending on Bill's information, either return to the Valley or continue east to Fort Kearney.

Passing the fort's cemetery, he descended the low bluff, passed the sutler's trading store, and headed for the parade ground at the center of the fort's quadrangle. It was just about dark now and lamps were beginning to illuminate windows in the officer's quarters to his right as Porter headed for the headquarters building at the quadrangle's west corner. Good, he thought as he rounded the headquarters building and saw the illuminated window in a small office at the rear. Bill's in.

Porter tied Brown Sal at the hitching rail, strode to the door, and knocked.

"Come in!"

Porter opened the door and entered the small room. There, at a small desk shoved against the wall to his left, sat Bill Moore, a short, balding man with a large bushy moustache, reading glasses perched on the end of his nose as he hunched over the desk. Glancing up at Porter, Bill stood up in recognition and extended his hand.

"Porter Rockwell!" he exclaimed. "Well, I'll be danged! You're a mighty far piece from your usual huntin' grounds. What brings you clear out here? Here, sit down," he said, motioning to a small chair. "Coffee?"

"I'd be obliged," replied Porter as he removed his hat and long cloak. "Been a long ride. Sure as thunder glad I caught you in."

"Well, you only just caught me," Bill said as he filled two cups from the large pot atop the small pot-bellied stove in the opposite corner. "Headed back to Omaha in the mornin'. This here war is sure a stirrin' things up. Fightin' between the Jayhawkers and Bushwackers in Kansas is spillin' over into my territory. I got authorization to hire two more Deputies to help." He paused. "Say! You interested?"

"Nah. Got plenty of action out our way," Porter replied after he took a long sip from his cup. "But I can use your help. We're outfittin' more'n three thousand emigrants this season in Florence. Our down-and-back trains are headed this way now. I'm out doin' a little scoutin' ahead of all this to see what might be lurkin' around to cause us trouble. You seen or heard tell of anythin'?"

Moore paused as he sipped his coffee. "Let me think. Injuns have been quiet of late. Don't expect they'll cause you any trouble. Of course, you'll have the usual riff-raff headed this way along the roads, but that'll be no different than every year. Just have your folks keep an eye out for them. No, I can't think of any specific threats you might face." He paused. "Now I did hear about somethin' not long ago goin' on down in Kansas along the Santa Fe road. Marshal Donaldson is still chasin' the Weldon bunch, but lately his hands been full chasin' fugitive slaves comin' into Kansas."

Porter interrupted Bill. "Weldon, you say? Dick Weldon?"

"Why yes! You know Weldon? Here," Bill said as he rummaged through a desk drawer, pulling out a sheet of paper. "Here," he repeated as he handed it to Porter. "Got a wanted poster on him and a parcel of warrants. Some for murder."

Grimly, Porter took the poster. "That's him, sure as shootin'. Right good likeness. Me and him met up a long time ago." He paused as his mind returned to those early encounters. "Been hopin' I'd run into him again sometime."

"Well, his territory is the Santa Fe. And the army has him on the run. Knowin' these outlaws are creatures of habit, I'd be surprised if you'd see him along the Oregon road. Or your road. Hope I never see his kind in my territory. So far, thank the Lord, I haven't." He paused as he drained his cup. "You goin' to stay the night? Be obliged if you'd join me for supper. Could use the company."

THE JOURNEY
1861

CHAPTER 1
At Sea

As dawn broke, on Tuesday, April 16th, the Ship's Company was awakened by the crew's movements and cries as the crew turned-to, preparing for the tow out to the bay and setting sail thereafter. By then, their third morning aboard, routines were settling down, with house-keeping chores and duties becoming second-nature. Sanitary pails and chamber pots were emptied and cleaned, bedding was folded away, floors were cleaned, and breakfast preparations were underway. Elders Spencer, Hanham, and William, as the ship's company presidency, had further organized the Saints by appointing leaders of five smaller "wards," or branches, of about eighty members, each responsible for the spiritual and physical well-being of its members. That way, duties could rotate equi-tably and fairly among the groups. In turn, the newly appointed leaders presiding over their wards assigned each family or individual the respon-sibility to look after another.

The tug boat, chugging and billowing smoke from its lone smoke-stack, arrived at about 9 A.M. Not wishing to risk another search, Mother Ould and the others went to their cramped hiding places below once more in case Mr. Ould tried one last search. Indeed, the tug carried two fresh detectives, but not Mr. Ould. They came aboard and, as the tug towed the *Manchester* out to her departure point, searched through the ship. William was less worried this time, for without Mr. Ould aboard, how would they recognize his family? Indeed, he wasn't sure who they were searching for. In any case, they did not find their prey, whoever it was, and departed with the tug. As soon as the tug was away, William went below to free his family.

About twenty miles out into Liverpool bay the tug released the *Manchester*, and, with a flurry of activity and shouted orders as the sailors climbed into the rigging to set sail, the ship began to move slowly with the winds, setting course northwest across the Irish Sea, around the Isle of Man, and on toward the North Channel and the expanse of the Atlantic beyond. Almost the entire ship's company was out on deck, cheering as the ship began to make headway. And what a glorious day! The winds were from the southeast, the sky clear and sunny, the residual breeze warm and comfortable, the sea swells gently raising and lowering the vessel. Spirits were high as the ship and her company of Saints were finally on their way. On to America and a new life in Zion! That evening, in song and humble, yet joyful prayer, the Saints joined together in a thanksgiving worship service on the main deck.

In the Church emigration offices in New York City that same day, Elders Jacob Gates and Nathan Jones sat together discussing plans for the *Manchester's* arrival. Elder Gates was the Church's agent in charge of this season's overland emigration. He was leaving the next day for Florence to direct preparations there for the formation of wagon trains bound for the Salt Lake Valley and for the large expected influx of emigrants. Elder Jones was his representative in New York City. They had just finished lunch and were discussing the late-breaking news of South Carolina's attack on Fort Sumpter just two days earlier, the Union stronghold in Charleston's harbor. The New York Tribune, with its war headlines, was lying on the table between them.

"There's no doubt now. We'll soon be at war with the South," said Elder Gates. "It's just as the prophet Joseph prophesied almost thirty years ago. Here. I'll read what he wrote."

Elder Gates reached beneath the newspaper and picked up his copy of The Pearl of Great Price, one of the Church's standard works, and thumbed through. "Here it is. It's dated Christmas Day, 1832."

Elder Gates held out the opened book to show Elder Jones, then read: *"Verily, thus saith the Lord concerning the wars that will shortly come to pass, beginning at the rebellion of South Carolina, which will eventually terminate in the death and misery of many souls."* He paused while he read ahead silently.

"Look here," he continued. "It even says the Southern States will be divided against the Northern States, and the South will call upon Great Britain for assistance. Now that's what I call a prophecy!"

"Yes, it is!" replied Elder Jones. "Elders Snow and Pratt have been preaching to many of our Eastern Saints from the revelation to fire them up some. Seems to be having an effect, too! I've already learned many are planning to emigrate to the Valley this season to escape the ravages of war. It will swell our numbers significantly!" He paused to pick up the Tribune, read a few moments, then continued.

"And, I'm worried war may not bode well for our emigration. It says here President Lincoln has called for seventy-five thousand volunteers to restore order." He paused once more to read, then continued. "The Massachusetts volunteers are already on their way to Washington, and the secessionist Baltimoreans are vowing they won't let them through Baltimore. There's sure to be bloodshed when they arrive."

"Any news of Federal volunteers mustering here in New York?" Elder Gates asked. "Are they likely to interfere with our emigrants when the ships arrive?"

"Hard to say. I've heard New York City is trying to raise a regiment, but I don't know where they'll muster. I'll keep a close eye out."

"Please do that, Nathan. I've already made railway bookings out of Jersey City for the European emigrants. If troops are mustering, they're likely to tie up a lot of railway trains, and I may not be able to get bookings from another departure point at this late date. So we can't divert the ships. I only hope the troops don't try to preempt ours."

"I share your concern, Jacob. I'll let you know as soon as I hear anything. What about provisioning at Florence? Do you think war will interfere with that?"

"President Young thinks so. That's one reason he's sending the down-and-back teams to Florence. I've already ordered most of the provisions required for three thousand emigrants, and these should be on their way to Florence by now. I wish I knew how many Eastern Saints to expect. I do know we'll likely be short of wagons. I'm stopping in Chicago on my way to Florence to order unassembled wagons from Peter Schuttler. His works ought to be able to provide over a hundred, at least. If that's not enough, I'm not sure what we'll do."

"Well, let's hope and pray the war will wait long enough so it won't interfere with our emigration this year. With a little luck, and the Lord's help, maybe it will," replied Elder Jones. "President Lincoln says the war will be over within ninety days, so maybe we're worrying too much."

"Perhaps," said Elder Gates. "But Brother Joseph's prophecy doesn't sound like it will be a short war. I only hope we can keep our emigrants out of harm's way."

Spirits aboard the *Manchester* remained high for the next several days. Now that they were at sea a sense of excitement sustained the Saints. One could almost feel, mile-by-mile, their new land drawing closer as they sailed with fair winds astern. Aboard, routines were refined. The day would begin and end with prayer services on the main deck as weather would permit. If not, they would be held between-decks. Galley rules were translated into Welsh, Swedish, and Swiss. A social committee was established with representatives from each of the five wards to plan and conduct evening activities. Laura volunteered to serve, delighting to participate in planning the music, singing, dancing, and games to be enjoyed each evening after prayer services. A Sanitation Committee of willing sisters was established to care for Saints who might become ill. Classes were established to assist the Welsh, Swedish, and Swiss Saints learn the basics of the English language. Returning missionaries were enlisted to give instructions on traveling by wagon across the plains, and, most important, sewing-groups were established to begin making tents and covered-wagon sheets from the sail-cloth purchased in Liverpool. In sum, every effort was made to keep the Saints occupied and busy.

James had no trouble at all in finding things to do. When freed from his assigned duties, he could be seen all over the ship, observing, asking questions, and, where allowed, helping the sailors in their duties. Much to his mother's dismay, by the third day he was climbing into the rigging as he helped the crew change sails with the changing course and winds.

It was also on the third day that the *Manchester* emerged from the North Channel, which separates Ireland from Scotland, and into the Atlantic. Almost imperceptibly, the sea swells began to grow higher as the last sight of the sheltering lands faded from view astern. The change in seas was quite evident to many in the company, however, as they soon succumbed to sea-sickness. Those predisposed to the malady first began the rush to the railings and the sanitary buckets, followed thereafter by many others as the ship's rolling and pitching increased, all to the amusement of the crew who seemed unaffected by the ship's motion. Fortunately, the weather remained fair, so most of the ill were able to find a measure of relief by remaining in the fresh air on the main deck. Supper that evening was sparsely attended, and few joined in the social activities on deck.

William, Mary Frances, Mother Ould, and Laura retired early, along with the majority of the Company. All four were affected by sea-sickness to some degree, Mother Ould especially. Indeed, she was one of those unfortunate souls predisposed to motion sickness. Neither James nor Franklin seemed to be affected, however, and both were on deck for the evening social activities. Taking advantage of the boys' absence, William and Mary Frances lay together on the upper berth, but their happiness at having time to themselves was short-lived as they both began to feel queasy. They cherished the few minutes alone together, nevertheless. Too soon, James and Franklin returned, and Mary Frances joined her mother and Laura on the berth below.

Few in the company slept well that night. Just before dark, the wind strengthened and swung from the southeast to the northeast, adding to the severity of the ship's twisting movements. The Saints tried to settle down for the night, but the cries of young children and infants were joined by the groans of retching and vomiting as a majority of the ship's company succumbed to sea sickness as the ship's motions intensified through the night. At about midnight, the galley's pots and pans broke loose and tumbled to and fro with the roll of the ship, adding their clatter to the din. Those who attempted to reach the sanitary buckets up forward likewise found themselves tumbling about. Most did not manage to reach them in time. When it seemed things could not get worse between-decks, the sanitary buckets broke loose, spilling their foul contents across the deck. The ensuing stench caused the few who had not yet succumbed to sickness to finally lose the contents of their stomachs as well. Finally, in desperation, many went to the main deck, braving the cold northeast winds and sea spray to escape the stench and discomfort below. Mother Ould and Mary Frances were too sick to move, so William and Laura, sick as they were, stayed behind to try to make them as comfortable as possible.

The dawn brought little relief from the ship's motion, but those able nevertheless got themselves up, William among them, and organized work parties to clean up the fouled between-decks. They found that keeping occupied, even cleaning up the effluent on the deck seemed to stabilize their stomachs. Soon, many of the others joined in. There was no breakfast that day.

By noon the winds slackened and the *Manchester* returned to more tolerable motions. All but a few of the company were able to get up and assist with the cleanup. By mid-afternoon, the bedding was out on deck for a thorough airing, and each berth and the deck was swabbed and sprinkled with lime. Gradually, the stench went away. About a dozen remained ill and weakened, however, Mother Ould included, and Elder Spencer petitioned the Captain to allow Dr. Chamberlin to look after them. The doctor responded promptly. After examining the sick, Dr. Chamberlin conferred with Elders Spencer, Hanham, and William.

"I don't see anything serious," he reported. "If you can get them up on deck, I think they'll all feel better. Pretty difficult night, was it?"

"That's an understatement!" replied Elder Spencer.

"The first rough night at sea always is. Sometimes it's the first night after we've broken out into the Atlantic, sometimes a few days later. This time of year we get a lot of noreasters, so it's no surprise it hit us the first day out. But with a few more days sailing, most of your group will get their sea-legs and settle down. The more time you can spend on deck, the less the chance of sustained sickness. Except for a week or so when we reach Newfoundland's Banks, the temperature ought to be moderate enough to conduct most activities on deck. I recommend it."

"That's good advice," replied Elder Spencer. "We'll take it."

"But I'll be honest with you," continued the Doctor. "It will probably get worse this time of year. What we've had the last day or so has just been a good blow. It wasn't a storm. When a storm hits, you'll have to close and secure all the hatches. You may be confined below for several days! I'd suggest you make plans for that eventuality as best you can."

The three members of the Presidency looked glumly at one another, nodding their heads.

The doctor was right about adjusting to the seas. Winds continued from the northeast for the next several days, increasing and decreasing in cycles, but fewer and fewer of the company were affected by seasickness. And, the lessons of that horrible night were put to good use; more care was henceforth taken in securing items between-decks, particular the sanitary buckets. Indeed, after that night, none objected to emptying the buckets more frequently, even though it meant rotating the duty more rapidly.

Appetites soon returned, and the galley assistants again became busy as they prepared meals. Over the next week, the weather allowed daily routines to become well established, and, heeding the doctor's advice, almost all activities were conducted on deck. Up at daylight, dressing and washing; breakfast; bedding on deck for airing while the between-decks were cleaned; and, finally, all available Saints on deck for prayer services and the day's activities. Divided into groups, the company went about their respective tasks, attending lectures and participating in community duties as assigned. At noon, the company broke for lunch, most often left-overs from breakfast, with one-half the group eating while the other half rested, then reversing. After lunch, activities resumed, until time to prepare the evening meal. All those not involved experienced a welcome free time. It was during this time of day that William went about collecting the fares as directed by Elder Cannon.

Supper was then served and afterward, all available Saints gathered on deck for prayer services and social activities, which was enjoyed by everyone until lights-out at 11 P.M.

By the thirteenth day, the weather turned noticeably colder as the *Manchester* approached the Banks of Newfoundland, making it increasingly difficult to conduct activities on deck. By late afternoon the ship sailed into fog, just scattered pockets at first, but then into a thick, oppressive blanket. Visibility decreased to a few dozen yards in the fog bank. Two lookouts were set on the bow, each blowing a horn in turn every 15 minutes and listening for either an echo or the horns of another ship. Activities on deck were discontinued, and most of the company went below to escape the cold and dampness. After the evening meal, William, accompanied by Franklin and James, who knew most of the crew by now, climbed to the quarterdeck and walked aft. There, standing with the helmsman and first mate, was Captain Trask.

"Good evening to you, Elder Jefferies. Everything shipshape below?"

"Yes. At least it appears so. Many of the company are growing a little nervous about the fog. Is it dangerous?"

"Not unless we run into an iceberg or another ship," replied the captain, smiling as though he had told a joke. Then realizing this was William's and the others' first experience with fog at sea, he continued more seriously. "I meant that in jest, of course. But those are our risks! We'll have no trouble maintaining course as long as the wind continues, but we'll have to be alert to either hazard. That's why we have watches on the bow. They're experienced mariners and can tell the direction of an iceberg by its echo or of an approaching ship by its horn. As soon as it grows dark, we'll also begin ringing the ship's bell. Sometimes a bell's sharper sound can carry farther than a horn. Reassure the others you're in good hands. Besides," he continued, "I have no doubt of divine protection, given that marvelous dedicatory prayer before leaving."

William glanced quickly at the captain, trying to discern if his last statement was made mockingly. The captain's stern visage assured William that it wasn't. Captain Trask appeared to be a God-fearing man who believed in what he had just stated.

Although the ship's movement with the steady north wind was well within comfortable limits for the now seasoned ship's company, it took longer than usual to settle down for the night. The sounds of the foghorns and ringing bell kept most of the company on edge and nervous. Even the infants seemed to sense the tenseness. By early morning, the sound of rain and sleet on the hatches awakened many, but few stirred from their warm berths, especially as the temperature had dropped noticeably during the night. Soon, however, the galley crew was up and preparing breakfast, and by 6 A.M., most of the Saints were up and preparing for the day. But only the most hardy ventured up on deck; it was just too cold, windy, and wet. The day's activities were limited to those that could be conducted between-decks, and the day passed with few leaving their area.

The next two days passed much the same. The fog thinned, but the rain and sleet continued steadily, so activities continued to be confined to the crowded between-decks. But the winds remained steady from the north and northwest, and at ten knots, the *Manchester* made good time on its way to New York City. So good, in fact, the crew were already predicting a quick crossing, with odds being offered that they would reach port on May 5th, only 21 days from Liverpool. On learning of this, the company's spirits raised expectantly. Only five more days! Thank the Lord for a safe and speedy crossing! At their next meeting with Captain Trask, the presidency reflected the company's expectant enthusiasm and excitement.

"I understand twenty-one days is almost a record crossing this time of year!" Elder Spencer exclaimed as they joined the captain in his quarters, seating themselves around his chart table. "This will be a real blessing to us!"

Though cordial as always, the captain didn't reflect their enthusiasm. "Yes. Well, I'm sorry to spoil your enthusiasm, but the crew is only up to their usual rumor-mongering," he said with a slight, knowing smile. "It's mostly wishful thinking on their part. And," he continued, "we have maintained good headway. But, we'll soon sail into the southerly wind patterns. That will slow us considerably. And, we haven't hit a real squall yet! I expect at least one before we reach Sandy Hook, just off New York harbor. It's the time of year for them. I stick by my original estimate of thirty to thirty-five days."

Sobered by Captain Trask's assessment, the presidency completed their visit and returned to the between-decks. They called a special meeting of group leaders to relay the news, and it wasn't long before the whole company seemed similarly deflated.

As if on cue, the next morning brought a change in the weather pattern. William stirred awake early, well before dawn, awakened not by the ship's movement, but by its lack of motion. And the quiet. Alongside of William, James likewise lay awake; William could feel his movements.

"Notice anything, James?"

"Aye. It's too quiet. Too still. Seems like we're not moving."

"Same thing woke me. No sounds. Seems like a different ship."

Others up and down the deck were likewise stirring, though few had yet gotten up. William held his watch up to catch the faint light from the lantern hanging near their berth.

"Only three o'clock," he stated, as much to himself as to James. "Another three hours before wake-up call."

"Funny thing," replied James. "Couldn't wait until we reach land so's I could get a good nights sleep, but now I can't sleep without moving."

The two turned over and lay still, hoping to fall back asleep. William could hear Mary Frances and Mother Ould whispering below, though he was unable to make out what they were saying. He could likewise hear movement and whispers from adjoining berths. As he lay trying to sleep again, he suddenly thrust back the quilt covering them, realizing that the bone-chill of the past week had gone.

"Definitely a change in the weather," William said out loud. "About time it warmed up. Should make a lot of us happier."

William and the others dozed fitfully over the next several hours, but no one slept soundly, until the cook's assistant moved up and down the deck, awakening those assigned to mess duty. Unable to lie still any longer, William pulled on his trousers and shoes and climbed down to the deck. He leaned over the lower berth and kissed Mary Frances lightly on the forehead. She was awake.

"Just going top-side to use the necessary," whispered William, as Mary Frances reached up and caressed his cheek. "Be back shortly."

William joined several others heading toward the ladder to the main deck. It was still dark, but warm and humid as William came out on deck. Looking to the east, William saw a thin line of light spreading across the horizon, about the width of a finger held at arms length. He moved to the sanitary facilities on the port side so he could continue to observe the lightening horizon. When finished, he wandered aft, still watching, hoping to see the light broaden into a glorious sunrise. But the thin line didn't broaden. It intensified in brightness, turned a deep red for a few moments, and then turned gray to match the lightening sky. Seems to be an overcast, William observed to himself. As he looked toward the quarterdeck, he saw Captain Trask climbing down the short ladder to the main deck. The captain was making his morning inspection rounds. He saw William and came over.

"Mornin', Elder Jefferies. Did you and the others sleep well?"

"As well as could be expected, I suppose. Ship seems awfully still."

"Yes. We're becalmed," Captain Trask replied, motioning above to the slack sails. "We're between wind patterns. I expect the wind to shift southward and, judging by the overcast, we'll get rain. Soon's the wind's up, we'll tack into it as best we can. Long's the wind's not directly from the southwest, we should be able to make headway. There," he exclaimed, then paused. "You can feel the wind rising now."

Indeed, William did feel the breeze, softly at first, but then gusting briefly and fading back into softness again until the next gust came. Over the next thirty minutes the gusts grew more intense and sustained, until a south wind blew steadily and briskly. The captain sent the hands aloft into the rigging to set the sails for tacking into the wind, and the ship moved slowly in response. Sailing toward the wind, the ship tacked at an angle away from the wind's direct thrust. Soon the seas began to rise again, and the ship settled into its familiar rolling and pitching motions as the company began its daily activities. Today the company would bring all the bedding out on deck for a thorough airing.

After several hours, the ship changed its heading, crossing through the wind's direct thrusts and sailing into the wind on the opposite tack. Two hours later, the ship changed its tack again, back to the original angle. The *Manchester* continued the same pattern throughout the day. The rains came mid-afternoon, just as the captain predicted, and the Saints scrambled back down between decks, taking their bedding and sewing projects with them.

As evening settled upon the ship, the seas grew increasingly rough. Lightning flashes began to light the distant horizon, and within the hour, a roll of thunder began to reach the vessel. The ship's pitching and rolling increased, becoming so pronounced that the galley crew could not prepare the evening meal. But there were few who had an appetite, and those who did grabbed left-overs from the noon meal and retired to their berths.

The ship's movements continued to increase in severity, and few ventured from the security of their berths. Those who did were tossed to and fro across the deck, joining the pots, pans, unsecured luggage, and sundry other items. The rolling thunder and lightning was now upon the ship, continuous in its intensity.

Soon the seas grew mountainous, towering above the vessel and crashing loudly against its sides as the ship thrust upward to a peak, only to drop quickly again into a valley. As the seas increased, the ship began to ship water around its closed hatches. A seaman dressed in yellow oil-skins opened the main hatch and, struggling to close it behind him, descended the ladder in a deluge of water, tumbling with its force as he reached the deck. Horrified at the water's volume, frightened Saints exclaimed their fears about the growing storm and the safety of the ship. The seaman picked himself up and, holding on to the berths, moved down the larboard and then up the starboard sides, checking passengers and warning them to stay in their berths.

"We're headed into a heavy squall," he repeated, "and it'll be a long one. Stay where you are." In response to questions about what else they could do, he replied, "Pray. Long and hard."

The seaman climbed back up the ladder, opened the hatch, this time trying to time it between the waves steadily washing over the main deck, and closed the hatch behind him.

The Saints had experienced several squalls since setting sail from Liverpool, but this one was growing in intensity, and fear showed in their worried expressions. The rush of the sea as it moved along the ship's side grew to a roar. Suddenly it grew silent for just a moment, broken by a monstrous wave crashing loudly over the main deck above, sweeping away the hatch covering. Water cascaded down the hole. The frightened Saints grew horrified as the water continued to flood the deck, the only pauses coming as the ship recovered from its forward pitch. But then it pitched forward again, and a new deluge cascaded down the hatch. The fore and aft ventilation hatches also began to leak severely as waves continued to sweep the main deck.

All but a few of the lanterns went dark, and in the dim light the Saints could see water awash on the deck before it drained through the scuppers to the hold below, only to see the deck flood anew as another large wave crashed on board, its waters pouring below. After what seemed like an eternity, the Saints heard seamen yelling at one another as they worked to batten down a cover over the main hatch. The deluges finally stopped, but water continued to leak, keeping the between-decks awash. Then the remaining lanterns went out and the Saints were pitched into darkness, with intense, almost continuous lightning providing the only illumination.

In the darkness, everything seemed more intense. The pitching and rolling grew more violent. Each time the ship pitched forward, pausing momentarily before beginning its recovery, the Saints held their breaths. But it was the side-to-side rolling that was the most frightening. Alternating with pitching, sometimes together, the ship rolled slowly and cumbersomely, taking forever, it seemed, before beginning to right itself. Each roll seemed to be longer and steeper than the previous one. Many swore the ship's masts rolled to a true horizontal before recovering. Several times the Saints felt sure the ship would continue rolling until it was upside down. Being trapped in a capsizing ship was truly a terrifying thought.

Tossed to and fro on their berths, the passengers struggled to hold themselves steady by bracing their feet against the ship's timbers, the boards and planks of the berths, and holding on tightly to anything solid. Spectral winds whistled shrilly through the ship's shrouds and rigging, frightening in their intensity. Continuous thunder claps and lightning flashes were unnerving. Children screamed with fright. Retching and vomiting sounds came from all directions. And the continuous cacophony of pots, pans, tin-ware, luggage, storage barrels and the sanitary buckets rolling about, added to the confusion and fear. Many a prayer, both silent and audible, were offered to the Lord for deliverance from this living nightmare.

William had left James and Frederick to themselves on the upper berth when the storm grew violent, and crawled into the lower berth with Mary Frances. Wedged between violently ill Mother Ould and Mary Frances, he encircled his bride with his arms and held tight. Mary Frances sobbed softly against William's cheek.

"Dear God, I'm so frightened! How can we survive? How can we stay afloat?"

William's only response was to hold her tightly. At this point, they both knew that they, along with the rest of the ship's company, were in the hands of the Lord.

Hours passed before the storm began to abate. It seemed like an eternity. Finally, though, the crashing and roaring of the seas and winds, the pitching and rolling of the ship, and the water leaking through the hatches, began to moderate. Still, no one was inclined to leave his or her berth, despite being soaked through to their skins and lying in berths fouled with vomit or worse. But someone was about, making his way toward William, hanging on as he moved, berth-to-berth, steadying himself against the still-pronounced ship's movements.

"Elder Jefferies! I am so sorry to disturb you, but it's my wife. She is having terrible pains and is afraid she may miscarry. Is there any assistance for her?"

It was Brother Ward. William recognized his voice and knew his wife was pregnant. He thought quickly. Who could help? Mother Ould had some experience as a mid-wife, but she was in no condition to help. Leaning out of the berth to look about in the darkness, he sensed chaos and quickly concluded Sister Ward's best hope lay with Mr. Chamberlin, the ship's doctor. But how to summon him? James came quickly to mind. The boy knew the ship well, the result of his insatiable curiosity about the vessel, and knew most of the crew by name. As though reading his mind, James leaned down from the upper berth.

"Why don't I go fetch Dr. Chamberlin?" asked James. "He's offered to help. I know where his quarters are and how to get there safely. We could be back in just minutes. Besides, the storm is winding down."

William agreed, and James quickly climbed down and headed for the aft ventilator hatch. A wise thinker, that James, thought William. The aft hatch was adjacent to the crew quarters, and James was just small enough to squeeze through, exposing himself only momentarily to the heavy seas.

Just as James predicted, it was only minutes before William heard the main hatch being cleared and opened. In the faint light coming from a lantern above, James could be seen scrambling down the ladder, followed by Dr. Chamberlin carrying the lantern. James knew where the Wards were berthed, and took the doctor there directly.

James' and the doctor's arrival encouraged others to leave their berths and begin moving about the deck, and soon the lanterns were relit. And what a sight greeted the ship's company! Water-soaked clothing and bedding was strewn everywhere, together with all the myriad items rolling across the deck to which the Saints had listened throughout the storm. The galley was stripped clean; nothing remained but the large stove. William and Elders Spencer and Hanham conferred and agreed to organize work parties to clean up as soon as possible. The crew was doing the same above, and they could hear the rhythmic squeak and groan of the bilge pumps as the crew worked them to empty the accumulated water in the bilges below.

The Presidency, together, tried to comfort Brother Ward as the doctor finished attending his wife. The doctor packed his instruments. Lying next to his bag was a small cloth bundle. He glanced toward Brother Ward and shook his head.

"I did all I could, but the baby miscarried. Not sure the storm caused it, but it surely didn't help. It was a boy, six, maybe seven months along. I gave Mrs. Ward some laudanum to help her rest. She seems to be fine, but she should stay in bed for a few days." Looking at the bundle, then Elder Spencer, he asked, "Do you want to hold a service for the child?"

Elder Spencer replied yes, they would hold a service. Dr. Chamberlin then gently handed the small limp cloth to Elder Spencer and straightened up.

"Well, while I'm here, I'll check the rest of the passengers. That was quite a blow we went through, as bad as any I'd seen." The doctor turned and started checking the passengers, berth by berth.

William had just begun organizing a work-party when James approached him.

"Elder Spencer would like you to join him. Seems Sister Fulcher didn't make it."

William followed James to a lower berth at the bow end of the starboard side where Elder Spencer and Dr. Chamberlin were bent over Sister Fulcher's body. Elder Spencer stood up at William's approach.

"She passed away sometime during the storm. Sister Leggett and her daughter were so busy holding on, they didn't notice anything unusual. Only when the doctor arrived did they discover she was dead."

William sighed dejectedly. Sister Fulcher was an elderly woman of great faith who insisted on emigrating, even though of poor health. William and his family had taken a special interest in her because she was old, frail, and lonely. They had spent many an hour caring for her as their special charge and they had grown to love her.

"We'll honor both the departed in our service," Elder Spencer said. "I have no doubt the Lord is comforting both souls in His Kingdom even now, Sister Fulcher because of her exceeding faith, and Baby Ward because of his innocence."

By midday the remains of the storm passed, and as the clouds began to break, welcome sun shown through. The Saints' work parties had repaired the damage between-decks, and the ship's crew the damage to the main deck and rigging above. The winds remained brisk, but they had moved to the east and the *Manchester* made good headway at a steady six knots, no longer having to tack into the wind. The entire main deck was draped with bedding and clothing set out to dry.

The funeral service was brief. The remains of both souls had been sewn in the same shroud, and most of the ship's company, joined by the ship's officers, gathered at the leeward rail to offer their respects. Elder Spencer gave brief remarks, and William offered the prayer, dedicating the deep to the burial of Sister Fulcher and Baby Ward until the morning of the First Resurrection when both would come forth. Elder Hanham, assisted by several others, lowered the shroud to the water where it caught in the ship's wake, bobbing briefly as it moved astern before sinking out of sight. These were the first deaths experienced since the Saints left Liverpool, and all seemed sobered by the thought that life was, after all, so frail. All lingered, looking astern even though the shroud had long since disappeared from view.

As the gathering broke up, Captain Trask turned to Elder Spencer. William stood near.

"My profound regret at your losses. It's a rare crossing when we don't experience one or two deaths. How have the others come through?"

"A few bruises and bumps, but I don't think anything more serious," replied Elder Spencer. "And we've still got a handful who just can't seem to get over their sea-sickness. Nor have they been able to adjust to the galley food. I'm afraid they're wasting away."

"Yes, that's a familiar pattern. The less they eat, the harder it is to recover. You have just a few, you say? Why don't you move them up to the officers' quarters for a few days. Perhaps they'll fare better if they eat from my mess. I'll send the first mate down to assist."

"That's most kind and solicitous of you, Captain Trask," responded Elder Spencer. "We're grateful for your help. How did the storm affect our progress toward New York?"

"I'm afraid it set us back some. I reckon we're about 50 miles further from New York now than before the storm. So we've lost about a day.

And, if the weather patterns prove to be as expected for this time of year, the winds from here on will be less predictable. I'd say we're about a week to ten days out. How are your provisions holding up?"

"We'll be fine for another ten days to a fortnight. We were able to replenish the water during the storm, so I don't see a problem with either food or water."

"Good," acknowledged the captain. "I'll do my best to be sure we make it to New York as soon as possible."

As the captain predicted, the winds were variable in their direction over the next several days, sometimes moving them along nicely at eight to ten knots, other times just three to five, and occasionally becalmed. But the weather was pleasant, and the company made good progress toward completing the wagon sheets and tents. Classes in English and in the skills needed during the wagon trek resumed. Though storms threatened on two more occasions, they both passed to the northwest with little affect on the *Manchester*.

The Saints' spirits improved greatly with the good weather and with anticipation that the end of the long voyage was near. Excitement built with each passing day. And much to Laura's delight, dancing and games resumed on deck after evening prayers. She had met several boys she had grown interested in, but the cold and the storms prevented the social activities that would allow relationships to develop, and she resolved to correct the situation. The Captain's kindness in moving the chronically seasick Saints to the officer quarters resulted in their rapid recovery, and after a few days, all were able to return to their families.

Sunday, May 12th, dawned cool and beautifully clear, but the ship was quite becalmed. Coming up on deck, the Saints were greeted with a rare and unusual sight. There, before them as far as they could see in all directions, lay the vastness of ocean as smooth and calm as a fishpond. What a stark contrast to the rolling and pitching seas they had experienced daily over the past four weeks! Word spread quickly, and soon the entire ship's company and crew were standing on the main and quarterdecks, awed by the view. They were enjoying the moment, savoring the sight and the stable, unmoving deck, when suddenly they heard a shout from the starboard bow.

"Look! Look! Off there!" a young man exclaimed, pointing. "I see smoke!"

Several others, including William, rushed in the boy's direction and peered with him at the horizon. William strained to see, and could just make out what he thought might be a faint plume of dark smoke on the far horizon to the west-southwest, when he heard the cry of a seaman aloft in the rigging with a telescope.

"Steamship on the horizon, four points off the starboard bow!"

The first mate, standing on the quarterdeck with his own telescope, acknowledged the observation. "Bosun, notify the captain, and prepare to launch the longboat!"

In a flurry of activity the crew untied the longboat lashed to the quarterdeck, and swung it over the side, awaiting instructions to lower it into the water. Captain Trask joined the first mate and peered through the telescope. Several minutes passed before he spoke.

"An American steamer. She's flying the Stars and Stripes. Bosun, run up the signal flags telling her we would like to rendezvous!"

"Aye, Aye, sir." the Bosun replied, and did as he was instructed, though William wondered how the steamer would see the flags with no wind to stretch them out. As if in answer, a light breeze began to blow, just enough to unfurl the signal flags.

The ship's company stood clustered in small groups, looking on excitedly. Discussions grew animated, many on the deck gesturing toward the smoke as it slowly grew larger on the horizon. The *Manchester* had been at sea for 28 days now, and this was the first vessel they had encountered during all that time. The black cloud of smoke gradually became a steamship as it altered course to head directly toward the *Manchester*. Soon they were able to make out paddlewheels on either side churning the sea. William and Elder Spencer joined the captain.

"Ah, there you are," the captain exclaimed as the two approached. "We're about one hundred miles from Sandy Hook, well into approaching and departing sea-lanes. With the winds down, I'm not surprised we'd spot a steamer first. I'll send the first mate aboard to get news. If the wind freshens, we should arrive at the quarantine grounds tomorrow evening." He turned to the first mate. "Launch the longboat."

The expectant crew lowered the longboat into the water, and five crewmen scrambled aboard. Four took up oars and the fifth stood by the helm. The steamer, now about a mile out, blew a long, low-pitched, resonant blast on its horn. Those watching on deck cheered and began waving at the approaching ship. Several passengers standing along the steamer's deck rail returned the greetings. About a half mile out the steamer began to slow as its paddlewheels first slowed to a stop, then began moving in reverse, churning the water into a frothy foam. The steamer's captain was well experienced. The steamer came to a stop exactly opposite the *Manchester*, about a hundred yards abeam. The great paddlewheels stopped, the billowing smoke dying to a single wisp rising from its single stack. What a sight she was! In contrast to the broad, tubby *Manchester*, the steamer seemed long, low, and sleek. It looked almost naked, with no sails, and practically no rigging. Only two masts, one forward, and one aft, rose from the decks at slightly raked angles toward the stern, framing the smokestack atop the low superstructure in the center of the deck. It was truly a strange and wondrous sight!

The *Manchester's* first mate climbed down into the longboat and the crew cast off toward the steamer. Just a few strong, well-coordinated strokes brought them alongside and the first mate climbed the lowered ladder to the deck where he was greeted by two men. The three disappeared. The *Manchester's* passengers looked on, enthralled at the events and awed by the steamship.

About fifteen minutes later the trio reappeared and the first mate climbed down to the longboat carrying a small bundle. As they cast off, the steamship blew two long blasts of its horn and the smoke began to belch once more from the stack. The paddlewheels began to turn, slowly at first, and then more rapidly, again creating foam. Slowly, the great ship began to move. The Saints aboard the *Manchester* cheered and waved as the steamer picked up speed. By the time the first mate returned to the Captain on the quarterdeck, the steamer was well on its way, black smoke hanging heavily in the air before slowly dissipating. William could smell it. Coal. This was one of the new coal-fired steamers.

"Captain, sir," the First Mate reported. "Captain Mayhoe, SS Golden Rule, sends his compliments. They're bound for Liverpool, general cargo and a few passengers. Says we may be delayed landing our passengers because the docks are full of war materials and troops. Seems the United States is at war. Here, he sent along these newspapers." The first mate handed the captain the bundle he carried under his arm.

The captain took the papers and turned to Elder Spencer. "Let me look these over first, then I'll send them along to you this evening. It appears you're arriving at a difficult time for your new country. Will this change your plans?"

William and Elder Spencer looked at one another for a few seconds, both men surprised and uncertain about what it all meant.

"No. At least, I don't think so," Elder Spencer replied. "I wouldn't think we'd be pressed into the army, being new to the country and all. I just hope we can avoid the fighting as we travel westward!" he declared. "Besides, the Lord has brought us this far. He won't abandon us now!"

"Well, I admire your faith," the Captain said, "and I wish you luck. Here. Why don't you take some of these now," he said, handing several papers to Elder Spencer. "I'll keep the rest and exchange with you later."

The wind began to freshen as they finished speaking, and the captain departed to attend to his duties. The *Manchester* began moving again, slowly. The day was still pleasant, and as it was the Sabbath, Elders Spencer, Hanham, and William arranged and prepared for a worship service to be held mid-afternoon on the main deck. Then the three retired to a quiet spot on the quarterdeck and began reading the newspapers. All were dated May 9th, just three days earlier. Twenty minutes passed. Elder Spencer spoke first.

"From all I can tell, the fighting is confined to the South. The city of Charleston and the surrounding area. We'll be heading west from New York until we reach Florence. Perhaps we won't be affected."

"I pray you're right." William was speaking. "In any event, do you think we ought to leave New York as quickly as we can? From these accounts, the city is in a general ferment about the war."

"Yes, we should," replied Elder Spencer. "I trust Elder Jones in New York is aware of the situation and is making arrangements for us to depart as quickly as possible. Do you think we ought to appraise the Saints about the war situation?"

All three paused to reflect on the question. William spoke.

"Perhaps at this point we ought not to add to any worries they already have. Why don't we wait? They'll learn of it soon enough." The others nodded their agreement.

The worship services, the last they would hold aboard ship since they were due to arrive at the quarantine grounds the next afternoon, was well attended. Even Captain Trask, his officers, and many of the seamen attended. Unlike any they had held since departing Liverpool, a feeling of excitement, happiness, and joy mixed with humble gratitude to the Lord for their safe passage prevailed at the meeting. Each speaker seemed to express the feelings of all as they recounted the trials and challenges they had undergone, the opportunities about to be fulfilled as they reached America, and the blessings and mercies bestowed upon them by the Lord. Captain Trask seemed particularly attentive, reaffirming William's impression that the captain was God-fearing and spiritually inclined. After the meeting adjourned, William sought him out.

"Captain Trask. Did you enjoy the meeting?"

"Yes. Yes, I did. And I must say, you Mormons are an impressive lot! I've carried many a shipload of emigrants over the past ten years, but none compare to what you have accomplished. Your organization, your discipline. And your faith! Do you realize we were sinking at the rate of almost a foot every two hours during the storm? The bilge pumps were not keeping up. If the storm had not abated when it did, then we would have gone down! I was getting mighty worried until I remembered the dedicatory prayer made before we left. One phrase came clearly to my mind: 'I bless this ship that she may sail true and safe, her journey sped by Thy protective hand.' It's almost enough to convince me to become Mormon!"

William clapped a hand on the captain's shoulder and replied. "We can assist you, dear Brother. We can assist you." Smiling, the captain turned and departed.

All through the night the winds continued to blow steadily from the southeast, perfect for the *Manchester's* run to Sandy Hook and ideal for sleeping. But just as sleep did not come easy on their first nights aboard, it did not come easy on what many hoped would be their last. Excitement at their imminent arrival in America, and the continuing adventure awaiting them beyond, precluded a sound rest.

As he had done since the storm, William climbed into the lower berth next to Mary Frances as Laura, displaced, climbed to the upper and lay next to her brother, very self-conscience of young Franklin lying just beyond James. The arrangement wouldn't be for the entire night, but only until the between-decks settled down and quieted as the ship's company began to fall asleep. Nor was it with any hope of consummating their growing desire for physical intimacy, inexplicably rekindled since the storm. Mother Ould's presence put a damper on that. But it was, rather, to enjoy the intimacy of just lying closely together and sharing the emotional and spiritual bonds that had developed since their wedding just weeks before. William, caressing Mary France's head against his chest, spoke softly.

"Are you sorry we came?"

Mary Frances tilted her face upward toward William's. "No. Are you sorry you married me?"

William smiled lovingly at Mary Frances's question, and kissed her lightly on the forehead. "No. It's being married to you that makes all this worthwhile. I love you, dearest."

The ship's company was up early, well before daylight, making final preparations for landing. And, as daylight broke, the Saints caught their first sight of America! There it was, at last, clearly visible along the starboard side! America, and the promised land beyond! A new sense of excitement spread through the company as the realization sank in that they had finally arrived, and all went about their tasks with a renewed vigor. After breakfast the galley crew packed the spare provisions for the trip onward. Families busied themselves packing their belongings, tasks that required bringing up from the hold most of the boxes, crates, and luggage stored there since that first day on board. Many a groan was heard as the musty smell caused by the hold's dampness greeted them when they opened their luggage. Wouldn't be time to air it out now! Perhaps later.

At about seven in the morning, a harbor pilot came on board to bring the *Manchester* into the harbor and the quarantine grounds. They were now forty-five miles from New York City, and the pilot brought aboard the City's papers, full of war news and the City's ongoing preparations for the conflict. Word quickly spread through the company about the state of affairs, but none seemed particularly disturbed. They were too relieved about arriving.

None, that is, except William and his two colleagues. They could not help but be concerned because of their responsibility to get the Saints safely through customs and immigration, and then on to the trains leaving New York. Yet there was little they could do for now. William's concern turned to unease as he caught sight of warships patrolling all approaches to New York's harbor. Preparations for war were extending even out to sea!

The wind continued favorably, moving the ship along at about five knots as she paralleled the beaches of Long Island, now clearly visible off the starboard side. The white beach sands contrasted with the low green slopes rising gently beyond. What a treat to see shades of green after nothing but the monotony of a gray sea for weeks on end! By early afternoon the ship arrived off Sandy Hook, its tall, graceful lighthouse, the major navigation point for approaches to the harbor. With the pilot standing next to him, the helmsman turned the *Manchester* northward for its run toward the Narrows and the harbor beyond. The wind freshened, now almost directly off the stern as the ship completed its turn. They were making good time. As the *Manchester* approached the Narrows, only a few ships like their own were headed toward the harbor, but many more were departing and heading south, sundry warships interspersed among merchant vessels. To the south. Where the war was.

Late in the afternoon, Elder Spencer approached William.

"Elder Jefferies, what would you think of assembling the Saints to prepare resolutions of appreciation to the captain and the crew? I can't help but be amazed at the contrast between this captain's behavior and the rude behavior of the captain of the ship on which I sailed to England three years ago!"

"Why, I think it's a splendid idea!" replied William. "He and his officers have been most solicitous. Why don't we do it now?"

Agreeing, they assembled as many of the ship's company as could be found on the upper deck, explaining their intention as they gathered. Elder Spencer appointed a committee which then retired for a short while to complete the task. Upon the committee's return, the resolutions were read aloud, and only minor changes were suggested. Then William went for the captain.

As the two joined the gathering, Captain Trask looked puzzled, and even a little apprehensive. Elder Spencer greeted him.

"Captain, sir, we've assembled together to express our profound thanks and great appreciation for the courtesies and kindnesses you and your officers have shown us during this long and arduous voyage. Allow me to read aloud our declaration of appreciation."

Elder Spencer held up the paper and began to read.

"First, that we deem it not only a duty, but a pleasure to express our approbation for your gentlemanly and courteous bearing, liberal acts, and solicitous spirit, by which you have sought to make our voyage as comfortable as possible.

Second, that we unitedly tender our thanks to you, with our best wishes for prosperity.

Third, that we remember with very kind feelings and much respect the officers of the good ship *Manchester*, for the propriety which characterized their conduct towards us, and also the crew, for their general civility.

Fourth, that we offer with one voice our great appreciation to Dr. Chamberlin, who has been most kind and attentive in the discharge of his duties.

And fifth, may you, and all on board who have shown a manly and unprejudiced bearing towards an oft-misrepresented people, be blessed in life, and saved in eternity."

As Elder Spencer finished reading, he rolled the document and handed it to the surprised captain as the Saints responded with three hearty cheers. For a moment, the captain seemed almost overcome with emotion, but quickly recovered. Placing the rolled resolutions under his left arm, he straightened up, cleared his throat, and spoke.

"In all my years at sea, this is a first! I have never before been paid respects in such a manner. Indeed, the opposite has usually been the case! But I must say, it is in large measure, only because you have worked in unity, that your voyage has been as pleasant as could be expected. You have my respect, and my wishes for happiness and prosperity during the remainder of your journey to Zion, and the realization of all the blessings you anticipate. It has been an honor and a pleasure to have you aboard my ship."

The ship's company responded with three more cheers as many lined up to shake the captain's hand.

Light began to fade as the *Manchester* entered the Narrows, passing between steep cliffs rising on either side, rich verdure covering the bluffs above. Almost the entire company lined the railings, William and his family among them, watching the cliffs slip slowly, silently by. Enjoying the earthy scent of Spring's vegetation and the sweetness of honeysuckle, they listened to the chatter and chirping of birds as they darted about in small flocks, first on the cliff tops, then on the water's surface as they swooped down to feed on the insects, then back up to the cliffs once more, other flocks following in turn. It was a glorious sight, bringing gladness to the heart. William's arm encircled Mary Frances's waist, and he pulled her close.

"Why, this is truly a paradise," he exclaimed, turning to kiss Mary Frances on her cheek. "A fairy-land couldn't be any more beautiful."

"Oh, William. I'm so happy we came! Any doubts I had while we were at sea have been swept away! What a glorious place to come."

"Aye, that may be," interjected Mother Ould, "but let's not forget we have many a mile to go yet, and from what I've heard of Utah territory, there won't be much honeysuckle!"

But not even Mother Ould's practicality dampened their spirits as they stood in silent awe at the magnificent foliage, and all shared a silent relief that the voyage was about complete. Particularly Mother Ould, for whom the crossing had been difficult.

Beyond the Narrows the bay widened again, and the *Manchester's* crew climbed aloft. Amidst a shouting of orders and instructions, they furled and stowed the sails. Then, as the harbor pilot found a spot among similar vessels waiting in quarantine for medical inspections before allowing the passengers to disembark, the captain ordered the anchor dropped. The ship slowly came to a stop. The sea-voyage was over.

.

CHAPTER 2
Arrival

The ship's company was aroused at 5 A.M. It was dark, but from across the harbor to the north, the Saints could hear the faint sounds of steam whistles and engines, indicating that the harbor was awake and in business. A cold breakfast was served, ablutions were quickly completed, last items were packed away, and by daybreak, work-parties of the crew and Saints hoisted and carried luggage to the upper deck. Coming out on deck, the workers were greeted by a warm, misty rain. Undeterred, they worked industriously and the baggage accumulated rapidly. Before the baggage was all assembled on deck, the chug-chug of a steam-powered vessel could be heard approaching. Soon a tugboat revealed itself through the mist. The tugboat captain expertly maneuvered along the *Manchester's* starboard side and the crew threw down lines to secure it alongside. A rope ladder was lowered and a uniformed officer came aboard carrying a valise. Expecting Elder Jones, the Church Emigration Agent in New York, William and his colleagues were standing next to the first mate as the officer came aboard. The first mate greeted him.

"Welcome aboard the *Manchester*."

The officer replied brusquely. "Thank you. I'm Dr. Stern, Immigration Medical Officer. I'll inspect the passengers."

Short, slender, and fastidious in appearance, the medical officer gave an impression of competence and efficiency. He looked over the deck, noting the growing stack of luggage, and turned again to the first mate.

"I'll want to get started as soon as possible. Will you assemble the passengers here, on deck?"

Elder Spencer interjected. "I'm Elder Claudius Spencer, ship's company president," he said, turning to William and Elder Hanham, "and these are my counselors, Elder Hanham and Elder Jefferies. We were expecting Elder Jones, our Emigration Agent."

Dr. Stern turned to Elder Spencer. "Ah, yes. Mr. Jones. He had planned to accompany me, but it appears that at the last minute complications developed about your landing at Castle Garden to register. It seems it is occupied by Federal troops. He asked me to convey to you that you should not disembark until he comes. In the meantime, I'd like to get on with my inspections."

"Quite so," replied Elder Spencer. "We'll assemble our passengers."

Castle Garden was New York's immigration landing depot, the predecessor to Ellis Island. Built in 1811 as a large, circular stone fort on an outcropping of rock just off the southwestern tip of New York City's Manhattan Island, its walls had been roofed to form a large, circular hall that could accommodate several thousand people. Before it became the immigration landing depot in 1855, it had been used as a music hall, opera house, and exhibition hall. It's location made the building easily accessible by water and by land, a convenient location where immigrants could be registered as they disembarked from their ships, and yet isolated until it could be determined if any carried communicable diseases. It also served as a place of refuge for immigrants. Here they were allowed to stay for several days, if necessary, until able to move onward, and could find a measure of protection from unscrupulous elements preying upon the vulnerable newcomers.

The three leaders turned and separated, William staying on deck and the others descending below to rally the Saints. It didn't take long for the emigrants to assemble on deck for the inspection; all were anxious to complete everything necessary in order to go ashore. The medical officer was just as efficient as his appearance suggested, and the inspections proceeded quickly. Only five of the company did not pass, and the medical officer instructed them to remain on board until they could be conveyed to a quarantine ward at Castle Garden. As soon as the work-parties finished their inspections, they returned to bringing the baggage on deck.

Soon the rain stopped, the mists lifted, the sky cleared, and the Saints got a panoramic view of the harbor for the first time. And what a view it was! The magnificent harbor of New York dwarfed any the emigrants had seen in England or on the Continent. There, directly ahead at the end of the twelve-mile long bay, bathed in the morning sunlight, spread the great City of New York, its imposing red- and white-brick office buildings clustered along the waterfront facing the Hudson River, stately mansions lining the East River, and fastidious town houses interspersed among the more common older residences. Myriad church steeples punctuated the skyline. On the eastern shore to the right was the prosperous-appearing city of Brooklyn, while on the western shore opposite, the industrial city of Jersey City spewed smoke from a forest of factory smokestacks. Harbor traffic moved briskly to and fro, sailboats, steam ferries, and steam tugs pushing and pulling barges, all dodging around the larger ships anchored throughout the harbor, their wakes reflecting the rising sun. The Saints couldn't help but be energized by this stirring view of their new homeland!

His inspections complete, Dr. Stern approached the three leaders standing near the boarding ladder awaiting Elder Jones' arrival. The baggage was on deck, ready to be off-loaded.

"Well, Mr. Spencer, I've completed my work and wish to depart. I've informed the captain that he is cleared to depart the quarantine ground."

Even as the medical officer spoke, the crew began throwing towlines down to the tug as it began maneuvering into position to tow the *Manchester* into the harbor. The medical officer continued.

"My skiff should arrive soon, and perhaps your Mr. Jones will be aboard. But I doubt you'll want to spend much time in the city! Martial fever has most of the city agitated and mistrustful of strangers. It's not a very friendly place to be for the present." Peering intently toward the city, he paused, then continued. "And, speaking of my skiff, I see it approaching now."

Dr. Stern pointed toward a small sail vessel several miles away yet, but clearly headed toward the *Manchester*. As it approached, they could see a single passenger standing at the bow.

"Ah, yes," commented Dr. Stern. "That looks like Mr. Jones now. You have my best wishes for your onward journey."

The skiff came alongside the vessel and the lone figure grabbed the ladder dangling alongside and climbed quickly. As the newcomer reached the deck, Dr. Stern saluted perfunctorily, and departed. The new arrival, tall, slender, and dressed in a dark suit and fashionable stovepipe hat, greeted the first mate and then approached the presidency. Elder Spencer extended his hand.

"Elder Jones, I presume. We've been expecting you!"

"Welcome to America!" replied Elder Jones. "Did you have a pleasant crossing?"

"As pleasant as conditions permitted. The captain and his crew were most solicitous. But what's this about difficulties with our landing? We're most anxious to disembark, as you can well imagine. We've been at sea for a month! Is it true army troops occupy the reception station?"

"Yes. Unfortunately, it is. The New York militia is using Castle Garden to muster troops. But I've talked with the proprietors, and informed them that until the Garden was cleared of troops, neither we nor any other emigration ship will land our passengers! They agreed to see what they could do. I hope you can land tomorrow, but that means you'll have to remain aboard one more night."

The *Manchester* began moving slowly toward the harbor as Elder Jones was speaking, the steam tug chugging loudly amidst billowing black smoke.

"But we've packed away our bedding and provisions!" exclaimed Elder Spencer. "Another night aboard ship will surely dishearten the Saints."

"That may well be, Elder Spencer," replied Elder Jones, "but I can assure you, remaining aboard is better than encountering those soldiers!

They're mean, ill-disciplined, and surly! Most are intoxicated! They're just plain ruffians. I don't know where the Militia found their recruits, but they're an army in name only. I wouldn't want our Saints to be subjected to their abuse!"

Elder Spencer, Elder Hanham, and William looked at each other, aware suddenly that their growing apprehension about war preparations were justified.

"I see," Elder Spencer replied. "Of course, you're right. What can we do that might help?"

"I can use assistance ashore. If we delay your disembarkation by a day, we can make arrangements to expedite processing through customs and immigration, and ensure your onward railway arrangements are complete. That way, you'll spend only the minimum time in New York before moving on. Will you accompany me?"

"Yes, surely," replied Elder Spencer. He turned to Elder Hanham and William. "You two will have to inform the Saints and help them settle down for the night. Have the kitchen crew unpack only what they can easily and quickly prepare for a light meal, but be certain you do not allow the company to remove the luggage from the main deck. We'll lose too much time tomorrow if we have to repack everything for removal!"

William spoke up. "As you are going on ahead, perhaps I ought to give you the money I've collected for our onward transportation. It's a considerable sum."

"An excellent suggestion," replied Elder Jones. "That will help." Turning to Elder Spencer, he continued. "Make whatever arrangements you need before departing, and join me on the steam tug as soon as we're in our mooring place. The tug-master will ferry us ashore. I'll arrange for landing barges to be alongside tomorrow morning before daylight."

The four dispersed to begin their assignments.

The tug towed the *Manchester* to within a quarter-mile of Castle Garden, a location where the Saints could observe bustling activity in both the harbor and the city itself. Activity in the streets just beyond Castle Garden caught their attention first as the sounds of a band playing martial music wafted clearly over the water, interspersed with hearty hurrahs from time to time amidst the waving of flags and handkerchiefs. The captain was preparing to leave the ship, and William asked him about the activity.

"Sounds like a recruiting rally," explained the Captain. "The Militia is trying to fill its ranks. I'd be careful about going over if I were you. Likely to find yourself signed up!" That would explain the presence of troops in Castle Garden, William thought.

The next morning dawned clear and bright, cheering the Saints after one last difficult night aboard; almost everything they carried to provide a measure of comfort remained packed in their luggage. Afraid the Saints might be tempted to reclaim their luggage after the delay was announced, William and Elder Hanham posted guards around the stacks after each family was allowed to unpack just what they absolutely required for the night. And their wisdom became apparent; soon after the Saints arose, the tug returned, carrying a customs officer and pulling a harbor barge. Asked to take charge of the luggage handling, William jumped aboard the luggage barge as the tug came alongside. He was greeted immediately by the customs officer.

"Looks like you're ready for my inspection," the officer replied. "Good. Shouldn't take long. Your Elder Jones suggested I come out here to examine luggage. It'll be quicker than unloading it at the Garden. Your train leaves from Jersey City, so as soon's you clear immigration, you can be on your way. The depot is just a short trip across the bay. Save you time."

The customs officer began his inspection, stopping here and there to open and prod among the Saint's packed baggage. He could tell clearly by the luggage that few of the immigrants were prosperous and thus unlikely to possess much of interest to U.S. Customs. The inspection progressed rapidly. As soon as the customs inspection was complete, the inspector signed the luggage release and cleared the luggage for unloading. Upon signal, the *Manchester's* crew lowered a stair gangway to the barge below, and the Saints began to move their luggage from the deck to the barge waiting below. When the barge was full, the Saints scrambled aboard and the tug pulled away toward Castle Garden's docks. None of the Saints turned to look again at the ship. What a relief to be off!

The journey to Castle Garden took about twenty minutes. After leaving the *Manchester*, the harbor barge and tug were in the midst of harbor traffic, dazzling the new arrivals with activity. What a place! There, off to the starboard, was the Brooklyn Naval Yard, warships lined against the docks as crews busily loaded materiel and troops. On the opposite side of the bay, harbor barges lined the docks of Jersey City, loading and offloading cargo into warehouses beyond the docks.

Castle Garden, its massive red granite walls dominating the tip of Manhattan Island, loomed dead ahead, with covered gun embrasures, rifle ports, and portholes clearly visible in its circular walls. Two large warships were tied to the Garden's docks, and as the Saints drew near, they could see lines of soldiers, backpacks and muskets slung over their shoulders, slowly making their way up the gangplanks. Some were in uniform, many were in partial uniform, and some remained in civilian clothes.

The tug-master expertly squeezed the leading luggage barge between the two warships, gently nudging the heavy wood-timber dock as the tug and barges came to a stop. Dock hands quickly tied the barge to the dock's capstans. Soldiers lined the railings of the warships on either side, peered closely at the immigrants and began whistling and yelling cat-calls. The Saints tried to ignore them, but it was difficult.

"Lookie there! All those Mormon women! How many can you get in bed at once, Elder?"

"Why they look positively ripe for the plucking! Sure like to have some of them in my bed tonight!"

"Where do I sign up for wives? Can I get me two like those over there?"

Elders Jones and Spencer were waiting at the dock, and stepped aboard, greeting William and Elder Hanham standing at the bow. Both Jones and Spencer looked harried.

"The troops are leaving, but you can see they're still rowdy," Elder Jones said. He had to speak up to be heard over the din of catcalls. "I've had a long word with their colonel, and he assures me they've slept off their drunkenness and they'll be civil. But we've had a devil of a time getting them out! None seem pleased to be going to war."

"Aye," added Elder Spencer. "And they've left quite a mess. We won't want to tarry long."

"He's right," replied Elder Jones. "The registrar has Captain Trask's manifest, so all you have to do is identify yourselves to the registrar and give your destination. We're the first group through this morning, so they're waiting for us."

Elder Spencer turned to William. "Elder Jefferies, take your family, and as many men and their families as you think you'll need to handle the baggage at the rail depot, and go on ahead. You'll register first. As soon as you all finish, I'd like you to accompany the barge on ahead to the railway depot to get the luggage weighed and loaded aboard the train. Then send the barge and tug back for us. We'll follow soon's we finish."

William nodded and turned back to the barge, jostling through the Saints crowded toward the dock to make his way. He located Mary Frances, Mother Ould, Laura, James, and Franklin, and gave them instructions. As they picked up their hand-luggage and moved forward, William sought out another half-dozen men who, after they received their instructions, gathered their families and likewise proceeded through the crowd. After they assembled on the dock, Elder Jones led the advance group toward the large sally-port entrance in the fortress' wall about a hundred feet distant. The remaining immigrants gathered their belongings and began to follow behind.

The on-looking soldiers awaiting their turn to board the warships grew more rowdy and undisciplined as the Saints passed, and began to take on the characteristic of a mob. As the line of immigrants filed through the soldiers, the whistling and catcalls began again. This time, though, the soldiers' jibes were accompanied by a shower of refuse. William, his head lowered and his hat pulled low, held Mary Frances tightly as they walked the gauntlet of trash. The line of immigrants neared the entrance just as the line of soldiers began edging toward them, hands extended in mock groping gestures. They drew close enough for William and Mary Frances to smell long-unwashed bodies and alcohol on their breaths. The soldiers edged closer, one or two grabbing at the luggage William, Laura, James, and Franklin clutched tightly in two hands. But they dared not look at the soldiers' faces, and kept their heads down, ignoring them, and hurrying along as quickly as they could.

Then William heard Laura cry out in alarm. He turned to see a particularly scruffy soldier groping at Laura's body as he yelled obscenities at her. She screamed again, and immediately James, Franklin, and William dropped their luggage and turned to pull the soldier away. But in his drunken stupor, the soldier fought back wildly, landing hard blows on the three as they tried to subdue him. All the while, his comrades cheered the drunken soldier on, creating a spectacle. In tears, Laura retreated to Mother Ould and Mary Frances who shielded her with their bodies. Their progress halted, the other immigrants huddled together closely, fearful of an onslaught by the jeering soldiers.

William, James, and Franklin were having a difficult time holding the soldier down, and just as it looked as though several of his comrades were about to join in the scuffle, a tall, heavy-set sergeant followed by two city policemen forced their way into the fray, knocking back the line of soldiers. The two policemen swung long clubs at the approaching soldiers, who, faced with injury, pulled back. The sergeant carried a short billyclub in his right hand and, approaching the drunken soldier, reached down with his left arm and jerked the soldier to his feet. The soldier stood unsteadily and began again to resist. The sergeant, his patience at an end, swung the billy-club in his right hand, hitting the man squarely on the side of his head. The soldier collapsed at the sergeant's feet. Scowling, the sergeant turned to the line of soldiers who had suddenly grown quiet, their mouths open in amazement as they looked at their comrade lying in a heap.

"Any more o'ye recruits ready for me club?"

The crowd quiet now, the sergeant turned to the ladies, and tipping his cap, offered apologies. "Sorry about me boys, Ma'am," he said to Laura, who was sobbing softly beneath Mother Ould's protective arm. "They got no manners, and no training. They's just raw recruits. We're shippin' out for South Carolina, and I'm afeared they ain't ready. They won't give you no more trouble."

The sergeant reached down, grabbed the unconscious soldier, and, helped by the policemen, dragged him away. The remaining soldiers, now chastened, drew back silently and let the immigrants continue into the Garden.

William and Elder Jones led the immigrants through the entrance and into a long, gently rising corridor. As they climbed, they passed empty gun platforms and ports facing outward. At the top of the corridor, the Saints turned and entered a magnificently large, circular hall. In concentric circles, three progressively higher roofs rose above the red granite walls, each about six feet higher than the other. A circle of windows rose from the outer circular roof, flooding the hall with bright sunlight, and a smaller circle of windows rose from the second circular roof, creating a dome of light. The roof-lines reminded William of a three-layer cake, each successive layer smaller than the one upon which it sat.

The hall was divided into two large compartments separated by a tall picket fence. In the center was a raised platform on which sat a series of bureaus, or desks. Leading to the desks from each compartment was a corridor partitioned by a low railing in which immigrants lined up to give information to the registrars. At opposite ends of each compartment stood two large iron stoves about five feet high, one for women, and one for men. In the outer walls stood the sanitary facilities, a series of privies that were open to the bay below, men on one side of the hall, women on the other. The floor was made of rough-sawn wooden planks. At both ends of the dividing picket fence were two water taps, ladles hanging from each.

As soon as William entered the large hall, he could tell it had been occupied by a large number of people. The smell of unwashed bodies was almost overpowering. In the wake of the occupying troops, trash lay strewn about the floor, the remains of meals, discarded packaging, cores of eaten fruit, pools of putrid vomit from intoxicated soldiers, and even urine. A large task force of men was cleaning up, but they had much to do. Stepping over and around the trash, the Saints filed into the hall, mercifully directed to the partitioned area in which cleaning had already been completed. But the smells remained. It was not a place to spend any time.

William and his family approached the low-fenced corridor that led to a row of desks, and were motioned onward. As they approached the desks, William and his family moved to the farthest. The following families stopped at the next available desks.

Their registrar was a pleasant-faced man, courteous and cheerful. He looked at them and smiled.

"Welcome to America! What a welcome change you are from those rowdy soldiers! I shudder when I think they may be all that stand between us and the Secessionists! Give me your names, please."

"William Jefferies."

The registrar paused as he looked down the list.

"Yes. I see it here. Is this your family?"

"Yes. My wife, Mary Frances, her mother, Mary Ould. That's spelled O-U-L-D. Her sister, Laura, and her brother, James. And this is Franklin Blair, traveling with us."

"Mr. Blair, we'll get to you shortly. Your destination?"

"We are headed to Zion. To Salt Lake City in the territory of Utah."

"Ah, yes. To Zion. That is quite a trip! Are you prepared?"

"With the Lord's mercy, yes. We're all traveling to Zion!" With this, William turned and gestured to the growing number of Saints assembling in the hall.

"I must say," the registrar said with a smile. "From what I hear, you are indeed prepared. Much more orderly and organized than other immigrants. I wish you a safe and pleasant trip."

He turned toward Franklin and began to address him, but William interrupted.

"Is that all? We're registered?"

"Yes. That's all. As I say, welcome to America."

For some reason, one he didn't understand, William suddenly felt a wave of relief and joy come over him. As they departed the registrar's desk, he turned to Mary Frances and embraced her tightly.

"We're here! We're in the promised land at last! We've done it! The worst part is over! Zion is just a land's journey away! In less than a fortnight, we'll be in Florence and ready for the last part of the journey."

Mary Frances shared his joy and enthusiasm, as did Laura, James, and Franklin. But Mother Ould, ever the realist, brought them back to solemn reality.

"Enjoy your feelings, William, but don't lose sight of what we have to endure yet. From all I've heard listening to Utah missionaries for ten years, the last part may well be the hardest."

"Oh, mother!" replied Laura. "From what I've heard, the wagon trek will be the most fun! I can't wait."

"I hope you're right, my dear. We'll see."

They waited for the other six families to join them before returning to the dock. By then, the warships had loaded their passengers and were preparing to depart. William's group was small, and the soldiers ignored them, now bored by the sport. The tug-master had maneuvered to depart with the luggage barge to the train depot across the harbor in Jersey City.

As soon as William and his group boarded the tug, it left for the short voyage across the Hudson River.

Dodging the mid-morning river traffic, the tug and luggage barge drew near the Erie Railroad's ferry terminal and rail station in Jersey City. Directly ahead, two ferry slips jutted perpendicularly from the shore into the river, one containing a steam-ferry offloading its passengers. Just beyond the slips stood the large railroad and ferry terminal, a wide three-story redbrick structure with hints of classical Georgian architecture. On the riverside, facing the slips, three arched and open doorways led into the station. The ferry passengers, carrying their luggage, were entering the building. The tug-master maneuvered to the right to go around the ferry slips, and headed to the loading docks running parallel to the terminal on its north side.

Rounding the slips, William could see that the brick terminal stood at the head of a massive, arched-roof, open-sided barn-like structure that extended a hundred yards or more beyond the station. A railroad train of ten passenger cars and three baggage cars at its far end stood in the structure, just behind a Baldwin 10-wheeler locomotive and fuel car. No smoke came from the large funnel smokestack atop the idling steam engine, but occasional puffs of steam emitted from domes behind the stack. Passengers were climbing aboard the train and two porters were loading luggage stacked on carts into the baggage cars.

As William's tug approached the docks where they would land, he could see a rail marshaling yard containing four parallel pairs of railroad tracks laid out between the dock and the structure. The tracks ran a quarter-mile or so beyond the yard where they joined with tracks running from the barn into a single strand leading away from the station and through a pass cut in the low hills about three miles distant. On the rails next to the barn stood a long train of ten passenger and two freight cars, the freight cars at the far end. On an adjacent set of tracks, nearer William, stood another long train, flatcars loaded with cannon and crates of war materiel. Several soldiers, muskets slung over their shoulders, stood watch along its length.

On the opposite side of the structure William could see a locomotive roundhouse, and in an open doorway facing the station, the nose of a steam locomotive. A small rail-yard switch-engine was idling near the round-house at the head of a line of freight cars, wisps of pale smoke coming out of its narrow smoke stack. Beyond the switch-engine were several parallel lines of rail cars, some passenger and some freight.

The tug and barge drew alongside the stone-faced dock, and dockhands caught the mooring ropes as they were thrown up, tying them to the moorings. William climbed a short flight of stone stairs and walked over to one of the hands.

"Where should we take our baggage? We've got quite a load."

The dockhand glanced casually down at the barge, drawing on his long-stemmed pipe. "Yup. You do. Ain't my department, though," he replied, then nodded in the direction of the terminal. "You'll have to see the stationmaster."

William tipped his hat and went off across the rail yard toward the terminal building, crossing the tracks and circling around the standing line of cars, studiously avoiding the sentries. Entering the barn, he noted three pairs of tracks within. The loading train sat on the middle set, blocking from view another idling Baldwin engine standing on the far set of tracks. William crossed the nearest set of tracks and entered the terminal, a long hall with offices and ticket windows at the far end, and a refreshment stand nearest William's entry. Running perpendicular to the hall's length were rows of back-to-back benches facing one another. Only a few were occupied, a line of people stood at one of the ticket windows. William continued down the hall toward the offices, stopping before a door labeled "Stationmaster." He knocked. After a pause, he heard a voice within.

"Enter!"

William opened the door and entered. Seated at a wall-desk adjacent to an open window sat the stationmaster, a clerk standing at his side.

"What is it?" the harried-looking official asked.

"I'm Elder Jefferies, advance party of Latter-day Saints ticketed to St. Joseph. I'm here with the luggage."

"Yes. Your Mr. Spencer was here yesterday," the Stationmaster replied as he shuffled through the papers on his desk. "Ah. Here it is."

He read silently for a few minutes, then spoke. "Four hundred and one passengers plus luggage. You get five emigrant passenger cars and two freight cars. Those who can afford it can pay the surcharge for first class when we attach the parlor cars. You're routed to Chicago through Elmira to Dunkirk on the Erie Railroad, where you'll change trains, to Cleveland on the Cleveland and Erie, where you'll change trains again, then on to Toledo on the Cleveland and Toledo line. After another change, you're on the Northern Indiana to Chicago. At Chicago, you'll take the Quincy and Chicago Railroad to Quincy. From there, you'll ferry the Mississippi to Hannibal, where you'll take the Hannibal and St. Joseph to St. Joe. That's a long trip. Let's see. I count about six train changes. Take about eight days, more or less."

"Yes, it is a long trip. We'd like to depart as soon as possible."

"Well, now, that might be a little tricky," the stationmaster replied as he searched through the papers once more. Picking one up, he continued. "I've got the Seventh New York Militia due in here in just thirty minutes. Near one thousand troops. Got to get them loaded and on their way to Washington 'fore we can get you folks gone. War troops get first priority."

William listened in dismay. More soldiers! What kinds of indignities would the Saints suffer this time!

"Troops, you say? My group will arrive here not long afterward! Where're we going to wait? Like to avoid the soldiers if at all possible."

"Yes. That may be a problem." He paused to think. "Tell you what. I'll have the yard master make up your train soon's the Rochester Limited leaves at noon. We'll put it on the line over against the dock," he said, pointing in the direction where the tug was tied up. "Might not be comfortable sittin' in the car all day, but it might be better than minglin' with the troops in the terminal. Meantime, unload your baggage and stack it next to the rails. I'll send a scale over. Soon's the train's made up, you can weigh your luggage and start loading."

The stationmaster turned to the clerk, issued instructions, and the clerk left. William expressed his thanks, and likewise turned and left. As he departed, the stationmaster called after him.

"If all goes well with the Seventh, ought to have you out of here by late afternoon or early evening."

William paused to tip his hat to thank him once more, and continued on out. He returned to the dock to begin unloading the luggage, again filled with dismay about the prospects of more encounters with the soldiers. Dear Lord, protect us against further insult, he thought to himself.

Unloading the barge and stacking the luggage alongside the rails, as instructed, went smoothly and quickly. The women helped where possible, and even two of the dockhands pitched in. Not long after beginning to unload the barge, they heard the shrill whistle of an approaching steam ferry. Pausing to watch it dock in the vacant ferry slip beyond the station, William and the others could see its decks crowded with uniformed soldiers. Without comment, the work party returned to unloading, glancing anxiously from time to time toward the ferry and the disembarking troops.

But the troops took no interest in the small group of Saints busy at their task. The soldiers disembarked in an orderly manner, forming up in companies as they reached the dock, and marching away as directed in disciplined formations to designated areas. There they stacked their arms in well-aligned pyramids and stood in loose formation nearby. By the time the Saints finished off-loading their luggage, the soldiers had completed disembarking and waited quietly and resignedly, filling the dock area some distance away from the Saints between the ferry slips and the terminal.

As soon as the advance party of Saints finished offloading, their tug and harbor barge left to pick up the Saints awaiting at Castle Garden. Then, as the vessels pulled away from the dock, two long whistles blew from the Rochester Limited to signal its departure. Thick black smoke billowed from the Baldwin's funnel stack in powerful bursts and steam hissed from the side of the engine in white clouds as the drive-wheels began to turn, the chug-chug-chug starting slowly and gradually increasing in frequency as the train began to move. Friends and family standing in the loading area waved farewell with hats, handkerchiefs, and hands. The Saints sat on the luggage in the warm, mid-spring weather, watching the Rochester Limited's departure.

As promised, the switch engine began assembling the Saint's train as soon as the Rochester Limited cleared the rail yard. Puffing and chugging less noisily than the departing Baldwin, the switch engine shuttled back and forth efficiently, collecting and assembling the five passenger and two freight cars on a siding. It took about an hour to assemble the train, and when complete, the switch engine maneuvered it to the rails adjacent to the dock where the Saints and stack of luggage waited. As luck would have it, the two baggage cars stopped neatly adjacent to the stacked baggage. The work party began weighing and loading the luggage as soon as the switch engine departed, separating the remaining food provisions from the rest of the luggage for easy access.

The loading proceeded smoothly, allowing William time to inspect the emigrants' passenger cars. Returning from the stationmaster, William had peeked inside the cars lined up next to the barn awaiting the soldiers, and was pleasantly surprised at their comfort. They were filled with upholstered and spacious seats, carpeted floor, and curtained windows. Looked almost like a parlor, William thought. So he was surprised and even dismayed when he climbed aboard the first of the emigrants' passenger cars and discovered spartan, strictly utilitarian accommodations. Their car was a long, narrow wooden box about fifty feet in length, ten feet wide, and seven feet high with a flat roof. A narrow isle ran between two rows of wooden benches placed uncomfortably close together. At two occupants per seat, William calculated it was designed to carry forty-eight passengers. With four hundred passengers divided between five cars, they would have to crowd about eighty passengers in each car, not a pleasant prospect!

A row of twelve uncurtained windows ran along each side of the car, and a narrow wooden shelf ran the length of the car above the windows. Small oil lamps were mounted at intervals along both walls below the storage shelf. At one end of the car stood a woodburning stove next to a wood box. A large water jug was anchored to a stand across the isle, a small tap at its base. At the other end of the car, a curtained corner hid the "convenience," a toilet that was nothing more than a wide pipe open to the ground at its base, rising about eighteen inches from the floor and covered with a circular wooden seat, about fifteen inches in diameter, in which a hole about twelve inches in diameter was cut from the center.

A fitted lid covered the device when not in use. The car looked much like the freight car into which they were loading the luggage, with the exception of the rows of windows along each side, and the seating. The other four cars were the same.

The luggage was finally aboard the baggage cars when the rest of the Saints arrived from Castle Garden. Again, the tug-master maneuvered the barge expertly alongside the dock and, when tied securely, the passengers began to disembark. It was mid-afternoon. Elders Jones and Spencer were among the first off the barge. Behind them came Elder Erastus Snow, one of the Council of Twelve. Accompanied by Elder Spencer, Elder Snow went over to look at the luggage and the passenger cars. Elder Jones approached William.

"Well, Elder Jefferies, it looks like you have everything well in hand," he exclaimed. "Any problems with the soldiers?"

"No. None at all. They've largely ignored us. They'll likely delay our departure, though. Stationmaster says we won't depart until they've gone, and I don't see any sign of their loading. He also advises us to stay with our train rather than mingle with the soldiers inside the terminal."

"I think that's wise counsel," replied Elder Jones, "especially after our encounter this morning. Let's go in and have a word with the stationmaster. Yesterday I booked twenty-two Saints from the New York City Branch who are joining us and I need to pay for their tickets. We'll return shortly."

William and Elder Jones walked around their train, crossed the vacant adjacent tracks, and skirted the row of loaded flatcars and the empty passenger cars beyond. They intended to give the troops a wide berth, but had no choice but to pass near them as they entered the terminal. Only a few paid them any notice at all, and they simply acknowledged the two men with nods. Inside, the terminal was crowded with officers and their families, seated together or standing in groups throughout the hall. A number of sergeants stood near the refreshment stand, and privates were loading and carrying boxes full of refreshments to the assembled troops outside. Elder Jones turned to William, a pleasant, surprised look on his face.

"Why, these troops are civil and well disciplined! What a change from the rabble we encountered this morning! They're obviously seasoned troops."

The stationmaster's door was open, and upon entering, the two men saw him, a clerk, and a captain in heated discussion. As before, the stationmaster had a harried, stressed look about him.

"Captain, I must have you load your men so I can get your trains on their way to Washington! I've got passenger and freight departures and arrivals this afternoon, and they'll be delayed unless you're gone! You're playing havoc with my schedules!"

"And, as I explained to you," replied the captain, patiently and a bit condescendingly, "we're not going anywhere until we get a wire from Washington that it's clear to proceed! We've had word of roving patrols of Rebel sympathizers between here and Washington, particularly around secessionist Baltimore. Their favorite tactic is to tear up rails. Now, I needn't remind you that we are at war, and we have priority over all rail traffic. Until our patrols around Baltimore and Washington have confirmed the Rebs are no threat, then we'll not depart."

So stating, the captain turned and departed, leaving the stationmaster and his clerk shaking their heads, perplexed about how to schedule their trains. Elder Jones and William approached the stationmaster cautiously. Seeing the two men, he snapped at them.

"And I suppose you're here to complain about your delays!"

"Well, no, but I guess its clear we can't expect a departure any time soon. We just wanted to check with you and let you know our party has arrived."

The stationmaster calmed, clearly appreciating he was not being burdened with another demand.

"Yes. Of course. Sorry. As you can see, we're a bit disorganized here. You say your party has arrived? All . . . " he paused as he consulted a sheet of paper on his desk. " . . . All three hundred seventy-nine of you? No. I see here you added twenty-two more."

"Yes. That is correct. Here's the added money for their fares." He pulled out several bank notes and handed them to the stationmaster who, in turn, handed them to the clerk. The clerk pocketed the bills, and made out tickets from a book on the desk. These he handed back to Elder Jones.

"Good. So you're all here and ready to go," said the stationmaster. "That's one less worry. Keep your passengers on or near your train. That way, you'll be prepared for a quick departure if I can see my way clear to get you out. Besides, it's a bit crowded in here," he replied, gesturing toward the terminal waiting room.

"We've got to feed our group," continued Elder Jones. "Can we fire up the train stoves? We have sufficient for a meal."

"Surely. Go ahead. But please refrain from using the convenience while you're in the station. Have your folks use the necessaries out back, a few at a time."

As they returned to their train, Elder Jones instructed William. "Better get your Company organized into the five cars and appoint galley crews. Take inventory of what you've got. If you have trouble making a meal, let me know and I'll arrange for extra provisions unless you depart beforehand. Your fares include one meal a day, so it'll be tomorrow before you'll have a meal courtesy of the railroad."

Passing the empty troop train reminded William of the contrast between the more luxurious cars and their own. He asked Elder Jones about the difference.

"We pay the emigrant rate, half the regular second-class fare. So, simply put, we pay less, we get less. It's the only way we can afford to move our Saints. You'll also likely find yourselves attached to slower freight trains, and on sidings to make way for express trains."

"Still," replied William, "with only five cars, that makes eighty passengers per car. It will be awfully crowded!"

"Yes, you're right, but we haven't enough to pay for an additional car. Some of the Saints who can afford it will upgrade to first class when parlor cars are attached, so that will relieve some of the pressure. But I've got another sixteen hundred Saints coming yet on the Underwood and the Monarch of the Sea over the next four weeks, and I've just learned that about one thousand more Eastern state Saints will be joining us! They've crossed from Europe over the last several years but couldn't travel to Salt Lake until now because of the recent unpleasantness with Federal troops in Utah. And now the war has fired them up! So we've got to marshal our resources carefully. The trip to St. Joseph may be relatively uncomfortable, but at least it will be over in about ten days. Still better than ten weeks by wagon."

Chastened, William conferred with Elders Spencer and Hanham upon returning, and they went about getting the Saints organized as Elder Jones suggested, and settled down as well as could be expected. Though crowded, families cooperated in making the accommodations as comfortable as they could with their limited resources. They had, after all, lived together under forced intimacy now for almost six weeks and had even grown dependent upon one another. Bedding padded the hard wooden benches, and families worked together to provide a measure of comfort and safety for their young children. Elder Jones arranged for supplies of bread and milk from local tradesmen, ever ready and anxious to sell their produce to passengers, supplementing the oatmeal and tea remaining in the Company's stores.

Late afternoon passed into early evening with no indication yet of when they might depart. In the meantime, the stationmaster's concerns about his schedule went largely unrealized. The Seventh New York proved cooperative and helpful, allowing both passenger and freight trains to come and go. Finally, as the sun set and lanterns were lighted throughout the terminal and station barn, the Saints heard a bugle sounding "assembly." Curious, they leaned out the open car windows or scrambled off their cars to get a view of what was going on.

And what a show! With the sounding of the bugle, the soldiers streamed from everywhere around the station and piers to their designated unit locations and quickly arranged themselves in formations. Company sergeants made verbal roll calls and called out appropriate reports to the Regiment's Adjutant who, in turn, reported the results to the Colonel. The Colonel assembled his staff of company commanders, gave them instructions, and they returned to their troops. One-by-one, the units picked up their arms and equipment, and upon command, began filing in sequence to the empty passenger cars.

This flurry of activity was accompanied by the sound of the Baldwin ten-wheeler locomotive still idling in the barn as it built a head of steam and chugged out to position itself at the head of the line of flatcars. As it did so, several groups of soldiers detached themselves from the others and climbed aboard the flatcars, positioning themselves among the cannon and crated materials as guards. The flatcars began to move, slowly but steadily, down the tracks past the switches, where the long train stopped. Then the switch was thrown, and the Baldwin backed the flatcars up the track to the line of passenger cars, coupling to them with a jolt. With the last "all aboard" call and a great hiss of steam and billowing black smoke, its whistle blowing a long departure signal and its bell clanging, the powerful Baldwin began a slow chug-chug as the assembled train moved out of the station. Amidst shouted hurrahs, wives and sweethearts walked alongside, blowing kisses and endearments to their men, until the train picked up too much speed for them to keep up. They then stood watching until the headlamp of the engine and the red tail light of the last car were no longer visible in the distance. Silently, they turned, gathered up their possessions, with heads low, and proceeded into the terminal to await the next ferry back to New York City. It was eight o'clock on a warm, pleasant, spring evening.

The Saints, on the other hand, grew excited. They were promised, after all, that as soon as the troop train departed, they would likewise be on their way. Clambering back aboard the emigrant train, they waited in anxious anticipation. After almost an hour, they grew agitated and restless as no sign of activity indicated they might be departing, young children crying as they sensed their parent's impatience. After all, they had been waiting patiently for seven hours! Then the rail-yard switch engine came to life once more, and began shuttling freight cars, one and two at a time, up and down tracks parallel to their own, until, finally, they backed up to the Saint's train of seven cars. With a great lurch each time cars were coupled, the switch-engine added eight freight cars and two parlor cars to the emigrant train. Finally, a large Baldwin eight-wheeler, less sleek, slower, but more powerful than the ten-wheelers proceeding it, steamed out of the round-house, slowly chugging across the marshaling yard until it aligned itself at the head of the train, jolting it once more as it coupled.

Conductors joined the train, and spread out among the cars to inspect tickets, moving from one row to another. The train crew inspected each coupling, ensured each set of wheels was lubricated, and after signaling the engineer, climbed aboard. Once more, they heard a departure whistle from the engine, felt a slight jerk, and almost imperceptibly the train began moving. Cheers erupted from the Saints, as they finally began their journey to Florence, the last stop before going on to Zion, waving animatedly at Elders Snow and Jones standing on the platform. For William, it was a great relief to sit and rest after a busy, hectic day superintending the luggage from the *Manchester* to the train's baggage cars.

CHAPTER 3
Amidst War's Alarms

William jerked awake suddenly, his fitful sleep interrupted yet again by the lurching of the railcar as the train wound its way slowly through the rolling hills between the Hudson and Delaware river valleys. It must be about two or three o'clock in the morning, he thought, unable to get to his watch. William was crowded uncomfortably against the wall, Mary Frances leaning on him, and Laura, in turn, leaning on Mary Frances. In the dim light cast by the oil lamps he could see that Mother Ould, crowded on the seat opposite with James and Franklin Blair, was likewise awake, fatigue and resignation reflected in her expression. The other passengers were strewn about the car in like manner, some lying in the aisle in an effort to find a measure of comfort, and even beneath the benches, though most of that space was taken by small children. And he had thought the accommodations aboard the *Manchester* were crowded! By comparison, the *Manchester* was luxurious.

He tried to doze off again, but without success. He had not been able to sleep well at all, given his discomfort, and he waited patiently as the train steamed along, stopping at the many small stations along their route: Hoboken, Hackensack, Passaic Springs, and Patterson in New Jersey, then crossing into New York and on through Ramsey, Ramapo, Southfields, Monroe, Chester, and New Hampton. His need to use the convenience had been growing steadily more urgent, but he dare not move lest he awaken Mary Frances and Laura. Mary Frances had a particularly difficult time getting comfortable and he didn't want to disturb her now that she seemed to be settled. Indeed, the effort to disentangle himself from the seat would surely disturb all six, and whomever else he would have to climb over to reach the curtained enclosure. He thought he could hold out for awhile yet.

The train pulled into Port Jarvis, a small town where the Erie Line intersected the Delaware River. The time indicated by the clock affixed to the station wall was four o'clock in the morning. The stop awakened most of the passengers, and as they stirred, the rest awoke. The station was deserted. The conductor warned them to stay close as the stop would be only long enough for the engine to take on water and fuel. Still, it was a chance to get off the train, stretch, and use the necessary, by now an urgent need for William. Soon, most of the Saints had disembarked. After thirty minutes the train was on its way again, picking up speed as it followed the New York side of the river valley to the northwest. But sleep did not return, and as it began to grow light, the passengers busied themselves trying to prepare for the day, and children climbed about seeking activity to assuage their boredom.

The train continued up the beautiful Delaware River valley through Pond Eddy, Narrowsburg, Cochecton, Hancock, Hale Eddy, McClure, and Binghamton. The valley's spring plumage cheered the weary, crowded Saints. As they traveled, they began to adapt to a routine to increase their comfort, the pleasant weather allowing them to take turns standing on the outside platforms at either end of the car. A few of the younger, more adventurous passengers even climbed to sit on the car roof, braving the soot and cinders from the wood-burning engine, James and Franklin among them, to Mother Ould's dismay.

By mid-morning, the train pulled into Binghamton after leaving the Delaware River and having climbed over the low rolling hills to the Susquehanna River and its valley. At Binghamton, several freight cars were detached from their train, others added, allowing the Saints to stretch their legs and to augment their spare provisions by purchasing bread, eggs, milk, and sausage offered by station peddlers. Their meal stop would be Elmira, New York, about three hours yet ahead. After being confined to the crowded train for over 12 hours, the stop was a welcome respite.

The Susquehanna River valley proved as pleasant as the Delaware, and the next leg passed quickly as the train rolled through Owego, Tioga Center, Smithboro, and Barton, stopping routinely to discharge and pick up passengers and cargo. About twenty miles from Elmira, New York, the Susquehanna turned south, but the railroad continued west along the Chemung River, a tributary of the Susquehanna running from Elmira. The train passed Chemung and Wellsburg, then approached Elmira.

Entering the town's outskirts, the Saints began to notice small clusters of blue-uniformed soldiers, rifles at their sides, standing guard at rail bridges and road intersections. The clusters became more frequent as the train steamed into town. When they entered the rail yard and stopped at the station, they were met by a large detachment of soldiers lined up the entire length of the platform. Beyond the station, the Saints could see a cluster of white tents where the soldiers had set up their bivouac. The train came to a stop, but the conductors restrained the passengers from disembarking, then left the train to speak to a sergeant who stepped forward to meet them. After a brief conversation, the three conductors returned to the cars. William stood with Elder Spencer on their car's platform between cars as their conductor returned.

"Seems they're looking for rebel sympathizers, spies, and saboteurs, though Lord knows how they'd tell. This town is a major north-south, east-west railroad intersection, and they've heard secessionists are heading this way. Want to inspect your immigrants."

"Well, I suppose it will be all right. I can assure you, though, that there are none among us," replied Elder Spencer. "Will it delay us long?"

"Nah! We'll be here several hours anyway. Got to change engines and make up a line of boxcars for Dunkirk. 'Sides, we'll be eatin' here. Over there, in the hotel beyond the station," the conductor said, motioning in its direction. "We'll just let the soldiers walk through the cars. Won't take long." So saying, he motioned to the sergeant who turned and gave orders to his troops.

A dozen or so soldiers gave their rifles to comrades and stepped forward, dividing into five groups, and climbed aboard the train. Two boarded William's car, one young and a bit nervous, but the other an old, grizzled corporal who seemed a bit put out that he had drawn the duty. The corporal entered first, followed by the young private.

"Lordie, Lordie, it smells in here," taunted the corporal after he had walked down the aisle a few steps. The Saints cleared the aisle so the two soldiers could make their ways. The corporal stopped from time to time to poke at a bag or to look closely at an individual, while the private just followed behind. The two hadn't gone more than halfway through when it became clear to both that there were no secessionist spies or saboteurs among the group. But the corporal warmed to his taunts.

"So this is what Mormons look like, eh? Looks like a bunch of igno-rant immigrants to me. Bet you don't even talk English. Hey, Mick!" he exclaimed derisively as he stopped before an older Welshman wearing his traditional old-country clothing. "You think you gonna make your-self a 'merican?" The older man looked down, ignoring the soldier.

With no rise from his baiting, the corporal grew bored and the two exited the door at the end of the car. A palpable sigh of relief escaped the passengers with their departure.

Inspection complete, the Saints were allowed to detrain, and as soon as they were all clear, leaving only a few behind in each car to keep an eye on the emigration company's possessions, the lead conductor sig-naled the engineer and the train moved off through the marshaling yard. Strung out in a long line, the Saints walked across the dusty street beyond the station to the hotel. The afternoon was warm and still, and many of the passengers removed their coats and wraps to become more comfortable. The woolens most had worn since leaving Liverpool were just too heavy in the humid spring air.

Entering the dinning hall, it was clear only half their number could be accommodated at one time. The wooden chairs filled quickly around the long, parallel tables set with crockery plates, cups, and eating ware, so the remaining Saints waited outside. Inside, negro porters immediate-ly began carrying out platters of food, placing them on the tables where the diners served themselves. The food was basic, but it was good: pork, potatoes, beans, greens, bread, butter, milk, and coffee. Hungry, the passengers ate quickly. After only twenty minutes, the porters returned and began removing the used tableware, leaving the condiments. There were no edible food scraps remaining. Lingering diners, rushed by the porters, quickly finished and left.

After brushing off the tables, the porters returned with fresh tableware, and only thirty minutes after the first group entered, the dining room was ready for the second group. They, too, promptly seated, and food was brought out. Again, on time, the porters returned to clean up, and soon the dining hall was ready for another group. It was an amazing and impressive performance. Four hundred diners in two groups were served in just one hour in a display of efficiency none of the emigrants had ever seen before! And they finished none too soon; the Saints had just completed their meal when an eastbound express arrived at the station and discharged its passengers to dine.

The Saints returned to the station, but the presence of so many soldiers made the emigrants uneasy and nervous. In general the soldiers ignored them, but a few seemed weary of monotonous sentry duty, and as a diversionary-sport began taunting the Saints. This went on intermittently, as the targeted Saints moved away from the offending soldiers in response. But then a new group of soldiers arrived to relieve the sentries, and the taunting began anew. This time several young women became targets. When the young women scorned their advances, the soldiers began to grow belligerent, and only intervention by a number of the elders quieted things down. It soon became clear that the Saints should leave the station for their own protection.

Their cars stood on the far side of the rail yard, not yet connected to an engine, while a switch-engine assembled additional freight cars to add to the train. But it was a slow process; each time a passenger or freight train steamed into the yard, the switch-engine responded to it rather than complete the task of assembling the emigrant's train. It had lowest priority. Nonetheless, Elder Spencer, William, and Elder Hanham agreed the Saints would be safer aboard the train and directed them to return. Two hours later, they steamed out of Elmira for Dunkirk, New York, on the shore of Lake Erie, the end of the Erie Line and a transfer to the Cleveland and Erie line to Cleveland.

Restless to be on their way, the Saints were happy to be aboard even though in crowded accommodations once more, and soon settled into a now familiar routine. The train continued up the Chemung River to Corning, then picked up a tributary to the Canisteo River. Following the Canisteo's valley, they passed through Addison, Cameron, and Canisteo. The light began to fade by the time the train left Canisteo and the river's valley to head southwest over the rolling hills, marking the northern end of the Allegheny Mountains. Travel slowed as the engine labored up the slopes, the smoke and sparks flowing out of the engine's funnel thickening with the climb and thinning on the descents. As darkness fell, showers of sparks created a remarkable sight for the Saints willing to remain outdoors.

Inside, the passengers tried to keep themselves as occupied as possible since none were looking forward to another night aboard the uncomfortable cars. The conductors lit the oil lamps, but the remaining dimness did not seem to affect the level of activity; few seemed interested in settling down. Those who could endure the evening chill and engine smoke remained outside, standing on the platforms or sitting on the roofs, well into the night, as they passed through Andover, Wellsville, Scio, Belvidere, Friendship, and Cuba. It was after midnight before the cars became quiet, only to come awake again an hour later when the Erie Line reached the Allegheny River at Hinsdale and the train stopped to replenish the engine's fuel and water. Within the hour, the train was on its way, again. This time, being able to follow the Allegheny River smoothed out the ride for awhile, and though exhausted, most of the Saints fell into a fitful sleep in the early morning hours, while the train labored, once more, over low hills on its way to Dunkirk through Great Valley, Little Valley, Catteraugus, Dayton, and Perrysburg.

William and Mary Frances had not been able to sleep. Huddled together against the wall on their bench, they sat quietly, occasionally exchanging endearments as one or the other shifted position. Despite the discomfort, both were happy to be together and to be on their way to Zion.

"Do you think Mother is right?" questioned Mary Frances. "Will the wagon trip to Zion be the most difficult? At least we'll be out in the air!"

William paused before answering. "I'm not sure. I've heard the same stories about the trek's hardships as your mother, but I'm thinking most of them happened years back, before the Church learned how to organize and prepare wagon companies. Not that there aren't some hazards, mind you! The calamity involving the Willie and Martin handcart companies, just a few years ago, is a ready reminder! Over two hundred perished in early snows, but they were ill-prepared for the journey. We'll be better prepared, I can assure you. Indian depredations, also, have been rare, I'm told. No, I don't really think there is much risk. But we'll be cautious. I fully believe the Lord hasn't brought us this far only to have us suffer misfortune before we reach Zion."

Assured, Mary Frances grew silent. Light from the eastern horizon was beginning to show through windows on the right side as they turned directly west. They watched quietly as the horizon grew brighter, the rising sun coloring the sky briefly before it rose. Soon after sunrise, the train passed through Forestville, and within an hour pulled into Dunkirk terminal. They had reached the end of their first leg.

The station was quiet. Only the telegraph operator was on duty, dozing at his table near a dim lantern, where he awaited the familiar clicks signaling a telegram destined for Dunkirk. William organized a work party to unload the luggage once more, and with many hands, it was soon stacked neatly on the platform. The broad expanse of Lake Erie spread before them, a light haze hovering in the early morning sunlight above its calm, windless surface. On this cool spring morning, the only activity they observed was a small group of men loading a boat at the low dock just behind the station house. After discharging the Saints and their baggage, the train pulled onto a siding where the engineers and train crew left to find breakfast. After a short while, a lone figure hurried toward them from the direction of town. It was the stationmaster.

"Well, well," he exclaimed as he reached the locked door to the station where William, Elder Spencer, and Elder Hanham were waiting.

"You're early! Made good time, did you? My, you've got quite a group," he continued as he unlocked the door and invited the passengers in. "Won't all be able to fit in here, but at least the women folk will have a place to sit."

William and his two companions followed the stationmaster into his office and waited as he shuffled among papers lying on a standing-height desk. He picked one out of a stack.

"Let's see," he continued. "Your group is headed for St. Joe?" He glanced at the three who nodded their heads. Elder Spencer spoke.

"We're scheduled to transfer to the Cleveland and Erie to Cleveland. Is the station near?"

"Not too far. It's just a few blocks back in town. You'll have to go over there to get baggage carts, though." He pointed back in the direction from which he came. "Just follow that street there. Can't miss it."

They thanked him and left the office. Outside, Elder Spencer turned to Elder Hanham.

"Stay with the Saints until I return. Elder Jefferies and I will go on ahead to check on arrangements. Shouldn't be long."

The two walked down the street in the direction indicated by the stationmaster, and saw rails visible a few blocks ahead. Arriving at the cross street down which the rails ran, they turned left toward the Cleveland and Erie station. Like the Erie Line station, it was quiet. Only freight cars stood in the yard, not a passenger car in sight. The stationmaster, though, was in his office, visible through the ticket windows. As they stepped up to the window, the stationmaster looked up at them.

"What can I do for you gents?"

"I'm Elder Spencer, Latter-day Saint Church. We've got bookings for 400 of our members to St. Joseph. We're over at the Erie station."

The stationmaster stood and came over. "Yes, you do. But I got bad news. Ain't any parlor cars available. Army's got 'em all goin' to war. May be some time 'fore we get 'em back. You see in the yard, all I got is freight cars."

"Yes, we noticed. Don't you have any idea how soon you'll get some?"

"Couple of days, at least. Looks like you'll have to put up in a hotel for a spell."

"Good Lord!" Elder Spencer exclaimed. "We can't afford to put our people up in a hotel! Very few can pay. Most are emigrants with just enough to get to our destination!"

"Seems you got a real problem."

"Isn't there anything you can do to help us?"

The stationmaster paused to think a moment. "Tell you what I can do. I'll telegraph on ahead to Cleveland and see what they got. Maybe they're better off than us. Take about half hour. Have a sit," he concluded, motioning to the waiting area and turning back toward his office.

William and Elder Spencer took opposing seats. Both were disheartened.

"I don't suppose a day or so delay would hurt," said Elder Spencer. "Still, several days could be a problem. Town seems quiet enough, and I've seen no troops. But it could place a strain on many of the Saints. Less than half have the means to set up in a hotel. I'm just afraid if some did and some didn't, then the inequity would cause hard feelings."

"Of course, you're right," replied William. "The stationmaster seems helpful enough. I'm sure he doesn't want four hundred emigrants camped in his station for several days. Maybe he can make suitable arrangements."

"I hope so," concluded Elder Spencer.

It didn't take that long for the stationmaster to send and get a reply from Cleveland. After about twenty minutes, he came into the waiting room.

"Looks like you've got a bit of luck! Cleveland has parlor cars they're willing to hold for you, but we have to get you there by late this afternoon. If you and your people are willing to rough it, I'll make up a train of freight cars for you. Got a freight train due in here in just two hours going on to Cleveland. I'll add you to it. Will that work?"

The two looked at one another, thinking it over. "How long is it to Cleveland?" asked Elder Spencer.

"'Bout seven hours, maybe less."

"What do you think, Elder Jefferies?"

William recalled the cramped accommodations they had endured for the last 36 hours. Could it be any worse? "I think we should," he replied.

Elder Spencer looked from William to the stationmaster. "We'll do it."

The mid-spring day had a touch of summer to it. Traveling smoothly along the lakeshore toward Cleveland, the Saints could see the lake's shimmering humidity through the freight cars almost-closed sliding doors. Inside, all were feeling uncomfortable and somewhat claustrophobic while the sun heated up surfaces around them. Open top-hatches at either end provided some airflow, but it didn't help much. And, the transfer in Dunkirk had been difficult. Though the distance between the two stations was not far, there were few baggage carts so most of the luggage had to be carried by the emigrants themselves. Though only for a short distance, lugging the heavy baggage had accentuated the moist heat, making everyone very grateful when they finally had it loaded aboard the cars. William was especially relieved as once again he had been in charge.

The stationmaster had been generous with the number of cars, but their condition was grim and required extensive cleaning by the Saints before they were habitable. Several had been used for livestock. The stationmaster had been able to furnish only a few amenities: a water cask for each car and several buckets each for sanitary facilities; the passengers held blankets up for one another for a measure of privacy whenever their use was required. What's more, the through freight to which they were attached arrived late, so it was midday before they were on their way once more. "It's only for a few hours," the Saints kept telling themselves, "it's only a few hours." But still, they suffered in the moist heat and primitive accommodations. William reflected upon his conclusion when the stationmaster suggested they travel to Cleveland on freight cars: Could it be any worse? Yes. It definitely could be worse.

But like all things, good or bad, it came to an end. At dusk the train steamed into Cleveland and the exhausted, harried, and disheveled Saints tumbled out of the freight cars in grateful release, welcoming the evening's coolness. The Cleveland and Eric Line would not be remembered fondly by any of these emigrants! Cleveland had been their original dinner stop, and though late, the dining room proprietor agreed to feed the company of very grateful travelers.

As promised, the railroad did, indeed, have passenger cars waiting for them. Real passenger cars, as upholstered and comfortable as those William had seen in Jersey City! Could the railroad be trying to make up for the miserable trip from Dunkirk? For whatever the reason, the Saints were nevertheless grateful for the change. They would travel in comfort only to Toledo and their next train change, just over 100 miles away, but it was a trip they savored. With a hearty meal and comfortable accommodations, the Saints were in much better spirits upon departing Cleveland than they were upon arriving. The five-hour trip to Toledo passed all too quickly for many of them as they pulled into the town in the early morning hours.

They were scheduled for a train change in Toledo and then on into Chicago. The delay in Dunkirk caused the Saints to miss their train and the next would not be until morning. The luggage transfer went smoothly this time, and 400 emigrants settled down in the station for the rest of the night, their rest interrupted hourly by the arrival and departure of both passenger and freight trains. Several were loaded with soldiers and war materiel headed toward Chicago.

At dawn, the yardmaster began making up the train that would carry the Saints to Chicago. He assembled the passenger cars first, and by early morning the stationmaster was ready to load the passengers. The cars they climbed aboard were emigrant cars once more, much the same as those they traveled on from Jersey City. Resignedly, the emigrants crowded aboard their five cars and tried to make themselves comfortable, not knowing how long before they'd depart. The stationmaster had seemed particularly nervous and anxious to get them loaded and out of the station. And, within the hour it became clear why as a long train pulled into the station and discharged a regiment of soldiers, almost a thousand. With feelings of relief they were out of the way, the Saints witnessed the flood of soldiers from the opposite side of the yard. The soldiers seemed too busy to notice the emigrants aboard the cars, and departed after their engine took aboard its fuel and water.

Several additional trains came and departed, each time interrupting the switch-engine's efforts to add freight cars to the Saints' train. Consequently, it was late afternoon before they finally pulled out of the station for Chicago. As they left town and the coastal plain on which it sat, the train entered the wooded, rolling hills of northern Indiana that soon became monotonous. Thick woods began just fifty yards either side of the railroad right-of-way, and the travelers were unable to see beyond the trees. Hour after hour, nothing but trees passed through their view. Darkness came almost as a relief.

But relief of monotonous scenery was soon replaced by the tedium of trying, however uncomfortably, to settle down for the night. The emigrant company had eaten early that morning before loading, but now they were hungry. Breaking out the spare provisions, galley crews prepared a meal of oatmeal, beans, and coffee. It would have to do until their meal-stop at Elkhart, Indiana the next day.

Sheer exhaustion accounted for the fitful sleep the Saints experienced during their fourth, long night since departing Jersey City. Five times, the slower mixed-passenger-and-freight train pulled onto a siding while express trains sped by, each time interrupting their restless slumber. Dawn found the train stopping briefly at Goshen, not far from their rest stop at Elkhart, and within the hour the train pulled into the station. The dining hall was ready for them, and with accustomed efficiency they were all served in just over an hour.

On their way back to the train after dining, William and Mary Frances savored a quiet walk together along the quiet streets adjacent to the station. Upon approaching the station, they saw several light wagons containing produce and bread goods lined up parallel to the tracks.

"Oh, William! I'm so tired of oatmeal and tea," exclaimed Mary Frances. "Let's get something fresh. I know Mother and the others would appreciate it."

William reached into his pocket and, drawing out his purse, counted his coins. "I suppose we can afford a little. Let's take a look."

They approached the center wagon, attracted to it because of its fresh paint and neat lettering, Anglemeyer and Sons, Produce. A ruddy-complected young man in his mid-teens, simply, but neatly dressed, stood near the wagon.

"Welcome," he said, politely, with a slight Dutch accent. "Would thou likest to see our goods? It's all fresh."

As they approached, the two saw that the wagon bed was loaded with root vegetables, summer sausages, eggs, bread, baked goods, and milk. Even though they had just finished a meal, the appearance of fresh groceries, particularly the baked goods, reminded them of how tedious train-fare had become. They looked longingly and carefully. William and Mary Frances conferred together.

"We've only got fifty cents to spare as we have a long way to travel," said William. "Will that get us eggs, sausage, bread, and a few of those delicious-looking cakes?"

The boy looked carefully at William and Mary Frances, recognizing them as emigrants.

"How far are thee and thy wife traveling?" he asked.

William explained where they had come from and why they were headed for the Salt Lake Valley.

"So, thou art Mormon! I know of thy persecutions and trials. We are Amish, and know a little of persecutions ourselves. Art thou an elder?"

"Why, yes! I'm Elder William Jefferies. And this is my wife, Sister Mary Frances."

"I am Levi Anglemeyer. It will be a while, but I also will be an elder. In our own faith. Pick out what thou wouldest like, and fifty cents wouldest be adequate."

Surprised and pleased at the young man's kindness, Mary Frances selected prudently, not wanting to take advantage of his generosity. When they completed the transaction, William thanked Levi.

"Thank you for your kindness, Levi. May the Lord bless you and your family."

The two returned to the train, by now ready to depart. As it pulled away, William stood on the platform and waved at Levi. The young man waved back. What a surprising, gratifying experience that was, thought William, especially after all the hostility that had greeted them landing in their new country.

Chicago would be the only major city the Saints would see on their journey west since leaving Jersey City. Beginning its frontier days as an Indian crossroads, frontier fort, and trading post, it had grown over the last thirty years into the major agricultural, industrial, and transportation hub of the northwest United States. In size and importance, it rivaled St. Louis, 300 miles to its south. It was also in turmoil at the beginning of the Civil War.

The city was staunchly pro-Union, but it also had a vociferous minority of secessionists. They were tolerated at first, but as war preparations intensified and neighboring Missouri continued to vacillate between secession and remaining in the Union, tolerance was strained. Moreover, the city became a major staging area for the Federal build-up along the Mississippi River at Cairo in southern Illinois where the Ohio River joined the Mississippi. A large Federal army presence in Chicago and the usual rumors of secessionist sabotage and espionage finally ended tolerance for secessionist sympathizers. A number of riots had destroyed pro-secessionist papers and mobs hung prominent pro-southern sympathizers in effigy. The Saints feared their passage would be difficult.

The sun was close to the western horizon as the mixed train carrying the emigrants turned northwest at the southern tip of Lake Michigan for its short run to Chicago, and the Saints began noticing once more groups of soldiers guarding railroad bridges and trestles. Near the larger trestles the soldiers established bivouacs of precisely aligned white tents that stood out in stark contrast to the browns and greens of the countryside. Nearing the outskirts of the city they passed through small villages, then larger communities with their dwellings and shops, all increasing in density as they entered the city itself. The train slowed to a crawl as it paralleled North Street in the small community of Crawford, crossing the heavily guarded bridge over the south river, then turned abruptly right to run north along a country road leading into the city. Soon the train began angling slightly to parallel the river for a short distance before it pulled into the railroad marshalling yard of Chicago's Van Buren Station.

The yard was full. Each track was occupied by a long line of freight cars onto which workmen loaded goods from freight wagons. Soldiers, individually and in groups, patrolled the yard. The emigrant's train finally stopped on a siding where their cars were disconnected. The rest of the train pulled away, and after a delay, a switch-engine coupled to the emigrant's cars. Pushing from the rear, the switch-engine maneuvered the short train toward the terminal, its seven cars swaying gently while crossing multiple tracks before finally turning directly into the wide, arched-ceiling barn that sheltered the terminal's seven-track loading area. Their train came to a stop before an imposing four-story, limestone terminal building aglow with hundreds of lighted lamps.

The Van Buren Station terminal was busy. All seven pairs of tracks were occupied by trains loading and unloading passengers. Three were troop trains, and blue-uniformed corporals and sergeants scurried around as their men stood in loose formation, muskets stacked in neat, aligned pyramids while awaiting orders to board. Civilians carrying their luggage hurried to and fro, dodging soldiers and baggage carts as they sought out their trains or headed toward the terminal. The Saints were instructed to remain on board until the church emigration agent in Chicago contacted them. William, Elder Spencer, and Elder Hanham de-boarded and stood together on the platform near the front of the train. They didn't have to wait long before a well-dressed gentleman approached.

"I'm Elder Tanner. Joshua Tanner" he said, extending his hand. "You're the emigration company presidency, I presume?"

"We are," replied Elder Spencer. They all shook hands as they introduced themselves.

"Well now! I'm certain you're all ready to get off the train! Been a long trip, hasn't it? I've engaged wagons and teams to haul you and your luggage over to the Chicago and Quincy terminal. It's in Crawford, just over a mile away. Your train departs early tomorrow morning. The wagons are waiting out front on Van Buren Street now. Soon's we can get carts to carry the luggage out, we'll get loaded. Meanwhile, have your passengers go into the terminal. But warn them to stay together! It won't be hard to get separated here tonight!"

William was dispatched to supervise the luggage transfer, taking with him James and Franklin and a dozen others to help. Elders Spencer and Hanham returned to the cars to give instructions and soon the Saints detrained and entered the terminal.

The terminal was much grander than the one at Jersey City. Entering the main hall from the train platforms through a long row of arch-topped double doors, the Saints entered a high-domed, marble-floored waiting hall bustling with travelers. The hall ran most of the city-block-wide structure's length, and down its center, row upon row of benches faced each other, providing seating for over a thousand travelers. And travelers were seated on every row. As at Jersey City, uniformed army officers awaiting departure sat and visited with their families, wives and sweethearts touching moist eyes with dainty white handkerchiefs. Ticket windows and offices occupied each end, and in the four corners stood grand staircases leading to the offices on the floors above. Beneath each staircase a lunch counter served meals, snacks, and beverages.

Elders Spencer and Hanham shepherded the Saints to a less-occupied section of seating as the emigrants looked about in awe at the high, arched ceiling, the hall's overwhelming size, and the large crowd. Such a large public building, in such grandeur, was a new experience for the emigrants.

Most of the occupants seated nearby moved to other areas upon seeing such a large group approach, leaving the group room to find space together. Grateful and relieved to be able to stretch after their four-day confinement, the Saints began to settle down and patronize of the food vendors.

William and the luggage crew struggled with the baggage deposited on the platform for loading. Few railroad luggage carts were available on such a busy evening, so they had to make do with the two they were able to procure. It took many trips between the large stack of luggage deposited on the platform and the fifteen wagons and teams waiting in front of the station, and several hours, to complete the task. But at last the baggage was loaded. William sought out Elder Tanner in the dim light thrown by myriad lamps hanging on the station's face. Elder Tanner was looking down the street as William approached, a concerned expression on his face.

"This is the last of it," William reported.

"Took awhile, didn't it?" He glanced briefly at William, then back again down the street.

Curious, William followed Tanner's gaze. Then he noticed it. Four blocks down Van Buren Street, about a quarter-mile to the east on the other side of the adjacent South River, stood a large group of people before a seven-story building. The nearby neo-classical office and merchant buildings lining both sides of the street were illuminated by torches carried by the group, their arched windows and pillars flickering in the shadows thrown by the torches. As he strained to listen, William could hear strident voices and shouts, interspersed with the tinkling sound of glass being broken. William suddenly felt anxious. He had seen these groups before. It was a mob!

"That's not good," Elder Tanner remarked. "Sounds like a mob. We will be going that way so I better have a look. Stay here with the wagons. Your clothes identify you as an immigrant, and we don't want to chance they might notice." Leaving William, Elder Tanner walked toward the mob.

As William waited, a group of about a dozen soldiers filed out of the terminal carrying their muskets and lined up in formation before a sergeant. The sergeant barked orders and the patrol turned and marched in quickstep down Van Buren toward the mob, crossing the canal bridge suspended by a single steel arch. Elder Spencer joined William as the soldiers departed.

"Saw the soldiers run out. What is it?" he asked.

"Seems there's a mob gathering down the street," William replied as he gestured. "Elder Tanner went to have a look. That's the direction we have to go, and he's concerned."

The soldiers reached the crowd, split up, and stood around it, but took no action. The sergeant began elbowing his way through the crowd and was soon lost from view. Shouting and yelling grew louder, as did the sound of breaking glass. Then the sound of wood splitting. Before long, the crowd pulled back, and a large object crashed through the glass of a second-story window and fell to the street before the mob. Cheers erupted, and additional objects followed in a shower of paper fluttering to the ground. The flames of a bonfire began to grow. The soldiers stood quietly just beyond the mob. Another cheer arose as a long object was hauled aloft at the end of a rope and tied to the top of a lamp pole.

"Oh no!" exclaimed Elder Spence. "Is that a man? They're hanging someone!"

With a sickening feeling, both stood there watching as the mob gradually quieted down, its fury spent. Within a few minutes, the crowd began to disperse and the soldiers formed up again, marching back toward the terminal, the figure left hanging from the lamp pole. Elder Tanner arrived before the soldiers. Elder Spencer cried out to him in alarm.

"Elder Tanner! Did they hang someone just now? What kind of lawless place is this?"

"No. Thank the Lord for that. The mob strung up an effigy of the newspaper proprietor. He's a southern sympathizer and his pro-secessionist newspaper has enraged most of the city, it seems. That's why the army didn't intervene. The mob burned his presses. It's fortunate we took so long loading the wagons! We could have been in the middle of it. Once a mob forms, no telling what it'll do. They could just as easily have turned on us if we'd been there! We've been blessed!"

It was late evening before the emigration company was ready for the mile trip to Crawford's Chicago and Quincy railroad terminal. The four hundred Saints strung out in a long procession following the wagon train carrying their baggage as they proceeded east on Van Buren, then south on Sherman Street. They were quiet and uneasy as they passed the still-smoldering fire in the street in front of the ransacked newspaper offices. The effigy of the newspaper publisher hung grotesquely from the lamp-post, illuminated from above. Below the effigy was a crudely written sign, "Death to Traitors." They would be happy to be out of this city.

The trip to Crawford and the terminal had proceeded smoothly once the wagon train turned south onto Sherman Street, where all was quiet and did not offer fearful images. Upon arriving, they discovered the emigrant train had already been made up, so the Saints were on their way to Quincy before first light, relieved to be out of Chicago. Elder Tanner had stood on the loading platform with William and Elders Spencer and Hanham as the train prepared to depart.

"Godspeed you and your company, brethren," he said, shaking their hands. "I'll be joining you in Florence the last of June. I'm shipping about a hundred wagons from the Schuttler works here in town over the next few weeks, and when the last emigrant company passes through, I'll join them for Florence." He turned to leave, then paused. "Oh yes," he continued, "Be alert during your trip across Missouri! Word is that secessionist and rebel groups are stirring things up, particularly in western Missouri. Several bands have shot up trains and torn up track. But, may the Lord bless you and keep you safe." Elder Tanner turned and departed just as the conductors shouted their "all aboard!" and the engine blew its whistle for departure.

Light was appearing on the eastern horizon by the time the Saints were beyond the city and its suburbs, but it had not yet spread to the southwest, the direction they were headed. Far ahead, low on the dark horizon, the Saints could see flickers of lightning.

"Looks like a spring storm ahead," commented William to Mary Frances. Her head lay on William's shoulder as William leaned against the short wall partition between two windows. The windows were raised a few inches to provide ventilation, yet hoping to keep out as much of the engine's smoke and cinders as possible. Laura was resting against

Mary Frances in what had become their accustomed positions. Likewise, Mother Ould and the two boys sat on the seat opposite, James leaning on Mother Ould, and Franklin on James. When the boys were out on the platform or the roof, where they went whenever they could, the remaining four could stretch out more comfortably on the crowded seats. But for now they were all resting quietly after the strenuous efforts of the night before, lulled by the car's gentle swaying.

Before long, Mother Ould would help the car's galley crew to prepare breakfast. The Saints had purchased bread, eggs, sausages, pork and milk from the terminal's peddlers, and they were looking forward to a good breakfast. All were surprised and pleased at the low cost of foodstuffs offered in Chicago. A lot lower than New York.

"How long before we change trains again?" Mary Frances asked.

"Don't think we change 'til Quincy. Then we take a ferry across the Mississippi to Hannibal on the Missouri side. I believe that will be our last change. Once in Missouri, we stay on the same train to St. Joseph where we catch a riverboat to Florence."

"Oh my!" sighed Mary Frances. "Just two more changes. When you say it like that, it seems we're almost there!"

"Aye. Would be nice. But today is just Monday. We've only been traveling since Wednesday evening. We'll get to Quincy tonight, but probably won't get a ferry until tomorrow morning. Then tomorrow we'll cross to Hannibal, board the train if it's made up, and on to St. Joseph tomorrow afternoon. Should make St. Joseph by Wednesday. I believe it's two days by steamboat to Florence, so that should put us there by Friday. Just four more days after today!"

Mary Frances sighed once more. "If it's like the last four days, it'll seem like a lifetime."

By mid-morning they had traveled well into overcast skies, the first they had encountered since leaving Jersey City. In fact, the weather had been exceedingly fair thus far, dry, cool nights and warm spring days. It got a little uncomfortable running along the shores in the humidity of Lake Erie, but the rest of the trip had been pleasant.

But few of the emigrants gave the impending weather much thought; overcast skies and rain were an expected way of spring life in the United Kingdom and northern Europe. Soon the train entered an area of scattered showers and the cars grew crowded again as passengers scampered down from the roofs and in from the platforms, only to return when they passed through the shower. But then the showers came more frequently, and finally they were traveling in a steady drizzle. Windows closed and the cars grew stuffy and muggy in the increasing humidity. Soon the Saints began to notice flashes of lightning, still distant yet. It was the storm William and Mary Frances had noticed on the far horizon several hours before.

Suddenly, the drizzle stopped as they came into an area of dark, rainless overcast. And then they saw it, dead ahead about ten miles away, a solid wall of thick, black clouds extending from the ground up as high as they could see. Lightning randomly flashed inside the wall of clouds and briefly illuminated the layers of cloud, while a deep rumble of thunder resonated through the still air.

"My lard!" exclaimed William. "I've never seen such a thing! What kind of storm is that?"

As they traveled closer to the storm, the rolling thunder became more constant and lightning grew more intense, illuminating the entire cloud-wall from within. Observing through moisture-laden windows, many of the Saints grew anxious, remembering the intense storm at sea that had many of them thinking they would surely perish. But now they were on land! How could a storm like this find them? But the train continued steadily on, approaching the black clouds. Fierce winds began swaying the railroad cars as they drew closer. The conductor came through the car, closing ventilation vents in the ceiling. One of the passengers, very agitated, stopped him.

"We've got to stop! We've got to stop! We can't enter that storm! It'll kill us all!"

The conductor, an amused smile on his face, paused to reassure the passenger. "Nah! Nothin' to it! Better to keep movin', though. That way, we get through it faster. We'll be safe."

Few believed him, though, as the train entered the storm. Rain suddenly came down in torrents, cutting visibility from the windows to nothing. On the left side, the direction of the wind, water began seeping in around the windows, and narrow, steady streams of water came though the roof vents. The rain increased in intensity against the windows, until it seemed they must surely shatter. Families seated on the left side quickly moved away, William and his family included.

By now the thunderclaps were deafening, the lightning a constant, flickering flash. Wind gusts threw debris against the train and windows. It grew black as night. Many of the Saints could be heard uttering prayers for deliverance. The storm continued. It seemed to last forever. Wind gusts swayed the cars so violently the Saints feared they were about to topple. But the train continued on, and as suddenly as they had entered the storm, they were out. One minute, in the depths of a devil-storm, and the next, out in the clear sun! Relieved and incredulous, the Saints gradually began to raise up and look about, their pale faces reflecting amazement that they had survived the storm, and relief that they had been spared.

But what a sight awaited them! Broken trees stripped of vegetation appeared everywhere, the ground was stripped bare of grass, and a wide swath of destruction paralleled the tracks just a few hundred yards away. Had they come through that? The Saints were silent. No one moved, the train now, once again, swaying gently, the familiar clacking of the wheels providing a reassuring calmness. The conductor opened the door and stepped in.

"Anybody hurt?" He started down the isle, looking from side to side. "We're past it now. You've just experienced a plains cyclone. Impressive, warn't it?"

The train arrived at Galesburg, their rest and meal stop, by mid-afternoon. The storm had been the leading edge of a warm front, and now the air behind it was hot and humid. The emigrants began shedding their heavy woolens and crinolines in effort to adapt to the change in climate, but found little relief. The town was pleasantly situated among the low, rolling hills of western Illinois. While approaching the town, they noted many prosperous farms, the owners in their fields turning the black, fertile soil behind pairs of plow horses.

William and his family had eaten with the first group seated, and now he was standing with Elder Spencer in the shade of a covered boardwalk waiting for the second group to finish. Elder Spencer was uncharacteristically silent, appearing pre-occupied and despondent, his gaze directed toward nothing in particular.

"Didn't enjoy the meal?" asked William, hoping to draw him out.

Elder Spencer looked up, startled. "No. Quite the contrary. Very good fare."

"You seem a little out of sorts. Is everything going well?" replied William.

"Sorry. I was just reminiscing about times past." He paused a moment, then continued. "Our beautiful Nauvoo is just a little over fifty miles southwest of here." He paused and nodded in the direction. "We had quite a prosperous trade relationship with Galesburg before things went bad for us back in '45 and '46. Used to come up here with my father from time to time. Folks here appeared to be fair-minded. Sure liked our goods. Paid well for them, too! But in the end they turned against us like everybody else."

Elder Spencer and his family had been among the dispossessed Saints who, unable to defend themselves against murderous mobs, abandoned Nauvoo in 1846 and emigrated to the Salt Lake Valley in distant Mexican territory under Brigham Young, Joseph Smith's successor.

He grew silent, pensive again. William sensed his pain and remained quiet. Before long, their attention was drawn to the second group, now finished and returning to the station. William and Elder Spencer joined them.

As the train continued its journey toward Quincy, William sought out Elder Spencer once more. He found him on the platform at the rear of the last car, standing silently. Elder Spencer seemed pleased to have William's company, but little conversation passed between the two.

Then William saw tears form in Elder Spencer's eyes as he viewed the passing countryside.

"That's Macomb," said Elder Spencer, pointing at a passing town. "Used to come here, too. The next town we pass will be Colchester. It's only a few miles from Carthage." He paused, fighting back the tears. After a few minutes, his chin quivering slightly, he continued. "Carthage jail is where they murdered Joseph and his brother Hyrum. Nauvoo is just another fifteen miles beyond." He looked down to shield his tears from view.

Fifteen minutes later, the train slowed as it passed through Colchester. Elder Spencer looked up as they entered, and pointed out a road toward the west to William.

"There. Carthage is just down that road." He paused for several seconds. "May the town be damned forever!" Anger now clouding his countenance, Elder Spencer turned abruptly and entered the coach. After watching Colchester pass from view, William turned to return to Mary Frances and his family, saddened by Elder Spencer's loss and the outrage suffered by their beloved Church.

Quincy had grown to become the largest town on the Illinois side of the Mississippi between Alton, 75 miles downriver to the south and just a few miles upriver from St. Louis, and Rock Island, about 75 miles upriver to the north. Normally a placid, quiet town, Quincy was now a bustling river port, crowded with steamboats loading war materiel streaming in from all across west-central Illinois and headed downriver for Cairo where the Federal troops were gathering and training.

Darkness overtook the Saints just after passing Colchester, and as they pulled into Quincy's marshaling yard they found it full of railcars. Those they could see were empty or being unloaded. Light from a dozen bivouac campfires, scattered throughout the rail yard, silhouetted soldiers and illuminated the motionless railcars in a reddish glow as the emigrant's train switched slowly from track to track toward the dimly lit terminal. Upon detraining, the Saints found that the steamboat ferrying them across to Hannibal would not be loading until morning.

After unloading their baggage, the Saints settled down in the waiting room and on the platform in the warm evening to await the dawn. From the terminal, the emigrants could see hundreds of campfires spread upstream and downstream along the river's shoreline as an Illinois volunteer infantry regiment, the 21st Illinois commanded by Colonel U.S. Grant, waited to board steamboats for their trip to Cairo. Listening carefully, the Saints could hear the sounds of laughter, singing, and musical instruments from the camp wafting toward them on the warm evening breezes. Dozens of steamboats lined the shore, silhouetted against the river with their decks illuminated by lanterns. The level of activity and sounds from the camps finally began to die as night grew on, growing silent in the wee hours of the morning.

The Saints awakened well before dawn to the sounds of the regiment's bugles playing reveille, and by the distant barking of orders soon after. Dying campfires were stoked, stirring sparks that flickered in the still-dark morning. Before long, the sounds of rattling tinware reached the Saints as the soldiers ate breakfast. By daybreak the Saints could see the regiment breaking camp, and by the time the rising sun reached the river's lower elevations, the regiment was standing in formation awaiting orders to board three steamboats moored to floating docks tied securely to the riverbank nearby.

The rest of the waterfront had also come alive, and amidst the neighing of horses and shouts of teamsters and stevedores, hundreds of wagons, many of them coming from the rail yard, lined up before the many steamboats, waiting in turn for their cargo to be unloaded and carried aboard. The steamboats began to fire their boilers as they were being loaded, and soon pale plumes of smoke began billowing from the forest of smokestacks. William wondered when their turn would come to load, and upon inquiring, was informed the Saints would load at the docks to be vacated by the Regiment.

Regimental loading proceeded slowly aboard its three vessels. Supplies and provisions were loaded first, carried aboard and stowed on the main deck by soldiers, tunics removed to provide relief from the morning's moist heat. By late morning, the troops, themselves, were ready to board. Responding to shouted orders, the troops divided into three groups, formed themselves into two-abreast columns, and with packs and muskets over their shoulders, began marching up the dock's gangplank and on to the steamboats tied beyond. The first aboard climbed to the upper deck and filed out to line the railings. Then they filled the cargo deck. When the troops were loaded, their officers boarded, gangplanks were raised, and by noon, amid the piercing sound of steamboat whistles and a great belching of thick, dark smoke, the steamboats began to steam away in turn, giant rear paddlewheels churning the river water to a white froth.

Now it was the Saints' turn. William and his work-party had loaded the emigration company's luggage and provisions aboard wagons during the course of the morning, and upon signal, they descended the slight slope to the river and the first of the floating docks where the steamboat Blackhawk was tying up after just arriving. The Saints followed the wagons and, like the soldiers, waited along the shore for cargo loading to finish, only to find themselves crowded by groups and individuals streaming out of town to board the vessel. Many of the Saints began to worry there wouldn't be space for them, and sought out Elder Spencer. Inquiring, however, he was assured there would be room. But it would be a crowded crossing. Troop mobilization had created a shortage of steamboats all along the river.

Having arrived first, the Saints were allowed to board as soon as a late arriving platoon of about forty soldiers finished boarding and took their pick of seating. The emigrants were instructed to climb to the middle, or hurricane deck, and soon found themselves crowded closely together along the eight-foot second-level covered deck, which ran around the steamboat. Down below on the cargo deck, open on its sides to the elements, the passengers continued to stream aboard, finding space where they could: atop cargo, sitting on railings, and even climbing onto the upper deck, or roof. Finally, when it seemed the steamboat could not possibly accommodate one more passenger, the gangplank was raised and the boat departed.

Moving out to mid-river, it picked up speed as it caught the swift spring current. Hannibal was thirty miles downstream, about a three-hour crossing this time of year.

During the course of the voyage, passengers spread out in an effort to relieve congestion. But space was scarce. Hurricane-deck staterooms were occupied by soldiers, and many passengers sat in the deck's corridors and staircases. The spacious cargo deck at the water's level, now crowded with goods, had filled quickly upon loading, but many soon abandoned it in the late-spring heat, hoping breezes on the upper decks would be more comfortable. William and his family managed to find space atop cargo crates at the bow, and because of the breezes were able to enjoy the voyage more than most as they looked upon the lush verdure along both shores.

As the steamboat moved down river, on the Illinois side, the land sloped gently upward from the riverbanks to rolling hills, whereas on the Missouri side, the low hills opposite Quincy turned to high limestone bluffs, then alternated with pastoral valleys and meadows through which small rivers and creeks flowed, emptying into the river.

The crossing was uneventful. Within the expected three hours, Hannibal's church steeples came into view, just downstream from a high limestone bluff that gave way to more gently rolling terrain. Soon the emigrants could make out the town itself, modest-sized three- and four-storied brick commercial buildings in parallel streets lining the shore, a row of warehouses arranged along the street fronting the river. White homes spread upward on the slopes beyond. Along the south edge of town a wide creek flowed into the Mississippi from the base of a line of low hills running to the west. The Mississippi's high bluffs began anew south of the creek junction. Railroad tracks from the west ran parallel to the creek and turned north into town along Front Street. The railroad station itself lay just to the south of downtown, on the other side of the creek along the Mississippi's banks. Only a few steamboats were arrayed along the shoreline: several along the shore at Front Street, and one at the shore next to the railroad terminal.

In contrast to the bustling Quincy, Hannibal appeared quiet and tranquil. Businesses were open, but few wagons or other vehicles occupied the streets. As in so many towns through which the Saints had traveled, small groups of blue-coated soldiers stood with their muskets around the town at key intersections. War commerce didn't seem to be having much affect on Hannibal.

The Blackhawk nosed onto the shore next to the railroad terminal, angling upstream against the current, tied off, then lowered the gangway. The soldiers filed off before the passengers were allowed to disembark. Forming up, they marched on to the train depot and a line of cars standing at the platform. The passengers then began disembarking. Baggage and cargo followed the passengers, and within the hour a large stack stood on shore adjacent to cargo waiting to be loaded. Then the new cargo was loaded, passengers re-boarded, and the steamboat left, leaving the Saints and just a handful of other passengers to grapple with their luggage.

Picking up what they could carry, the emigrants began streaming up the shore's slope to the train station. William had made a trip up to the station to arrange for wagons and returned to Elder Spencer's side. The Elder still appeared morose, and gazed blankly out at the river.

"Got good news!" reported William. "Station-master says they don't have emigrant cars, so he's putting on regular parlor cars! Train's just about made up. Station-master says we should be on our way before dark."

"That is good news," the Elder replied. William thought surely the news would cheer him up, but it didn't seem to have much effect. "Want to spend as little time as possible in Missouri," continued Elder Spencer. He seemed as though he wanted to say more, but didn't. William didn't reply. Then, after a minute, the Elder spoke again. "Sorry I seem so desolate, but I just can't help it! It's been fifteen years since we were driven out of Nauvoo. And even longer since we were driven out of Missouri! But Illinois, and now Missouri, is just too full of unpleasant memories. Seems there's still a bad spirit about it. Can't seem to shake it."

William knew he could offer little solace, so he kept quiet. He hoped the Elder would soon snap out of it. It saddened William to see Elder Spencer so despondent. Together they turned and walked to the train station where the Saints were waiting to load, William pleased at the prospect of parlor cars despite Elder Spencer's melancholy.

The waiting room was filled with soldiers, most lounging on the benches. A young lieutenant stood talking with an older sergeant near the door leading from the waiting room. Another smaller group waited on the platform, some standing about while others sat on its edge. The Saints had dispersed along the platform, keeping to themselves and avoiding the soldiers as much as they could. William and Elder Spencer sought out the stationmaster and found him in his office. He glanced up as they entered, acknowledging William.

"Wagons'll be here in a few minutes." He returned to his work. But Elder Spencer interrupted him.

"Town seems awfully quiet. Not at all like Quincy," he said. The stationmaster looked up again at the two men in turn.

"Don't know much about these parts, do you? Well, not surprisin' seein' you're immigrants. Quincy's Union, through and through. Most folks here are 'secesh'." Noticing their questioning looks, he paused, then continued. "Secessionists, to you newcomers. But, they keep quiet about it, if you know what I mean," he said, nodding toward the Union soldiers in the waiting room. "Not inclined to sell to the Union army or any of its agents. More likely to sell to Confederates, but ain't many of them hereabout, not with Federal's occupyin' the town." He paused, then nodded again toward the waiting room. "These here soldiers are with the 26th Illinois out of Quincy. Replacements, headin' down the Hannibal and St. Joe. The regiment's guarding the railroad between here and there. In fact, they'll be on your train."

The wagons arrived as promised, and William's work-party got the baggage moved from the riverbank to the freight cars at the front of the train. Soon a large engine backed up to the train and coupled to the cars with a loud, startling clash. The conductors gave the signal to load, and the passengers climbed aboard, the soldiers and civilian passengers in the first two cars, and the Saints in the passenger cars following.

The emigrant Saints luxuriated in the comfort of parlor cars. The sun just touched the western horizon as the train pulled out of the station and darkness overtook the train as it gradually climbed away from the Mississippi and began crossing rolling fields and hills. When the lamps were lighted, the warm glow they radiated created an almost festive mood. Such a pleasant contrast to the dim, smoky lamps they were used to! In one car, the Saints broke into song, and soon the others fol-lowed. If there had been room to dance, they would have enjoyed a splendid cotillion!

The emigrants gradually began to tire and settle down as the night passed, but William couldn't. He was restless, and although not sure why, apprehensive. He disentangled himself from Mary Frances and went out onto the forward platform to avoid disturbing her and the others. Riding in the lead emigrant car, the platform on which William stood connect-ed to the rear platform of the soldiers' car ahead. It was peaceful out there. The slow-moving train created a pleasant breeze, and the gentle swaying and rhythmic clack-clacking of the wheels seemed to calm him. William was startled as the door to the soldiers' car opened and a young officer came out, the same lieutenant William had seen in the station. The lieutenant also seemed startled as he saw William standing to one side of the adjacent platform.

"Sorry," muttered the lieutenant. "Didn't know you were here. Name's Wills," he said, extending his hand.

"Quite all right," replied William. "I'm William Jefferies," he said, taking the lieutenant's hand. "Can't sleep either?"

"No. This's my first detail. Not sure what to expect. Damn Rebs been stirrin' things up between Hannibal and St. Joe. Missouri's got as many Unioners as Secessionists. Hard to know who is who." He became silent. Several minutes passed before the officer spoke again.

"So, you're Mormon!"

William looked at him carefully, trying to discern if the statement had hostile or curious intent. He had experienced too many of the hos-tile kind. But he didn't sense hostility.

"Yes. I am. So're the rest of us. We're emigrating from England and Wales, most of us. Some from Scandinavia, too. We're on our way to Florence to outfit for the crossing to Salt Lake City."

"To Zion," interjected the officer. William looked at him in surprise.

"Why, yes! You know of our Zion?"

"My Ma. She was Mormon. She and her family settled in Hamilton when they came out of Missouri, about ten mile downriver from

Nauvoo. Pa lived in Warsaw, only five mile away. Courted Ma somethin' fierce, way I hear it. Her Ma and Pa were none too happy, but Ma ran off with Pa anyway. Pa and her family never did get on after that. When the unpleasantness started in '44, Pa started ridin' with the Carthage Greys. Most folks think it was the Greys' did in Joe Smith. Anyway, Ma's folks got burnt out and left. Ma thought Pa had a hand in it." He paused, then continued in a low voice, almost to himself. "Probably did. Ma was awful unhappy after that. Took sick and died. Think it all broke her heart." He paused a moment, then continued. "Pa and me didn't get on well after Ma died."

William didn't know what to say in the awkward silence that followed, the only other sounds being the distant chugging of the steam engine and the clacking of wheels. But he was curious about the young man.

"Ever think about finding your grandparents? They in Zion?"

"They were headed that way the last I heard. Course, can't do much of anythin' until this rebellion is over. Signed up for ninety days."

"Then what?"

"Don't know. Pa and I never been close, though he got me my commission. But don't think I'll go back to Quincy. Have to see what plays out."

The two remained silent, each engrossed in his own thoughts. William spoke first.

"You think we'll run into trouble?" asked William.

"Hard to say. Lots of partisans here about. From both sides. My troop is headed for Macon, 'bout an hour ahead. Maybe we'll find out something there."

The train made slow progress, but within the hour they spotted a distinct glow on the horizon down the track. The lieutenant noticed it first.

"Sky's awful light up ahead. Like somethin' burnin'."

The lights they saw were indeed fires. As the train approached Macon, they saw that all roads leading into the city were brightly lit by large bonfires and torches, giving an almost surreal quality to the town. Groups of soldiers stood in the shadows, their muskets at the ready. The town looked like it was under siege. Rude breastworks had been erected around much of the downtown area, and the Saints could see at least three cannon deployed around the perimeter. The entering train paralleled Vine Street along the south edge of town. The train slowed and approached the rail yard and station. Both were heavily guarded by soldiers who appeared nervous and alert. The lieutenant turned to William as the train came to a stop.

"Better get back and warn your people to stay on the train. Let me find out what's going on. But it don't look good."

William walked quickly back through the car, cautioning all to stay put, and found Elder Spencer on the next platform.

"The officer in the car ahead says we ought to stay aboard." Motioning toward the lieutenant just entering the station, he continued. "He's going in to find out what's happening. Best we take his advice, I think."

Elder Spencer agreed, and sent messengers to the remaining cars with the instruction. Elder Hanham soon joined them. The three stepped off the train, remaining close alongside as they awaited Lieutenant Wills. He came out after several minutes and headed directly for them.

"A group of Rebel partisans raided the town just two hours ago!" he reported. "You're not to get off the train. The stationmaster feared we might have been attacked on the way in, but I told him we seen no sign of trouble. But the Major doesn't want to take any chances. My troop is going to get off here, but he'll be sending a more experienced one along with us to protect the train. I'll lead it. Go back to your people and caution them to remain calm. And to turn the lamps down! You don't want to become targets."

By the time refueling was complete, a group of thirty soldiers had boarded the train and stationed themselves on the platforms at the rear and between the cars. The freight car doors were slid open, and soldiers sat in the doorways, muskets at the ready. Several more perched atop the wood-car, and more yet stood with the engineers in the engine's cabin. The train pulled slowly out of the station, the engineers keeping the throttles back and watching ahead carefully. They didn't want to outrun the powerful front lantern's reach in case the guerrillas had torn up the tracks or placed obstacles in its path. Every rail bridge and road crossing for the next fifty miles was guarded by detachments of soldiers, bonfires and torches burning brightly to illuminate any saboteurs who might try to approach undetected. It was as if the whole countryside was under siege!

Time passed slowly for the Saints on the slow-moving train. It was almost unfair, they thought: they finally had a more comfortable train, but they couldn't rest soundly because they were anxious about being caught in the cross-fire of this new civil war's sides. Would they make it to Zion after all? Surely after preserving their lives in the midst of so many hazards since they left Liverpool, the Lord wouldn't allow them to fall prey to a war that was not even theirs!

But not all were anxious. To the contrary, the young men, James and Franklin among them, were excited. Bored by the tedium of the long train ride since leaving Jersey City, the boys seemed enthralled by the adventure.

"I can't believe it!" said James excitedly. "We're right in the middle of a real war!"

That remark caused Mother Ould to take a firm hand to James. Grabbing him by the scruff, she marched him back to his seat and in no uncertain terms, instructed him to stay put. He obeyed. Mother Ould was seldom aroused to anger, but the few times James saw it convinced him he didn't want to be its cause. Franklin meekly joined James.

The trip to Chillicothe, the next refueling stop, took five hours, about the same as the trip from Hannibal to Macon. It passed uneventfully except for one emergency stop caused by an anxious lookout on the engine who thought he saw riders ahead on the tracks. The lieutenant dispatched a patrol to check, but it found no evidence of riders. They did, however, startle a large herd of deer. Relieved, they continued their journey.

No bonfires greeted the train as it pulled into Chillicothe's station, but there were torches. Hundreds of them, it seemed, carried by two large mobs gathered at opposite ends of First Street. The street ran parallel to the tracks, and from the train the Saints could see the mobs clearly as the train pulled onto the siding adjacent to the station. The mob closest to the station carried aloft the Union's Stars and Stripes, but the mob at the opposite far end carried the Stars and Bars, the Confederate battle flag. Shouting with fists and whisky bottles raised, the two mobs threw stones and bottles down the street at one another. They seemed to be summoning enough courage to approach. Approach they finally did, but after meeting and exchanging blows, both fell back again to their respective ends, strength and resolve tested. The mobs continued to mill about, their members drinking and yelling at the opposite side and threatening to approach once more. To the Saints peering from the train who had experienced mob violence before, it was a frightening scene.

The station, itself, was defended by a small detachment of soldiers commanded by a sergeant. It was clear they could not defend long against a determined onslaught if either of the mobs decided to come their direction. Lieutenant Wills was the first off the train and ran over to the sergeant. After conferring, he turned and returned to the train where William, Elder Spencer, and Elder Hanham were waiting. None of the Saints dared go out on the platforms, but stayed in the relative safety of the car's interior with their heads down.

"Sergeant says the whole town started gettin' liquored-up about nightfall, and the skirmishes started around midnight. He and his men are a little nervous, but he thinks if the mobs keep going at each other, they'll either fight and get it over with, or drink themselves silly and pass out. I'll detail some of my men to stand guard while we refuel. We'll be on our way soon's we can."

To the anxious Saints, refueling took an inordinate time. Elder Spencer was especially agitated, at times looking frightened as he paced nervously, glancing often in the direction of the mobs. William grew concerned about him.

"We'll be finished soon," William said to reassure the Elder.

"Won't be soon enough!" he replied anxiously. "You don't understand, Elder Jefferies. You've never faced mobs quite like this before! I have! What's more, we're only a few miles away from Caldwell and Daviess counties. This is the area in which we were driven from our homes twenty-two years ago! These mobbers are likely the sons of those who ran us out! You can be sure they share their fathers' anti-Mormon feeling!"

As if on cue, several men ran shouting from the station to the closest mob. "Mormons on the train! Mormons on the train!" The shouts carried down the street to the other mob as well. Both mobs quieted down as its members conferred among themselves. Then, several drunken members of the closest mob turned and began yelling in the direction of the train. "Mormons! Mormons on the train! Let's get the sons of bitches!" Their shouts seemed to energize the mobs anew, but instead of turning to face one another, they both began edging toward the station and the train.

The Saints froze in fear. Seeing what was developing, Lieutenant Wills quickly ordered all his men to detrain and take up position in a line across the path of the approaching mobs. Then he walked down the line, quietly issuing instructions to his men. When finished, he retreated to one side and ordered them to prepare to fire. Each soldier cocked the hammer of his musket and brought it up to his shoulder, pointing it toward the mobs. The lieutenant drew his pistol, and with it in his right hand, walked toward the approaching mobs. Seeing the soldiers preparing to fire seemed to sober the mobs some, and they stopped. The lieutenant walked right up to the leaders standing in front.

"I order you to disperse. As of now, you are under marshal law. If you advance further, I will order my men to fire." He raised his pistol and pointed it directly at the head of the man he thought to be the leader. "You will be first to fall!"

Most of the mob retreated a little, many of them staggering drunkenly. The leader blinked several times, but then seemed to gain strength as he noticed the lieutenant's youth.

"Aw, hell! You wouldn't dare. Why, you're just out of short pants!" he laughed. "You ain't got the guts!"

The lieutenant continued to stare at him steadily. "You don't think so? Just watch."

The lieutenant cautiously retreated backwards toward the soldiers, pistol still held steadily before him, angling off to the sidelines. When he had cleared the mob he turned to his soldiers.

"Odd numbers, kneel and prepare to fire. On my command!"

Each alternate man kneeled down on one knee and repositioned his musket against his shoulder. Once in position, the lieutenant continued.

"Ready . . . ! Ready . . . ! Fire!"

In stunned disbelief the Saints watched as the kneeling soldiers fired their weapons in a great volley of smoke. Without a glance at the mob, the soldiers quickly lowered their muskets and began reloading as the standing soldiers moved forward and, in turn kneeled, ready to fire. The mob, in equal disbelief, turned, and as a body, began running away, discarding their torches as they ran. The more drunken stumbled and fell as they struggled to escape. The lieutenant ordered his men to stand down, and upon the order, they lowered their muskets. In a matter of minutes, the street was deserted, discarded torches slowly burning themselves out. Amazingly, it was also devoid of bodies. The lieutenant had wisely instructed his men to fire over their heads.

The train was well on its way to its last stop, St. Joseph, before exhaustion from the tense moments in Chillicothe finally overcame the Saints. It was beginning to grow daylight. William, Elder Spencer, and Elder Hanham had been moving among the families they had come to know and love over the past eight weeks, reassuring and comforting them as best they could. When it seemed calm, William and Elder Spencer met, intending to visit briefly before rejoining their families.

"It's been quite a night," said Elder Spencer, understating the trauma they had suffered. "I must thank that brave lieutenant. He and his men saved many of our lives this evening, I have no doubt. Wasn't he marvelous? So calm and deliberate! And so young! I wish we knew more about him."

"I visited with him a bit before we got to Chillicothe," William replied. "His name's Wills. He's from Warsaw, just north of Quincy. He and his men were destined for Macon, but you know the events since then."

"Thank the Lord! It was providential the lieutenant continued on with us, wasn't it?"

"Providence, indeed! But that's not all," continued William. "And you will appreciate this, Elder. His mother and her family are members of the Church and were with you here in Missouri. They settled just south of Nauvoo after the exodus. His father was not Mormon, and rode with the Carthage Greys!"

At that news, Elder Spencer's eyes widened and he grabbed the back of a nearby seat to steady himself. Even in the lamplight, William could see the color had drained from his face.

"Do you mean to tell me the son of one of the mobbers who murdered the Prophet saved us from a mob?" He paused. "Can it be true?"

The Elder seemed confused, shaking his head slightly as he reflected upon what he had just learned. Then he spoke, his eyes moist.

"I have been humbled. My heart has been so filled with hate the last two days, I lost sight entirely that it's the Lord's place to judge, not ours." He paused as his chin quivered. "And we must forgive all who offend us. I am ashamed it took such a hard lesson to teach me that. I must thank Lieutenant Wills for what he has done for us. Not despite his heritage, but because of it."

The remainder of the trip to St. Joseph continued uneventfully. The soldiers began to relax with the coming of light, confident the partisans wouldn't dare attack the train in daylight. That wasn't how they worked; it was at night you had to fear partisans. But the day dawned grey and overcast. The train had overtaken the mid-spring rains, and short, intermittent squalls and drizzle accompanied the train on its run into St. Joseph. By the time the train began its gradual descent from the higher plains to the Missouri River plain, it was raining in earnest with occasional lightning flashes further to the west. The train reached the river and turned north to run alongside it for the last ten miles to St. Joseph. They were almost to the depot before the Saints began to make out its buildings through the rainy mist. It was too hazy to see the town lying beyond.

St. Joseph is located in the outside curve of a major bend in the Missouri River where the river's high eastern banks descend to the level of the river. Situated on the gently sloping river plain between the river and rolling hills about three miles east, it was a pleasant site. It had grown prosperous as a major river port and a jumping-off point for emigrants headed west along the Oregon and California Trails, offering almost a week's shorter trip than wagon trains departing from Independence and Westport further to the south. It was also where the Saints would board a steamboat for their last leg to Florence.

The railroad depot was located on the south edge of town, about a half-mile from the town's center, and about a quarter-mile from the Missouri and a line of steamboats tethered to the shore. Among them was their steamboat, the side-wheeler Omaha. Once more, the luggage work-party unloaded the baggage from the freight cars onto wagons hired for the trip to the river.

But it was miserable work. The rain continued steadily through the morning, making each round-trip along the muddy road between the depot and the Omaha increasingly difficult. Finally, the teamsters grew impatient, and began dumping the luggage on the shore without waiting for it to be unloaded and carried aboard the Omaha. At that, the stevedores refused to work any longer in the rain. Dismayed that their baggage was abandoned and getting soaked, the Saints were left with the task of getting it into the shelter of the steamboat. Working quickly, they slogged through the deepening mud to carry the luggage aboard.

By late afternoon the emigrants had their luggage aboard. The rains stopped just after noon, and though scattered thunderstorms continued to pass over the area, quite a number of the emigrants walked into town to shop. As the light began to fade, they returned to join those remaining aboard. But everything was wet. Most passengers went up to the hurricane deck to sit in the salon running the deck's length between the staterooms, Mother Ould, Laura, and the boys included. But even there, it was damp and steamy. William and Mary Frances chose to stay outside, near the bow, sheltered by the broad, overhanging top deck and enjoying the relative space and privacy.

Privacy was short-lived, however. As on the Mississippi, war had created a shortage of steamboats along the Missouri, and before departing in the early evening, nearly every available space aboard the vessel was occupied by passengers, luggage, or cargo. The salon grew hot and uncomfortable as the passengers continued to await departure. But most of the Saints were reconciled to the delay. After thirty-eight days and nights living and traveling in cramped, uncomfortable accommodations, what was another two days? They all tried to settle in, however uncomfortable, for two more nights, nonetheless grateful to be on their journey's last leg.

The trip upriver was uneventful, an anti-climatic end to what had been a very eventful six weeks for most, and even a grand adventure for some. Especially the youngsters. As expected, the night passed uncomfortably on the crowded steamboat, uneasy slumber interrupted by several stops along the river to load fuel and to discharge and take on passengers and cargo. But even overcrowded, the boat offered more space than they had endured over the last eight days aboard trains. The next morning dawned damp and drizzly again, but by now most were beyond caring. The heavy woolens the emigrants wore had not been completely dry since they departed Chicago and encountered their first thunderstorms. When it had not been raining, the heavy spring humidity kept their clothing damp. And, traveling on the river only aggravated the dampness. Would they ever dry out again?

Traveling up the river in rain and mist turned out to be terribly monotonous. Thick haze hanging over the river prevented the passengers from enjoying what would have been a scenic trip, and thus the second day passed as slowly and tediously as the previous, meals providing the only break from dreary waiting. The Saints had endured restraining stretches like this aboard the *Manchester*, but at least there they were able to participate in activities. On this confining vessel, there was room to do nothing but sit and wait. Would the trip never end? A stop at a small river town allowed the passengers to get off and stretch for a short time, but the continuing drizzle made even this relief uncomfortable. Darkness finally overtook the steamboat once more, and the Saints tried to settle down for one last night, exhaustion providing blessed sleep for most.

By early morning on their last day, the weather front finally passed. As dawn gave way to daylight and the rising sun, the Saints were greeted by a dazzling display of color as the sunrise's deep reds gave way to orange and crimson as the sun finally broke clear of the departing clouds. And what a change the improved weather made in the Saints' spirits! The air cleared and dried, and the morning turned into a cool pleasant day. The Omaha passed the mouth of the Platte River, only twenty miles from Florence. Just a few hours more! All of a sudden their arduous trek seemed momentarily forgotten as the Saints grew excited, almost giddy, knowing their long rail and steamboat trek was about finished.

Then came Council Bluffs, distant to the east across the river's broad flood plain, one of the sites to which the Saints had come that terrible winter of '46 after they had been driven from Nauvoo. Less than an hour ahead would be Florence, on the west bank, site of the old Winter Quarters, the departure point for Brigham Young and his lead expedition that spring of '47. Finally, as they rounded a large bend in the river, there was Florence, dead ahead, a small town sited on slopes rising to the west from the river. Many a tear was shed, not because of its beauty, for it had little, but out of relief that the five-thousand-mile trek they had endured to get to this point was over. Here, the Saints would gather, temporarily creating a little Zion while they prepared for the final, thousand-mile trek to the real Zion, Utah Territory and the Great Salt Lake Valley.

That same evening at the rear of a dim, smoke-filled saloon standing near the river along St. Joseph's First Street and its intersection with Felix Street, Dick Weldon, Isaac his son, and Jake and Jesse, two henchmen, sat sullenly nursing their drinks. Weldon had grown portly in his middle age and his shirtfront was stained with the drippings of many meals and tobacco juice. His long, dark, slicked-back hair gave him a slightly sinister appearance. He sat still. Isaac was thin, wiry, and fidgety, squirming in his chair and chewing at the nub of his fingernails. His right leg was bouncing in a quick, nervous rhythm. Jesse, a short, squat man, sat in a stupefied trance. Jake rolled his empty shot glass expertly between his fingers. He was tall and slender. All but Weldon wore low-crowned hats, and all four had several weeks' growth of whisker stubble that made their faces look dirty. Playing cards were strewn across the drink-stained round table, left where they had been flung after the last hand. None of the group was talking.

They were the only customers. Not many patronized this saloon; it didn't offer anything but cheap liquor. Only the most down-on-their-luck drinkers among teamsters, rivermen, and the town's dregs came here. That's why Weldon liked it. No one to ask questions. It was too early yet for other patrons. The barkeep was idly wiping shot glasses with a dirty rag behind the short bar placed a few feet away from the right wall. No fancy back-bar here; in fact there was no back-bar at all. Only an occasional steamboat whistle and the sounds coming from boats being loaded along the Missouri River's waterfront a short distance away punctuated the silence.

Exasperated, Weldon reached over and with his hand swatted Isaac across the back of the head. Isaac's head jerked.

"Damn, boy! You wear me out! Sit still! I'm tryin' t'think!

Isaac glared at his father morosely and settled down. Jake used the outburst as an opportunity to interject. He'd been thinking, too.

"Seems like we'd been better off stayin' along the Santa Fe road. We knows it right well. Could of pickup up a small emigrant group. Still plenty goin' west."

"Yea," replied Weldon. "And the Federals knows us right well, too! We came mighty close west of Lawrence. Mighty close! If'n Rose hadn't warned us, we'd be dead by now or headed for a Yankee noose at Leavenworth! Nah. Need to stay away from the Santa Fe for a spell. 'Sides, this here war's goin' to bring a whole lot more Yanks. Time to look elsewhere."

Isaac, resuming his squirming, spoke up.

"Jes' as long as it's somethin'! Can't stand doin' nothin'! St. Joe ain't a place I want to stay. Too many Yanks here already! Whyn't we jes' join up with ol' Gov'ner Price? He's raisin' Reb troops now!"

Weldon glanced at Isaac and shook his head in despair. "Boy, I know you're a little tetched, but you're sounding plain loco! I tol' you already; you want to get us killed? No surer way t'get killed than joinin' up. We'd be nothin' but cannon fodder."

Jake nodded his head in agreement.

"Nah. No fightin' for us," continued Weldon. "Leastwise, not yet. If'n we was to fight, we'd join up with one of the Reb partisan bunches. That way, we fight when we wants, not when the cursed abolitionists and Yankees want. I heared young Quantrill's been talkin' about raisin' some folks. Now he's one I might think about joinin' if'n the terms was right."

Jake spoke. "Yer crazy to be even thinkin' on such nonsense. I don't want to be shot at by anyone, Yank or Reb. If'n the Santa Fe's gettin' too hot, then let's head out along the Californy road. Heard tell all the Yanks out West and along the road are headed back East. With them gone, seems pickin's ought to be pretty easy out that a way."

Weldon looked at Jake thoughtfully. "Jake, sometimes you surprise even me. Maybe there's hope for you after all! Been thinkin' some on that myself."

Weldon paused as though formulating an important thought, then continued.

"In fact, those Mormons goin' through here last week been givin' me an idea. I been askin' around and found they's on the way to Florence, upriver a mite from Omaha. Outfittin' to head west to the Great Salt Lake. Zion, they calls it." He paused again, a smirk forming on his face. "Sure spoilt their first Zion, didn't we?" Weldon chuckled as Jake and Jesse, finally coming out of his trance, laughed.

"Like I say," Weldon continued. "I been thinkin'. This here war's makin' things mighty dear. Now if'n a man could come up with some goods real cheap, then he might make some money sellin' 'em to those that needs 'em but ain't got 'em. Like Mormons fittin' out for a long trip."

"You think?" interjected Isaac. "Like what?"

"Like somethin' we can get real cheap if'n we can't steal it. I was thinkin' hams. All emigrants carry hams and this here's hog country. Bet I could get a mess o' last year's harvest. Smoked or not. Whichever is cheaper. Then get us a couple wagons, some mules, and we're freighters with a consignment!"

"Boss, that jes' might work," said Jake. "'Sides, it'd give us a chance to look over those Mormons. They's always been good pickin's."

"They was a few years back, for certain." He paused and chuckled again. "That'd also solve my problem with the boy. He'd help us if'n he thought we was goin' straight." He shook his head as he continued. "Ever since he pulled out on us couple years back down New Mexico way he's been getting' awful high falutin' on us. His ma been talkin' us down, I expect. Say, where is he anyway?" he concluded, looking around toward the door.

"Who? Adam?" replied Isaac. "Sent him down to the stables to look after the horses. Not likely he'll be back anytime soon. Since we picked him up from his ma this time, seems like he don't want to be with us much."

"Well," replied Weldon with a chuckle. "Maybe he'll be more sociable when he thinks we're honest workin' men. Yea," he said after a pause, as much to himself as to the others, "this might just work. It might work real good!"

Just over one-thousand miles west in Utah Territory, as Weldon and his gang sat in the seedy St. Joseph saloon planning their strategy, Porter Rockwell slowed his horse's pace and leaned over almost parallel to the ground, examining the road carefully as he proceeded slowly. Then he stopped, dismounted, and walked a few paces to a dusty patch of ground adjacent to the well-traveled road marked with hoof prints and wagon wheel tracks. Frank Karrick, a companion, reigned-in just behind Porter, but did not dismount. He watched anxiously as Porter kneeled, reached down, and rubbed his right hand very lightly over marks on the ground.

"This is as far as I could track them," said Karrick with dismay. "Tracks just seemed to disappear."

Porter didn't reply, but rubbed his hands together to clean off the dirt, pushed back his low-crown hat, stood, and walked several yards further before kneeling again and examining the ground. The two were on the main road running south from Great Salt Lake City to California . The two had passed through the Santaquin settlement just an hour before, but did not stop.

"Not surprised," said Porter. "They took off the mule shoes here. We'll just stay on this road. Likely they're headed out of the Territory." He paused and glanced southeast at Mount Nebo, the highest peak along this stretch of the Wasatch mountain range. Noting that only the top quarter of the mountain was still bathed in sunlight, he continued. "Be dark in about an hour. We'll stop up ahead and get a fresh start in the morning. Unless they know we're on to 'em, we'll likely catch up late tomorrow." Returning to his horse, Porter unrolled the large cape secured behind his saddle, and swinging it over his shoulders, mounted and began riding south. Karrick quickly joined him.

Rockwell and Karrick had been riding hard for the last day and a half since the two left Porter's Hot Springs inn at the southernmost part of the Great Salt Lake valley. Karrick was a successful young freighter who ran freight wagon trains between Salt Lake City and Sacramento, and had recently lost eight mules and a grey stallion to rustlers. A competent tracker himself, he had tracked the thieves this far south until he lost the trail. Brigham Young, one of Karrick's acquaintances in Salt Lake City, recommended the freighter engage Porter. "None better," Young had assured Karrick. The freighter hoped so.

The two rode hard the next day. By mid afternoon, Porter broke the silence of their determined pace. "Keep a sharp eye out here on. Don't want to lose the surprise."

By late afternoon, still no rustlers. Then, about an hour before sunset, the two riders topped a slight rise forming the east side of the Sevier River flood plain and Porter suddenly reined up. Karrick had to react quickly to avoid colliding with him. Porter quickly reversed direction for a few hundred yards, and stopped again. Karrick followed him. Porter reached into a saddlebag as he dismounted and drew out a telescope. Motioning to Karrick to keep low, Porter returned to the rise and kneeled behind a small cedar shrub, Karrick close behind. Opening the telescope, Porter looked straight down the road to the right bank of the deep, swiftly flowing river about a mile distant. Looking in the same direction, Karrick could just make out the whisp of campfire smoke and a number of tethered animals.

"Got 'em!" Porter whispered loudly. "Two men, three horses, and five . . . no, seven . . . no, I see eight mules."

"Thunderation!" exclaimed Karrick. "It's them! Let's go!" he said as he turned to head back to the horses.

"Not so fast!" cautioned Porter as he reached to grab Karrick by the arm. "Want to surprise them. It'll give us the edge."

"Whyn't we just ride in and shoot 'em! They rustled my livestock! In California, that's a hangin' offense!"

"They kill anybody?"

"No. Not that I know of."

"Did they do harm to any of your teamsters?"

"No. They appeared to be agreeable fellows. Just up and took the animals when my teamsters wasn't payin' attention."

"Well, I never shoot a man less'n he killed someone himself. I want to give these gents a chance to give up peaceably."

"And how do you plan to do that?" asked Karrick.

"Give me about half an hour. Sun will be close to settin'. I'm goin' to swing west and come up on 'em from that direction. After a half hour, you mount up and ride on 'em normal like, just like a traveler headed home. Ask 'em for a cup of coffee. I'll do the rest."

Thirty minutes later, Frank Karrick did as he was instructed. But the closer he rode and the clearer he could make out his eight mules and grey stallion, all worth almost five thousand dollars, the angrier he got. He just couldn't abide a thief! As he approached the campsite, one of the men stood up from the campfire where both were hunkered down. A tin skillet and coffeepot were sitting on rocks at the edge of the flames, bacon and beans simmering in the skillet. The man who stood had a large revolver stuck in his belt. His companion, who remained sitting near the fire, reached over to pick up a sawed-off shotgun and placed it across his folded legs. Neither of the two men said anything. But Karrick did as he dismounted.

"Mightly nice lookin' livestock you got," he said, nodding upstream a little where the animals were grazing on the spring grass. "They for sale?"

At the mention of the livestock, the two men grew suspicious. The one sitting by the fire also arose, cradling the shotgun in his left arm, his right hand on the stock. The other moved his hand toward his pistol, but didn't reach for it.

"Why you ask, stranger?" asked the man holding the shotgun.

"I been lookin' for some of my own that's gone missin'," replied Karrick, who reached for a small pistol in a shoulder holster. "I think these is them!"

Before Karrick could reach his pistol, the man with the shotgun leveled it at him. "I reckon you're right, but you ain't gettin' these back. Don't pull that shoulder pistol. You'll be dead afore you get it out."

Karrick froze. Where was Rockwell?

The other man drew his own weapon, but didn't aim it at Karrick. It hung lose in his right hand. He turned to his partner.

"This ain't goin' right, Luke! It ain't goin' right at all! What we goin' to do now? We can't kill the man! No stock is worth that!"

"Shut up and let me think!" the other replied.

Just then, Porter stood up to the left of Luke, like an apparition rising from the dust. In his hand leveled at Luke was a short-barrel .36

caliber Navy Colt. The three distinct clicks the revolver made as Porter thumbed the hammer back made their own statements. No others were needed. Luke, startled, stared briefly at Porter, then lowered his gun. "I ain't hankerin' to get killed. Where the devil you come from?" He shook his head in bewilderment and placed the shotgun on the ground and raised his hands. His partner followed suit.

Just after noon on the Missouri River, May 24th, the steamboat nosed onto the shore a little upriver from the town near where the mill-stream entered the Missouri. The gangplank was lowered and four hundred weary, travel-sore, and dirty Saints gratefully came ashore. After seeing Mary Frances and the family off the boat, assisting with the hand-luggage, William joined Elders Spencer and Hanham. The three stood quietly, watching a carriage from town, a little to the southwest on the slope rising toward a low line of hills approach the steamboat. A line of wagons followed the carriage. Elder Spencer walked toward the approaching carriage and the others followed behind. It stopped near Elder Spencer and a man alighted and walked toward the three. He was dressed in comfortable work clothing and wore a low-crowned, broad-brimmed hat. He held out his hand as he approached.

"Welcome to Florence! I'm Elder Jacob Gates, emigration agent. You must be Elders Spencer, Hanham, and Jefferies, lately of the *Manchester*."

"Indeed we are!" replied Elder Spencer, taking his hand. "And we are pleased to be here! It's been a long, tiring journey."

"We've been expecting you, of course. I hope the trip hasn't been too unpleasant! I'm sure you're ready for a rest. Well, we'll give you a few days, but then we've got a lot to do!"

"We expected so. Just tell us what."

"Yes. Of course. But first, would you gather at least the heads of households? I'd like to welcome them and give instructions for now."

Most of the men were engaged in assisting the boat's crew offload the luggage; all were anxious to get settled after the long journey. The three turned and separated to gather the men, and within a short time a large crowd assembled near Elder Gate's carriage. He climbed on the carriage to rise above the onlookers.

"Dear Brothers and Sisters! I'm Jacob Gates, emigration agent. On behalf of the Church, and the local citizens, I welcome you to Florence! I know you are all weary and would like to get settled as soon as possible, so my remarks will be brief."

The assembly grew silent and crowded closer to hear.

"You're the first company of the season, so you'll have the pick of accommodations. There's a hotel in town offering accommodation, and we've hired a number of houses at reasonable rates for those wishing larger quarters. My clerk, Elder Taylor, is following on one of the wagons. He has a list. For those who desire to set up camp, free of charge, the grounds are up there, this side of town" He turned and indicated the broad, sloping meadows north of town, rising gently from the riverbank to the low hills about a half-mile distant to the west. "If you need tents, they are available at reasonable prices in the Church store, or you can purchase one from the local merchants. If you plan to travel with one of the Church companies, then we can issue your tent and some housekeeping supplies today."

He paused to allow Elder Hanham to catch up with his Welsh interpretation for the large number of Welsh Saints. Smaller groups of Scandinavian Saints clustered, listening to interpretations by their English speakers. Elder Gates continued.

"There are still a few abandoned dwellings in the area, but they are in disrepair. However, if any wish to occupy them, they are free to do so.

The wagons and teamsters," he gestured toward the approaching wagons as he spoke, "will help you get to whatever accommodation you choose. We'll call a meeting in the schoolhouse day after tomorrow, on Sunday, to provide further instruction. In the meantime, do as much as you can to make yourselves comfortable. Again, welcome to Florence!"

The group slowly dispersed and returned to unloading the baggage. Elder Gates approached William.

"I understand you have clerking experience."

"Yes, I do. I kept the emigration accounts on the *Manchester*," William replied.

"Good. Elder Jones is very complimentary of your efforts. I have a proposition for you. I intended to appoint Elder Charles Penrose as clerk of the Church store, but he'll be delayed in New York. He's assisting Elder Jones procure provisions. Would you be interested in clerking until he arrives? I expect him in about three weeks. In exchange, I'll offer room and board to you and your family. The rooms above the store are quite comfortable."

"Why yes! I'd be pleased to," said William.

"Excellent! Load your luggage on my wagon. Elder Taylor will take you and your family up. I'm grateful for your assistance."

William was elated at his good fortune, and the sentiment was shared by his family, including young Franklin. They would soon be dependent upon the Church for the westward trek, but William wanted to maintain their independence as long as possible. He, James, and Franklin joined the others unloading the luggage.

The last of the luggage was unloaded from the steamboat in just over an hour, and soon thereafter, William and the boys had theirs loaded on Elder Gates' wagon. The wagon pulled away, and William and his family walked along side, joining a growing line of wagons headed toward town or the camping grounds to the north. Climbing the short slope and entering town from the north, they proceeded down Main Street.

This was the first good look any of the emigrants had of a frontier town. It was not impressive. Main Street was two dusty blocks long. All the buildings, with the exception of the bank, were of rough-sawn board and batten construction with a boardwalk in front. To their right on the west side stood three single-story stores, two of them separated by a small saloon and café. Beyond the third store, a vacant lot standing between them, stood the bank, a two-story building constructed of stone. A post office shared the bank. On the other side of the street to their left stood an additional three stores, two more small saloons, a café, and the hotel. The bank and the hotel were the only two-story buildings in town. On the higher slopes west of town, laid out in neat squares, were about one hundred houses, mostly single-story with a few two-story dwellings scattered about. All but a few were constructed of sawn logs; the newer homes were board and batten. Some were whitewashed; most were unpainted.

Visible further south, along the river side of Main Street's extension, stood a livery stable and several blacksmith shops, and what looked to be a warehouse. Directly across the road from the blacksmiths stood a ten-acre corral containing a small herd of cattle. Along the south edge of the corral stood a separate corral for horses and mules. A large wagon yard containing about 50 wagons was located beyond the horse corral.

Florence was a small town, but it was busy as William and his family followed Elder Taylor and his wagon south along Main Street. Wagons stood before the stores on both sides of the street, most unloading supplies and provisions that had either arrived on the steamboat or by wagon from Omaha. In front of the hotel stood two wagons containing the luggage of fellow passengers who sought accommodations there. They would likely be crowded in the single hotel.

Reaching the bank building, Elder Taylor turned west on First Street and paralleled the north fence of the corral. They continued on, ascending a slight slope, and stopped before a two-story cut-log building standing on the corner of First and Elm, the street running along the west side of the corral. Barrels and crates of provisions, spare wagon parts, and trail equipment were stacked in front and on the covered porch.

"This is it!" called out Elder Taylor. "The Church store. We'll sell what we can to the independent companies, but our main purpose is to supply the Church companies when they provision. Here. Grab this. I've got to go back to pick up consignments," he said as he began handing down the trunks. "Your rooms are upstairs."

The first floor was a large, single room, a fireplace at one end, a staircase at the other, and doors at the front and back flanked by a pair of windows each. It was crowded with merchandise, mostly barrels of flour, rice, oatmeal, cornmeal and beans; hams and bacon sides hung from the rafters. Dry goods were scattered about as well, bolts of flannel, wool, linen, and linsey-woolsey, a mixed linen and wool fabric. Folded tents and wagon sheets stood in stacks, tinware, hats, and shoes still in boxes. Making their way through the crowded store, William and the others climbed the stairs carrying their hand-baggage.

The building was really just a story and a half. Upstairs was little more than a large attic divided into two rooms with a door between. A fireplace stood at the far end above the fireplace below, and each room had a small window on either side in the low wall. There was room to stand upright only in the center. It was sparsely furnished: one small table, two stools, and two straw-filled sleeping ticks in each room.

"Well," said Mother Ould. "I think we can make ourselves comfortable here. Don't you think? William, perhaps you can find us two more sleeping ticks. Mary Frances, why don't you and Laura walk back to town and get groceries. James, you and Franklin can get the luggage up here, and we'll just make ourselves at home!"